The Bunco Babes have something
to get off their chests . . .

The Babes were now chanting her name. "Geor-gia!
Geor-gia!"

Oh, hell. Why not? She turned to her sister. "I'll flash
if you'll flash."

Frida laughed. "You're on."

They stood up side by side. Frida went first. Up went
the white T-shirt and off came the bra. Georgia hesitated
only a second. She clumsily worked on the buttons to her
silk top. One of the buttons popped off and fell on the
floor but she didn't care. She'd worry about finding it
later. She snapped open the clasp at the front of her bra
and flashed the Babes.

"Take that, Spencer Moody!" she cried.

The Babes were laughing so hard, a couple of them fell
out of their chairs.

Just then, she heard a noise coming from the foyer.

She glanced over to see a tall, brown-haired man with
laughing green eyes staring straight at her. Or rather, staring straight at her boobs. His gaze slid to Frida, then back
to her.

"You're right," Dave Hernandez said, sporting that same
damn smile he'd given her just a few hours ago. "You and
your sister look nothing alike."

Other Berkley titles by Maria Geraci

BUNCO BABES TELL ALL

Bunco Babes Gone Wild

MARIA GERACI

BERKLEY BOOKS, NEW YORK

THE BERKLEY PUBLISHING GROUP
Published by the Penguin Group
Penguin Group (USA) Inc.
375 Hudson Street, New York, New York 10014, USA
Penguin Group (Canada), 90 Eglinton Avenue East, Suite 700, Toronto, Ontario M4P 2Y3, Canada
(a division of Pearson Penguin Canada Inc.)
Penguin Books Ltd., 80 Strand, London WC2R 0RL, England
Penguin Group Ireland, 25 St. Stephen's Green, Dublin 2, Ireland (a division of Penguin Books Ltd.)
Penguin Group (Australia), 250 Camberwell Road, Camberwell, Victoria 3124, Australia
(a division of Pearson Australia Group Pty. Ltd.)
Penguin Books India Pvt. Ltd., 11 Community Centre, Panchsheel Park, New Delhi—110 017, India
Penguin Group (NZ), 67 Apollo Drive, Rosedale, North Shore, 0632, New Zealand
(a division of Pearson New Zealand Ltd.)
Penguin Books (South Africa) (Pty.) Ltd., 24 Sturdee Avenue, Rosebank, Johannesburg 2196,
South Africa

Penguin Books Ltd., Registered Offices: 80 Strand, London WC2R 0RL, England

This is a work of fiction. Names, characters, places, and incidents either are the product of the author's imagination or are used fictitiously and any resemblance to actual persons, living or dead, business establishments, events, or locales is entirely coincidental. The publisher does not have any control over and does not assume any responsibility for author or third-party websites or their content.

NOTE: The recipes contained in this book are to be followed exactly as written. The publisher is not responsible for your specific health or allergy needs that may require medical supervision. The publisher is not responsible for any adverse reactions to the recipes contained in this book.

Copyright © 2009 Maria Geraci
Cover design by Tamaye Perry
Cover images by Shutterstock
Book design by Tiffany Estreicher

PRINTING HISTORY
Berkley trade paperback edition / November 2009

Library of Congress Cataloging-in-Publication Data

Geraci, Maria.
    Bunco babes gone wild / Maria Geraci.—Berkley trade paperback ed.
        p. cm.
    ISBN 978-0-425-22996-5
1. Female friendship—Fiction. 2. Dice games—Fiction. 3. Florida—Fiction. I. Title.
    PS3607.E7256B85   2009
    813'.6—dc22   2009022001

PRINTED IN THE UNITED STATES OF AMERICA

10 9 8 7 6 5 4 3 2 1

For my own wild bunch—
Stephanie, Kevin, and Megan

Acknowledgments

This book was so much fun for me to write and I have so many people to thank for helping the process go so smoothly. First off, I want to thank my fantastic critique partners—Melissa Francis and Louisa Edwards. This is a huge year for us and I wouldn't want to go through it with anyone but you two.

I want to thank my first readers—Lissa McConnell, Carmen Dick, and Maureen Winger for letting me know when I get it right. I'm deeply appreciative to the fabulous team at Berkley—Allison Brandau, Kathryn Tumen, and my wonderful editor, Wendy McCurdy.

A big thanks goes to Elizabeth Middaugh at Nancy Berland Public Relations for all your promotional help. I also want to thank Delroy "Ricky" Neath at Yard Media for my fantastic website. And to my wonderful agent, Deidre Knight, whose support and encouragement keep me going.

I have to thank my parents, Carmen and Fernando Palacios, for all their love and support. And of course, to my husband, Mike, who's always there for me and who celebrates each and every little victory alongside me. No acknowledgment would be complete without men-

tioning the fabulous Labor and Delivery nurses at TMH.
You all make me feel like a rock star and make delivering
babies almost as much fun as writing.

And last but not least, to the Bunco Broads of Tallahassee—I love you all.

It is a truth universally acknowledged that when a woman gets a boob job, she must show it off to her closest friends.

If Georgia Meyer were a man (or a lesbian), she'd have died and gone to heaven. But she wasn't either of those, so staring at a complete stranger's breasts while standing behind the counter at her sister's coffee shop, no matter how "firm and uplifted" the breasts in question now were, was making her a little uncomfortable. The fact that the breasts belonged to one of her sister's best friends and that the coffee shop was closed should have put her at ease. But it didn't. For one thing, her sister Frida seemed to have a lot of "best friends," and second, the Bistro by the Beach had these large plate-glass windows that any passerby could easily look into.

She mentally shrugged. Maybe they did things differently here in Whispering Bay, Florida. After all, it *was* a beach town.

"They're so perky!" Frida crooned, nudging Georgia on with a roll of her eyes. This must be Georgia's cue to say something.

"Yeah, totally awesome," Georgia replied, hoping she sounded more enthusiastic than she felt. Since she'd never seen the boobs in question before the "firming and uplifting," she really couldn't make a fair comparison, but the petite, dark-haired owner of the now-fabulous tatas seemed pleased with her response. So did the two other "best friends" standing by her side.

"Thanks!" Pilar Diaz-Rothman gushed, carefully covering up the prized twins with a sturdy sports bra.

"Are they sore?" Frida asked.

"A little. But it was totally worth it. I finally have boobs that point north again."

"What does Nick think?" Frida asked.

"He's crazy about them, of course," interjected Shea Masterson, a tall, stunning redhead who appeared to have been the generous recipient of her own upper body surgery.

Pilar grinned. "He was a little freaked at first that I went through with it. But he's totally on board now."

"Nick is Pilar's husband," Kitty Burke, the last of the Charlie's Angels trio, explained. Kitty was tall, like Shea, and while she lacked Shea's Heidi Klum–like model looks, or Pilar's more compact exoticness, she made up for it with a wholesome prettiness and a warm smile. Definitely the Drew Barrymore of the group.

"So, Georgia," Shea said, "you're coming to Bunco tonight. Right? Great outfit, by the way. Is that Alexander McQueen?"

Georgia blinked, not quite sure which question to respond to first.

"Don't mind Shea," Pilar said. "She has two little girls under the age of five so she's experienced at bi-processing."

"That's multitasking, but in your brain," explained Kitty, sensing Georgia's confusion. "Pilar likes to make up words to fit the occasion."

Boy, things sure were different down here in Whispering Bay. Maybe it was all that sodium floating in the air.

"You must really know your designers," Georgia said, pleased that Frida's friends had noticed her Alexander McQueen high-waisted navy silk trousers and matching top. Georgia took pride in her appearance. It was one of the things Spencer loved about her. She fought back a frown. She wasn't going to think about Spencer. Not now. Not for the entire weekend. Maybe not ever. "And I'm afraid I'm not sure about the Bunco thing."

Shea turned to Frida. "You didn't invite your sister to Bunco?"

"I didn't know my sister was coming to visit until she walked through the door ten minutes before you three did."

"I wanted to surprise you," Georgia said, trying not to squirm beneath her older sister's level gaze.

"Where are you from, Georgia?" asked Kitty.

Georgia hesitated. It was one of those generic questions people always asked one another. Despite years of practicing a pat answer it still sometimes took her off guard.

"You know, Georgia and I are from everywhere," Frida said, saving Georgia from responding.

"That's right!" Pilar said. "You guys were raised by hippies. That is *sooo* cool."

Groupies, not hippies, Georgia wanted to clarify. Although in her mother's case, there probably wasn't much difference between the two. Instead, she said, "I've lived in Birmingham for the past five years."

"Georgia's the chief financial officer for a major electronics company," Frida said proudly. "She graduated from Stanford."

"Impressive," said Pilar, giving Georgia a thumbs-up.

Georgia felt herself blush. "It's a small company and I'm really a glorified bean counter." Although, a damn good one she had to admit, even if it was just to herself.

"Moody Electronics is the Southeast's largest-growing company. Georgia was selected one of Birmingham's top ten businesswomen last year," said Frida. "Which explains why she never comes to visit me. She's too busy working."

Georgia ignored the dig.

Pilar sighed. "I know how that goes. I'm an ambulance chaser," she confided to Georgia. "Only I really don't chase ambulances. I read contracts all day. But for the past few years my life has revolved around billable hours."

"Not anymore," said Kitty. "You're cutting back at work, remember?"

"That's right," said Pilar, looking chastised. "I keep forgetting."

Kitty smiled at Georgia. "Are you on vacation?" Frida gazed at her expectantly.

"Sort of," Georgia said, hoping she wouldn't have to elaborate. "I'm here for a long weekend. All work and no play . . ." she added with a shrug.

"How's Spencer?" Frida asked. "Is he coming too?"

"He wanted to," Georgia said, having no other option now but to blatantly lie, "but he couldn't get away."

"Spencer is Georgia's boss," explained Frida. "He's also her fiancé."

"Congratulations!" said Shea. "When's the wedding?"

Georgia wondered the exact same thing. "Actually, we're not officially engaged yet."

Frida's brows scrunched together. "But I thought—"

"The timing's not right." Georgia gave Frida's friends what she knew was a shaky smile. But she couldn't help it. She'd always sucked at subterfuge. "Spencer has children from his previous marriage, and they're both at a very fragile age. We need to make sure they're in the right place first."

Her sister's friends went quiet.

"He's a wonderful father," Georgia rushed. "I wouldn't want it any other way."

"Well, you have to come to Bunco," Shea said. "It just so happens one of our regular members isn't going to make it, which means we need a substitute. Naturally, being Frida's sister, you get first dibs."

Kitty frowned. "What about Christy? Christy Pappas is number one on the sub list," she explained to Georgia. "Not that I don't want you to come, it's just that—"

"What Christy doesn't know won't hurt her. Besides, the three of us make the rules and I say family goes before the sub list," said Shea.

Pilar nodded. "Shea's right. Family comes first. You're just sensitive on account of you living with Christy's cousin-in-law," she said to Kitty.

"Kitty has a new boyfriend. A really *hot* new boyfriend," Frida supplied.

"Please, don't worry about it. I don't even know what Bunco is," said Georgia.

The Charlie's Angels trio looked flabbergasted.

Pilar was the first one to find her voice. "It's a dice game. A *really* fun dice game. We play every Thursday night. We're the Bunco Babes," she said, as if that explained everything.

"Actually, we're only part of the Babes," Shea said. "There's twelve of us all together. You have to have twelve to play Bunco. But the three of us are the founders. We make up the rules and we insist you come."

Come to think of it, maybe Frida had mentioned this Bunco thing a few times, but Georgia had never paid much attention. She'd hoped to spend some alone time with Frida tonight. Socializing with a bunch of giggly women wasn't Georgia's idea of a good time, but there appeared to be no graceful way out of it. And it would make Frida happy. "Sure, I'll come. Thanks."

"Great!" said Shea. "My house. Seven p.m. sharp."

"Shea makes these awesome frozen margaritas," said Kitty. "You'll love them!"

She watched as Frida said good-bye to her friends and locked the door to the Bistro behind them. Frida took off her work apron and tossed it into a laundry bin beneath the counter. It had been six months since Georgia had seen her sister, but Frida never seemed to change. She wore almost no makeup and let her curly auburn hair go natural. No blow-dryers or flat irons for her.

"What's really up?" Frida asked. "You look terrible."

"Gee, thanks."

"You know what I mean. Something's not right."

"How's business?" Georgia glanced around the small cafe. The gold-colored walls featured hand-painted murals of sea-scapes and mermaids. The wooden tables and chairs were scarred and each table had a vase with fresh-cut flowers from the outside garden. There was a smallish kitchen area behind the counter where the customers placed their orders. Frida served coffee, homemade bagels, muffins, and pastries. She opened at the crack of dawn and closed by eleven a.m. But Georgia knew that Frida's day started at four and didn't end until well after two p.m. when she finished cleaning and organizing her kitchen. Frida's insinuation that Georgia was a workaholic was like the pot calling the kettle black. Running a small-town cafe was a hard business, and from what Georgia could see, the payoff wasn't anything to brag about. But Frida seemed content.

"Business is business," said Frida. "Slow one week, crazy busy the next. It all depends on the weather and the tourists. Now answer my question. Why are you here?"

"I thought you'd be happy to see me."

"You know I am. And Ed's going to be thrilled. He loves when family comes to visit."

Ed Hampton was Frida's husband. He was an artist (as yet undiscovered), a fact Georgia found ironic considering her and Frida's upbringing. Ed helped out in the coffee shop during the morning and painted the rest of the day. He and Frida lived in a small apartment above the Bistro. Despite his lack of ambition, Georgia was fond of Ed. Although she couldn't help but think that Frida could have done better. They'd been married for twelve years and had no children. Georgia had never asked her sister about that. She'd always assumed it was by choice. "Speaking of Ed, where is he?"

"He went to see a potential client," Frida said, her voice turning enthusiastic. "There's a local restaurant that wants to feature Ed's paintings. This could be a terrific opportunity for him." She glanced at her watch and frowned. "I'm sup-posed to meet him so we can have an early dinner with the manager."

"Go on then. I know my way around upstairs. I'll just take a quick shower and unpack. I hope I'm not going to put you out," Georgia added. "I know your place isn't big."

"Of course you're not putting me out. You're my sister. You're always welcome. You know that."

"Thanks."

Frida studied Georgia's face. "You're sure there's nothing wrong?"

For a brief moment, Georgia thought about telling Frida everything. It had been a long time since they'd talked. About anything important, that is. But if she did, Frida would can-cel her dinner with Ed, and Georgia didn't want that. She put on a bright smile. "You're always bragging about how great Whispering Bay is. I thought I'd take you up on a few days of sun and fun."

"Okay, I'll buy that." Frida narrowed her eyes at her. "For now."

2

|||||

Georgia took a hot shower, unpacked her suitcase, then carefully folded her clothes into the empty bottom drawer of the pine armoire in the spare bedroom. The apartment consisted of a small living area, two bedrooms and a bath. There was also a large loft that Ed used as a studio. It was as big as the rest of the rooms combined and had a large window that overlooked the Gulf. Georgia didn't understand why Ed didn't use the spare bedroom to paint in. In her mind, the loft was the obvious choice for a living room.

It was almost five and Frida and Ed hadn't returned from their business dinner. It was too early to get dressed for this Bunco thing, plus there was the fact that it was hot in the apartment and she hadn't brought clothes to just hang out and sweat in. Frida and Ed kept the thermostat at seventy-eight. Frida had explained to her that keeping the thermostat at a moderate setting not only saved on the electric bill, it was environmentally correct. It felt warmer than seventy-eight, though. Maybe because the building was old, and then of course, there was the whole "hot air rises" principle. Georgia resisted the urge to reset the thermostat. When in Rome and all that.

She rummaged through Frida's drawers and found a pair of khaki shorts splattered with paint and an oversized T-shirt to wear. The T-shirt had a picture of a globe on it with blue lettering that read *Every Day Is Earth Day*. She was about to blow-dry her hair when her cell phone rang. She glanced at the number on the screen.

It was Spencer.

Maybe she shouldn't answer.

But that was childish. She was going to have to talk to him sooner or later. He was her boss as well as her boyfriend. She could ignore her boyfriend, but she couldn't ignore her boss.

Spencer Moody was the epitome of Georgia's perfect man. Tall, handsome, smart, and successful. He'd graduated from the University of Alabama, where his father had gone, and his father before him. He was blond, blue-eyed, dressed impeccably, and had a good ol' boy southern charm that never failed to win over clients. The first time he'd laid his deep, slow drawl on her, Georgia had been lost. Just hearing Spencer's voice gave her the shivers.

She hit the accept button on her phone and braced herself. "Hi," she answered coolly.

"Where are you? I just got to your place and found a note saying you were going out of town. What the hell's going on?"

Hmmm . . . no shivers today.

"Read the note, Spencer."

"This isn't like you, Georgia. We have a staff meeting in the morning, for God's sake."

"You can run the company for one day without me. Denise can fill in for me at the meeting." Denise was Georgia's assistant. She knew the Friday-morning drill almost as well as Georgia.

"It's two days. Not one."

"And your point is?"

"My point is that you just can't take off without telling me. I'm your boss, remember?"

"I told Crystal." Crystal was Spencer's secretary. She could be a little ditzy sometimes, but Georgia had trouble believing she wouldn't have given him the message.

"She didn't say you were going out of town."

"I haven't taken a vacation in the five years I've worked for you. I think I'm entitled to a couple of days off. But if you think differently, then maybe it's time I—"

"Now, babycakes, don't get all crazy on me. You know I would never begrudge you a few days off. Take a week. Hell, take two. Just don't scare me like this."

She hadn't thought that Spencer would worry about her. But then, after the scene last night, she hadn't been thinking period. "I'm sorry, you're right. I should have spoken to you."

"Where are you?"

"At my sister's place."

"You're in Florida?"

"I only have one sister, Spencer." *That I know of.*

"Why don't you join me?" she asked. It was impetuous, but maybe that's what they needed to shake up their relationship. She'd come down to Florida to think and regroup, but a romantic weekend getaway suddenly seemed like a good idea. Thinking was definitely overrated.

"I'd love to, sugar, but you know the kids and I have plans this weekend."

"Am I ever going to come first in your life?"

"This is exactly why our relationship hasn't gone to the next level. It's the same sort of emotional blackmail Big Leslie used to—"

"Do *not* compare me to your ex-wife."

"Okay, okay, you're right. I'm sorry. Is this about last night?"

She could hear her voice rising, but she couldn't help it. "Spencer, who gives their girlfriend a calculator for their five-year anniversary?"

"I admit the calculator was a mistake. But in my defense it *was* top of the line. I asked you what you wanted. Remember? You told me to surprise you."

"That's not the surprise I had in mind."

"I'm not ready for the kind of commitment you want from me. I'm sorry, but I'm just not. One of the things I love best about you, sugar, is your ability to see things logically. Look at it from my side."

Okay, she'd look at things logically. "You're forty years old. Do you think you can tell me when you *will* be ready?"

"This isn't because of that timetable thing you have, is it? Babycakes, you're young. There's plenty of time for you to pop out a kid."

"I'm thirty-two!"

"Exactly. You're an infant and you don't even know it. When I was thirty-two I was stuck in a loveless marriage. I have to be sure I don't make another mistake. There's Spencer Jr. and Little Leslie to think about."

"Your kids will adjust. Big Leslie remarried. They've adapted to that, haven't they?

"This selfish side of you is very unattractive, Georgia."

Selfish?

Before she could think of a response, a dull rapping noise caught her attention. After a few seconds, it went away.

Was it selfish to expect an engagement ring from the man she loved? Apparently, Spencer thought so. He thought she was being unreasonable. Georgia had always hated whiny, manipulative women. Maybe she'd acted too hastily. She'd stormed off like some petulant child instead of working their problems out like a mature, sensible adult.

Oh, God. What had she done?

"Georgia, are you still there?" he asked.

"Spencer, you're right. I'm—"

The rapping started up again. Only this time it was louder, making it impossible to carry on a conversation.

"Hold on," she said into her cell.

She padded barefoot across the small living room to the top of the staircase. The noise was coming from downstairs. Someone must be knocking on the door to the Bistro. Maybe Frida and Ed had forgotten their key. Or maybe it was another of Frida's Bunco friends coming to show off their latest round with BOTOX.

She went down to investigate.

There was a man standing outside the glass door. He spotted her and waved.

It must be a customer. One who couldn't read. She pointed to the Closed sign hanging from the window.

"It'll just take a minute," he said loud enough for her to hear through the door.

Georgia thought about it. It couldn't hurt to open the door a tad. Just to see what he wanted.

On the other hand, the man was a complete stranger and she was all alone. He could be a killer. Or a robber. She could open the door and he could pull out a knife. Or a gun.

She took a closer look at him. He had scraggly brown hair and a soul patch beneath his bottom lip. Dark sunglasses hid his eyes. He wore board shorts and a T-shirt, like he'd just stepped off the beach. There were no telltale signs of a hidden weapon. No suspicious bulges anywhere she could see. But he was a big guy—not fat—but definitely muscular. He probably outweighed her by at least seventy pounds. It wouldn't take much for him to overpower her.

She shook her head. "Come back in the morning."

She started back upstairs, but he rapped on the door again. This time he used his fist.

What part of no didn't this guy understand?

She glanced through the window to the parking lot. There was a white pickup truck that hadn't been there before. On the side of the truck was a sign with the logo Hernandez Construction.

It would be pretty stupid of him to park a truck with a distinguishing sign like that in front of a place he was planning to rob. The Bistro was located on a busy street. Busy for Whispering Bay, that is. Too many potential witnesses would be able to identify that truck. She'd seen enough reruns of *Law and Order* to know how that went.

Besides, she still had her cell phone in her hand. If he made any suspicious moves, she could always call for help.

Her cell phone . . . She'd forgotten she had Spencer on hold. She put the phone to her ear. "Spencer?"

There was silence. *Crap*. He must have hung up.

She unbolted the door and inched it open. "Step back," she ordered.

He looked surprised by her command. "Hi, there. I'm missing my wallet," he said. "I thought maybe I left it here."

"Stay right where you are." She aimed her cell phone at him. "If you try anything funny, I'm dialing nine-one-one."

He grinned. "You're kidding, right?"

"I'm serious as a heart attack, buddy. Now step back."

He put his hands up in the air. "Whoa, calm down." He pointed to her cell phone. "You got a license for that thing?"

"You got a license for that joke?"

"*Wow*. Listen, I just want my wallet. You remember me, don't you? You served me coffee this morning."

She served him coffee?

She slammed the door shut and locked it as fast as her shaky fingers could turn the knob.

"Hey! What was that for?" he demanded.

"You're lying," she shouted. "I wasn't here this morning."

"Sure you were. Look, lady, I just want my wallet. I sat at the table next to the window looking out at the water. Will you check? Please," he added with a forced smile.

Georgia thought about walking away and leaving him there, but something in his voice made her reconsider. He didn't seem like a bad guy. Of course, appearances could be deceiving. Perhaps if she made an attempt to look for this wallet of his, he'd give up and go away.

She kept her phone in the air where he could see it and made her way to the back table, searching the floor and the surrounding area, but there was no sign of a wallet or anything else. It looked like Frida had scoured the place.

She walked back to the door. "Sorry. There's no wallet."

"Maybe one of your employees found it. Do you have a Lost and Found? I really need my wallet."

He was persistent. She'd give him that.

"Okay, I'll look again, but just so you know, I've seen *Silence of the Lambs* and I know how you guys operate. You make one move toward that door and I—"

"Yeah, I get it. You'll shoot me with your phone."

She ignored his sarcasm and pushed the speed-dial button to Frida's cell.

For a second, he looked alarmed. Then he crossed his arms over his chest and stared at her like he was daring her to call the police.

Frida picked up on the second ring. "What's up?"

"Sorry to interrupt your dinner, but there's a guy here who says he might have left his wallet this morning and—"

"I was hoping he'd come back for it. I found it while I was cleaning. It's under the counter."

"Oh. Well, how do I know it's the same guy? I mean, he could be an imposter or something."

Frida laughed. "Georgia, I think you've been living in the big city for too long. Tall, good-looking guy? Nice smile?"

Georgia studied him through the glass door. He was definitely tall. And maybe *some* people would consider him good looking. But he was too rough, too . . . macho looking for her taste. As for the nice smile part. That was an indisputable no. His smile was way too smug to be described as nice. According to her scale, that was only one out of three.

"I guess he *might* sort of fit that description. Okay, thanks."

She found the wallet where Frida said it would be and reluctantly unlocked the front door. He put his hand out to reach for it, but she shook her head. "Hold on. I'm not just handing this over to you until I know it's really yours."

"Why am I not surprised?" He sighed. "Go ahead and do your thing, Kojak."

"You don't have to get snippy about it."

She opened the worn brown leather wallet and looked inside to find a twenty-dollar bill and some ones. There were also a couple of credit cards, a Social Security card—

"This is a big mistake, carrying your Social Security card inside your wallet," she said. "You're just begging to be a victim of identity theft."

"So you admit it's my wallet?"

"Not so fast." She pulled out the driver's license. "This wallet belongs to a David Hernandez."

"That's me. Dave Hernandez." He pointed to the white pickup truck. "And that's my truck. See? My name's even on the side." He waved his hand impatiently. "Now hand it over."

She read the address. "You live in Tampa?"

"That's right."

She looked at the card again. *Safe Driver* was written at the bottom. "It says you're a safe driver."

"That's me, Mr. Safety."

"What does that mean exactly? That you've never been in an accident or that you've never gotten a ticket?"

"No accidents." Then he added, "That I know of."

Something in his tone made her pause. Was he making fun

of her? She continued to study the card. He was also an organ donor. Which was kind of nice, actually.

She mentally shook herself. *Focus, Georgia.* She scanned through the rest of the information. David Hernandez, six-two, brown hair, green eyes—

"Can you take off your sunglasses?"

She could tell he wanted to protest, but he whipped off his glasses anyway. "Satisfied?"

His eyes were definitely green. They contrasted dramatically against his olive complexion. Maybe he was kind of good-looking. On second thought, his eyes were almost too green. He probably wore colored contact lenses.

She read on.

Birth date, August 20. According to the year, he was now thirty-seven. "When's your birthday?"

"I had a birthday two days ago."

Okay. She'd admit it. The guy standing in front of her was the owner of the wallet. "Happy birthday," she said, feeling lame.

He smiled, and she instantly wished she hadn't asked him to take off the sunglasses. So maybe he *was* tall, good looking, *and* had a nice smile. But he was still too much of something she didn't like. Not that it mattered. She was a pre-engaged woman.

She handed Dave Hernandez his wallet. He shoved it into the back pocket of his board shorts. "Thanks."

"I'm sorry about giving you a hard time, but you can never be too careful."

"Are you always this suspicious?"

"It's just, the bit about seeing me here today. That's impossible, so I thought you were lying."

"Sure you were here today. Don't you remember me? I ordered a black coffee and a lemon poppy seed muffin. You told me you'd just run out so I got blueberry instead."

He thought she was Frida?

She crossed her arms over her chest. "That wasn't me."

"Then it must be your twin."

Her twin?

"That was my sister, Frida. But you must need glasses because the two of us don't look anything alike." They weren't even full-blooded sisters, but this guy didn't have to know that.

His gaze skimmed over her. "Same height, same blue eyes, same red hair—"

"My hair isn't red!"

"Sure it is."

"You must be color blind."

He looked amused. "What do you call it?"

"Brown."

"If it makes you happy," he said with a shrug.

"It doesn't make me *happy*, it's a fact."

"Whatever. I was just making an observation." Now that he had his wallet, she assumed he would leave, but he stood there, lingering. "So, I'm Dave," he said, expectantly.

"Oh, yeah, I'm Georgia. Georgia Meyer."

"Pretty name. Like the state?"

"No."

She didn't elaborate and he finally got the message. "Thanks again," he said, backing away from the door. "It would have been a bitch to replace all the stuff in my wallet."

She watched him get in his truck and drive off, then she locked the door and climbed the stairs to the apartment.

She tried calling Spencer back, but his cell went directly to voice mail.

Damn it. If it hadn't been for Dave Hernandez, maybe she and Spencer could have resolved their argument.

She glanced at herself in the bathroom mirror. Her hair had dried on its own and was doing some sort of weird curly thing. On a whim, she lifted a section off her shoulder and brought it up to the mirror under the bathroom light. Dave Hernandez was crazy. Her hair was brown.

Okay, she'd admit there was a subtle cinnamon hue to it, but only if you looked closely enough.

It most definitely wasn't red.

And she absolutely didn't look anything like her sister.

3

||||||

Georgia smoothed down the pleats on her cream-colored slacks. She wore a lime green sleeveless silk top and her matching-colored Manolo Blahnik satin buckled sandals. She'd managed to salvage the hair disaster by scrunching it up with styling gel. In contrast, Frida wore a jean skirt with frayed edges, a plain white T-shirt, and flip-flops. "Am I overdressed for this Bunco thing?" Georgia asked.

They were standing at the door of Shea Masterson's large Mediterranean-style ranch located just a couple of blocks from the ocean. A white Lincoln Navigator sat parked outside the three-car garage. There were two small pink bicycles and beach toys scattered inside. Georgia could hear laughter and music coming from the house.

Frida gave her a long sideways look. "You're not nervous, are you?"

"Should I be?" Maybe she *was* a teensy bit nervous. She'd

never done well with the "girl" thing. But it wasn't that big a deal. If she was acting jittery, it was because she hadn't been able to get back in touch with Spencer. She'd tried calling him again on his cell, and then at his home. But both times she'd gotten his voice mail.

"Don't worry! Everyone will love you." Frida grabbed her hand. "C'mon. We don't need to knock at Shea's house. Not on Bunco night."

They walked in through the foyer and into a spacious living room. A pair of expensive-looking leather couches made an L shape in the center of the room. There was a massive stone fireplace with a plasma-screen TV above it and lit candles on the mantel. Three wooden card tables were set up around the room with matching chairs. Each card table had three dice in the center and decorated name cards. She noticed her name was written in script on one of the cards.

Frida led her to the kitchen filled with women. Georgia recognized the three she had met earlier this afternoon.

Shea gave her a hug. Georgia felt awkward, but she hugged her back.

"I'm so glad you came!" Shea said, placing a frozen drink in Georgia's hand. "Here, take a sip and let me introduce you around."

Shea clapped loudly and the kitchen went to a semi-standstill. "Everyone! This is Frida's sister, Georgia. She's visiting from Birmingham and she's going to play with us tonight."

They all came up to her, one by one, welcoming her. There were too many names to remember (thank God for those name cards on the tables).

Georgia took a sip of her drink. It was a frozen margarita

but it had an extra bite to it. "Thank you for having me," she said to the group.

A woman with short dark hair whose name was Liz smiled at her. "How long are you going to be in town, Georgia?"

"Just for the weekend."

"Too bad you can't stay till Labor Day," said Shea.

"That's when our Black Tie Bunco Bash is taking place," Kitty said.

"Black Tie Bunco?"

"It was all Shea's idea," said Pilar. "She's a genius."

"It's a long story," began Frida, "but basically, the town's senior center is being torn down by this evil land baron, Ted Ferguson—"

A few of the Babes began to hiss.

Georgia froze in shock. Ted Ferguson, evil land baron? Georgia had never met Ted in person, but she'd spoken to him on the phone numerous times. He was a personal friend and old fraternity brother of Spencer's. And thanks to Georgia's financial advice, as of two months ago, a business associate as well.

"Anyway," said Frida, not noticing Georgia's reaction to Ted's name, "the Gray Flamingos, that's our local senior citizen watch group, in partnership with us, the Bunco Babes"—she waved a hand around the room—"are heading up a committee to raise funds for the town's new recreation center."

"Black Tie Bunco is the big kickoff," said Pilar. "It's going to be great. There'll be lots of food, drinks, dancing, and of course, Bunco. It's all for charity and we've already sold more than two hundred tickets."

"That's wonderful," said Georgia, not knowing what else

to say. She took a gulp of her drink. Getting through tonight was going to require large quantities of alcohol. "I'm sorry I'm going to miss it."

A large man and two little girls walked into the kitchen. Both girls had strawberry blonde hair pulled back in pigtails tied with green ribbons and wore identical pinstripe sundresses.

Shea introduced Georgia. "This is my husband, Moose, and my two munchkins, Casey and Briana."

Moose? Georgia tried not to stare. But she could see how he got his name. The guy looked like a linebacker on steroids.

"I'm taking my babies out of the corruption zone," Moose said to his wife, but the announcement had obviously been for the Babes' benefit. It produced the excepted giggles from the crowd. "We'll be back by ten." He lifted the smaller of the girls up and took the other one by the hand. "You ladies have fun!" he shouted on his way out the door.

Georgia couldn't help but feel a rush of envy. A beautiful home, a devoted husband, two sweet little girls. What more could a woman want? She took another swig of her margarita. If only she was patient enough, she'd have it too.

"That Moose is one terrific father," said Tina Navarone, a woman with shoulder-length brown hair and glasses. "I wish Brett would take more time with the kids."

"How's Brett doing?" asked another of the women.

"He's doing great," Tina replied, crossing her fingers in the air. "No sliding backward."

"Brett is Tina's husband and he's a compulsive gambler," Frida explained to Georgia. "But it's all under control. He goes to weekly meetings of Gamblers Anonymous."

Georgia tried not to appear shocked.

"Oh, it's okay," Tina said seeing her reaction. "All the Babes know. We know everything about each other, don't we?"

"Almost everything," Pilar said, catching Shea's eye.

This created another round of laughter.

Georgia downed the rest of her drink. It was worse than she imagined. She just didn't get it. The inside jokes. The sorority mentality. Didn't these women have better things to do on their Thursday nights?

She thought about the way she spent her own Thursday nights. She worked till six, then she'd go by the gym for her one-hour workout. On the way home, she'd pick up dinner, take a long relaxing bath, and wait for Spencer. Thursday was Cub Scout night with Spencer Jr. and he usually couldn't get away before nine. Once Spencer arrived, they would have a glass of wine together and go over the agenda for the Friday-morning staff meeting. Sometimes Spencer would spend the night, but most nights he'd head back to his place by eleven. She'd spend the next hour reading the *Wall Street Journal*, or catching up on work she'd brought home. Lights out by midnight.

It might seem boring to most people, but not to Georgia. She enjoyed making Moody Electronics the financial success it was today. She had everything she'd ever hoped for as a little girl. A great job, a high six-figure income, a beautiful wardrobe. The only thing missing was the big brick house on top of the hill with a husband and a couple of kids inside.

Kitty slipped another margarita in Georgia's hand.

Just in time, she thought. Georgia drank down half of it. "What's in this?" she asked Shea. "It's delicious."

Shea smiled mysteriously.

"No one knows," said Frida.

"That's why they're called Shea's Secret Frozen Margaritas," said Brenda, a mid-thirtyish woman with chin-length blonde hair who blinked a lot.

Tina giggled. "Brenda, are you drunk?"

"Of course not!" protested Brenda. "I've only had two of these."

"Crap," muttered Shea, her head stuck inside a kitchen cabinet. "I'm out of tequila!"

"Does that mean tequila is one of the ingredients in your secret frozen margaritas?" asked Mimi Grant, a pretty brunette.

"Well, duh," said Pilar. "Did you think it wasn't?"

"I don't understand," continued Shea. "There were two bottles of tequila here this afternoon." She narrowed her eyes. "Damn it! I knew I should have checked her luggage!"

"Whose luggage?" asked Frida.

"Persephone, the nanny I fired two hours ago."

"When did you get a nanny?" asked Tina.

Brenda blinked. "You had a nanny named Persephone? How did we miss this?"

"She only lasted three days," said Shea, looking mournful. "She had excellent recommendations and she interviewed great, but deep down my gut was telling me something was wrong, so I checked my nanny cam and caught her drinking a Corona from Moose's hunting stash. I had to let her go immediately, of course."

"No good can ever come from those nanny cams," said Brenda. "I saw a whole show about them on *Dr. Phil*."

"What are you going to do now?" asked Pilar.

"I don't know, maybe try to see if I can get someone through an agency—"

"No, I mean about the tequila. How are you going to make more margaritas without tequila?"

"I hadn't thought about that yet."

"One of us could make a liquor run," said Tina.

"We've all had at least two margaritas," Shea said. "So maybe we shouldn't drive for a while. Plus, it's after seven and Cooper's Liquor Store is closed, which means we'd have to drive into Destin." She glanced at her watch. "I guess I could give Moose a call and get him to bring us some."

"But Moose has the girls. We don't want to interrupt his daddy time," said Pilar.

"I could call Steve," offered Kitty. "He'd be glad to bring us some tequila."

"Steve is the hottie we were talking about this afternoon," Frida explained to Georgia. "He's Kitty's new boyfriend."

"His company is going to build the new rec center we told you about," said Pilar.

"That's nice," muttered Georgia. She took another big sip of her drink.

"I'll go call him," Kitty said, slipping out of the kitchen. She came back a few minutes later. "Steve is out with a friend eating dinner. He says he can come by in about an hour."

Shea looked disappointed. So did the rest of the Babes.

"Sorry," said Kitty. "He was bummed he couldn't help right away, but he really owes this guy. Plus, it's sort of a business dinner."

"Can't you substitute something else for the tequila? How about this?" Pilar held up a bottle of clear liquid. "I found this in Moose's hunting trunk."

Kitty frowned. "Moose keeps booze in his hunting trunk?"

"And you searched through it?" Frida asked.

"Desperate times call for desperate measures," Pilar said. "Besides, if it's good enough for Persephone, it's good enough for us. Right, girls?"

The Babes nodded.

Shea studied the bottle. "This is Moose's moonshine. He thinks I don't know he keeps a bottle of it out in the garage. Just for when he goes quail hunting, of course. Good thing Persephone didn't find it."

"You really should get him to lock this stuff up," said Kitty. "You wouldn't want the kids to accidentally get into it."

"I say we use it," said Pilar.

"I can't just put any old liquor in my margaritas," said Shea. "It would alter the taste too much." She unscrewed the bottle and took a whiff. "Huh. It doesn't smell like anything." She poured a small amount out into a cup and took a sip. "It's kind of strong, but I don't think it will ruin the taste of my margaritas. I guess it wouldn't hurt to make a couple of batches with this. Just until Steve shows up with the tequila.

4

Dear God. What was Frida saying? Georgia had heard more gossip in the past hour than she had her entire life. Whispering Bay might be tiny, but it had nothing over Pine Valley or whatever that soap opera town was called.

"Georgia," her sister repeated in what seemed like slow motion. "We're rolling for fives. Remember?"

"Fives. Got it," Georgia said, sliding into the foldout chair. She stubbed her toe on the edge of the metal leg. Where were her Manolos? Oh, yeah, she'd kicked her sandals off a couple of games ago. With all this getting up and down and switching tables she'd been afraid she was going to twist her ankle in the four-inch heels.

"So guess what I heard?" said Liz, her words slightly slurred. "Christy Pappas is going to start her own Bunco group. Right here in Whispering Bay."

"Where did you hear that?" asked Tina.

"From Bettina Bailey. She's going to be in the group. And . . ." She paused dramatically. "They're going to play on Thursday nights. Just like us."

Shea moaned.

"Bettina is Shea's neighbor," Frida told Georgia. "She's hated Shea ever since Shea beat her out for homecoming queen."

Homecoming queen? Wasn't that back in high school? Georgia stared down at her glass. It was empty. Pilar came around with a fresh pitcher. Georgia gratefully held her glass out for a refill.

"Her husband, Bruce, is vice president of the bank and on the city council," added Kitty. "He's a real pompous know-it-all." She hiccupped, then giggled.

"Bettina probably strong-armed Christy into it," said Pilar. "I mean, Christy is sweet and all but she'd never have the gumption to start a group on her own. Besides, she's always wanted to be a Babe!"

"Yeah, but none of us is quitting and most weeks we don't need a sub," said Tina. "I guess I really can't blame her."

Frida shifted in her seat. "It's not that we don't like Christy," she explained to Georgia. "But she's not part of our original group, and like Tina said, no one is about to quit, so she's sort of doomed to being a sub forever."

"Is there something wrong with her starting another group?" Georgia asked. No one seemed to hear her question, or deem it worthy of being answered. She took a sip of the limey margarita. It wasn't nearly as good as the first four or five batches Shea had made—four or five batches? How many of these had she had? Oh, well, she took another long sip. It was definitely drinkable.

Brenda snickered. "I thought Christy had more self-esteem. I mean, how good could this group be? They're basically Bunco-Babe-wannabes. It's sad, really."

The group murmured in agreement. Shea passed another round of margaritas through the room.

"Bettina Bailey is so jealous she can't stand it," Brenda said. "Ever since Kitty showed Bruce up at the town meeting last month she's been after blood."

"Do you think they'll find ten other women who want to play?" asked Frida.

"Oh, yeah," said Pilar. "Everyone wants to play Bunco. But not everyone can be a Babe. Too bad for them."

The group laughed.

Georgia's head began to throb. "Are we still playing?" she asked.

"This is what's called a gossip break," said Pilar. She frowned and stared at her glass. "Hey! Who drank the rest of my margarita?"

"You did," said Kitty, still hiccupping.

"I say we take another kind of break," said Shea, her blue eyes twinkling. Or were they glazed?

"What kind of break?" asked Liz.

Shea began to giggle. "I say we try to convince Pilar to show us the goods. Her new six-thousand-dollar goods!"

Much laughter and clapping ensued.

"Did you really do it?" asked Brenda, wide-eyed.

"Yup!" said Pilar. She stood and unbuttoned the first three buttons on her cotton shirt, then raised the tube top bra up to expose her breasts. "They're a little swollen still, but I love 'em," she added, her voice turning husky with emotion. Georgia could have sworn she saw tears in Pilar's eyes, as well.

"They're beautiful!" exclaimed Mimi. "Who did them?"

"The same guy who did Shea's three years ago. He also did Bettina's boobs and her tummy tuck after she had the twins. She denies it, but there isn't any part of her that hasn't been nipped, tucked, or sucked."

"Man, I wish I could get my boobs lifted," said Mimi. "Breastfeeding did a number on them. But we really need a new roof on the house and Zeke wouldn't go for it anyway. He's such a tightwad."

"But he's a cute tightwad," another Babe who Georgia thought was named Lorraine pointed out.

"Roof, schmoof," said Pilar. "What's more important? Your boobs or a few leaky tiles? Zeke Grant needs to get his priorities straight."

"I've been thinking about getting mine done too," admitted Brenda. "But I want them rounder, not bigger. Do you think he can make them rounder?"

"We can't know until we see 'em," said Pilar.

Brenda looked startled. "You want to see my boobs?"

"Why not? I've just shown you mine."

"*Bren-da, Bren-da . . .*" the Babes began to shout.

Brenda laughed. "Oh, all right. What's a quick peek among friends?" She lifted her shirt and flashed them.

After that all hell broke loose. Everyone was flashing. It was a blur of nipples and pale-colored flesh. There were big boobs, little boobs, somewhere-in-the middle boobs. Sort of like an R-rated version of Dr. Seuss.

"You're next, Georgia!" someone shouted.

Next for what?

"Oh, no, I couldn't," she said, realizing what they wanted.

"Someone get Georgia another margarita!" cried Kitty.

Another margarita? How many had she had?

"No, no, really, I can't . . . can't have another drop," she heard herself slur. Georgia wasn't drunk. She couldn't be. She never got drunk. It was too . . . undignified. At least she didn't think she was drunk. But then drunk people didn't realize they were drunk at the time, did they? She was definitely tipsy though. Very tipsy. No more margaritas for her tonight. Maybe not ever.

"If you won't flash your boobs, then tell us why you dropped everything and came down to visit," said Frida. *"The real reason."*

Damn it. Frida was clever. It was either flash the twins or play twenty questions with her sister. Her head was throbbing now.

Or was it spinning?

She should wait until they were alone. She really didn't want to blab about her personal life in front of a bunch of strangers.

"Okay, I came down here because I'm mad at Spencer."

Shit. Why had she said that?

"Who's Spencer?" someone asked.

"Georgia's fiancé, only he isn't really her fiancé yet. Right?" said Pilar.

"Right." She glanced around the room. All eyes were on her. Waiting for her to tell the story. She supposed it couldn't hurt to tell them just a little. "We were celebrating our five-year anniversary last night at this French restaurant where we had our first date. It was really romantic. And I thought . . . I thought he was going to propose," Georgia admitted.

"And he didn't?" asked Liz, sounding breathless.

Georgia shook her head. "Instead of a ring, he gave me a

Texas Instruments calculator." Surprisingly, it felt good to finally say it out loud.

Shea gasped. "He gave you a *calculator* for your anniversary?"

"Yup. But in his defense it *was* top of the line."

"Creep."

"Bastard."

"Asshole."

Georgia nodded. She didn't know who had said all that, but she definitely agreed. One hundred percent.

"That's not the worst part. I was so angry, I lost it and gave Spencer an ultimatum," she continued, feeling emboldened to go on. "I told him to shit or get off the pot."

"Good for you!" shouted several of the Babes.

"What did he say?" asked Frida, looking worried.

Georgia eyed her margarita and thought about taking another sip. "He said he was constipated."

"Moron."

"Son of a bitch."

"Loser."

"Don't worry, honey, you can do better than this Spencer person," said Liz.

"Yeah," chimed in Kitty and Pilar.

Georgia had never spilled her guts like this before. It was actually quite . . . liberating. No wonder Frida liked these women so much. They were brilliant!

"The worst part is he's also my boss."

"Oh, no," said Tina. "That's not good."

"I know," said Georgia. "And there's even a more worst part." Was that even a sentence? She shrugged and continued. "He called me selfish on the phone."

Frida sucked in a big breath. "He said you were selfish?"

Georgia nodded miserably.

"You need to call him right now and quit," someone urged.

"That's right," said Pilar. "Fuck him *and* his job. You're a Stanford grad! You can get a job anywhere."

Pilar was right. Georgia had headhunters calling her all the time. What was she doing wasting her time at Moody Electronics?

"Where's my purse?" she demanded.

"Thatta girl!" cried Pilar.

Someone shoved her purse in her lap. She pulled out her cell phone and punched in number one, Spencer's speed-dial number.

This time he picked up. "I suppose you're calling to apologize," he said.

Apologize? Ha! "As a matter of fact," she began, then burped. "Oops, sorry, that was an accident. No, I'm not calling to apologize."

"Georgia, are you drunk?"

"No!"

"I think we should talk tomorrow."

"Too late for talk."

"You're obviously not in the right state of mind. Is it that time of the month? Because I have to say, I've never really believed in all that PMS crap as an excuse for—"

"Fuck you, Spencer."

There was a moment of dead silence. "What did you just say to me?"

"I said *fuck you*. Oh, and fuck your job too because I quit!"

She didn't know if he responded or not, because the cheering in the background was deafening. Someone pulled the phone out of her hands. The Babes were now chanting her name. "Geor-gia! Geor-gia!"

Oh, hell. Why not? She turned to her sister. "I'll flash if you'll flash."

Frida laughed. "You're on."

Frida went first. Up went the white T-shirt and off came the bra. Georgia hesitated only a second. She clumsily worked the buttons to her silk top. One of the buttons popped off and fell on the floor but she didn't care. She'd worry about finding it later.

She snapped open the clasp to the front of her bra and flashed the room. "Take that, Spencer Moody!" she cried.

The Babes were laughing so hard, a couple of them fell out of their chairs.

A noise from the foyer drew her attention.

She glanced over to see a tall, brown-haired man with green eyes staring straight at her. Or rather, staring straight at her boobs. His gaze slid to Frida, then back to her.

"You're right," Dave Hernandez said, breaking out into that same damn smile he'd given her just a few hours ago. "You and your sister look nothing alike."

5

|||||

"Oh my God!" someone shrieked. Was that her? It couldn't be. She never shrieked. But she did scramble to cover her breasts with her hands. "What are *you* doing here?" she demanded.

"Bringing liquor reinforcements," Dave said, "but I think we're a little late, huh, Pappas?" He nudged the man next to him.

That's when Georgia noticed he hadn't arrived alone. Great. She hadn't just flashed a complete stranger. She'd flashed two complete strangers. The other man was a little taller than Dave, with dark hair and dark eyes. The sardonic expression on his face gave nothing away.

Frida already had her shirt back in place. She didn't seem nearly as upset as Georgia thought she should. Georgia pulled the edges of her silk top together trying to keep her breasts covered as she discreetly clasped her bra, but the damn thing was a lot easier to undo than hook back up. Obviously, it must have been designed by a man.

The guy with Dave turned out to be Steve Pappas, the hot new boyfriend of Kitty's that Georgia had heard so much about. Despite the awkwardness of the situation, Georgia had to agree with the description.

"Everyone," Kitty said, in a loud voice that slurred, "This is Dave Hernandez, a good friend of Steve's."

Dave nodded to the group, but he never took his gaze off Georgia. She purposely ignored him as she began buttoning her blouse, but it wouldn't come together properly. Then she remembered about the popped button. She dropped to her hands and knees to search the floor, causing her stomach to do a nosedive.

Shit. She'd have to be careful to avoid any more sudden movements.

"Can I help?" a male voice asked.

She looked up to see Dave Hernandez leering down at her.

"I'm looking for a button."

He gave the floor a quick perusal. "Just buy another one and sew it on."

Georgia narrowed her eyes at him. "For your information this is a three-hundred-dollar designer blouse, which means I can't just go 'buy' another button. And I don't sew."

"You paid three hundred bucks for a shirt?"

Georgia decided to ignore him.

He inspected the floor more thoroughly. "This what you're looking for?" He bent over and scooped up her missing button.

"Yes!" She carefully pocketed it. "Thanks." She waited for him to move on, but he just stood there.

"Are we looking for something else? Maybe some other article of clothing?"

"In your dreams," she muttered. Then, and only because she was so miserable she didn't care, she added, "I'm trying to figure out a way to stand up without making the room spin."

"Let me help you." He squatted next to her and placed an arm around her waist, then slowly helped her straighten.

Instead of letting go, he kept hold of her, like he was afraid she'd fall down or something. "You can go away now," she said, wiggling out of his reach. He seemed to find her statement funny. "Look, I'm just a little embarrassed, okay?"

"Embarrassed?" His smile deepened, causing two little grooves to pop out on the sides of his cheeks. "Darlin', I've seen a fair share of breasts in my day, and believe me, you have nothing to be ashamed of."

"I didn't say I was ashamed!" she said hotly. "But it just so happens that I'm a pre-engaged woman."

"Pre-engaged? Is that like being promised? Like in high school?" The laughter in his voice made her want to hit him.

She glared at him instead. "At least I *was* pre-engaged. I just called Spencer—that's my boyfriend—and told him to fuck off. Do you think that will make a difference?"

His brows shot up. "I'd say, yeah, the pre-engagement is definitely off."

"Whatever," she said miserably. "You should have knocked before you came barging in."

"We did knock," he said. "For like five minutes. We only

came in because we heard screaming." He lowered his voice to a conspiratorial whisper. "I've seen *Silence of the Lambs* and I know how those guys operate."

"Ha-ha. I guess you think you're funny. Just because you're Mr. Experience when it comes to women's breasts doesn't mean I'm any less embarrassed to know I've just flashed them to a virtual stranger."

"I didn't mean to imply I was that experienced," Dave said, suddenly looking sheepish. "I grew up with five sisters and only two bathrooms in the house. That sort of gave me a leg up on most guys, you know?"

Before she could respond, Shea clapped her hands together to make an announcement. "I don't feel so good. Maybe we should call it a night. But I don't think anyone should drive home."

"I think we should call our husbands to come get us," said Brenda, looking dazed.

Women began scattering for their purses, looking for their cell phones.

Frida snapped her phone shut. "Ed isn't picking up," she told Georgia. "He must be painting. He never pays attention to anything else when he's in his creative mode."

"I'll be happy to give you a lift," Dave volunteered.

"You wouldn't mind?" Frida asked, her eyes looking kind of slitty. When had Frida started looking like a cat?

"I don't think that's a good idea," said Georgia.

"Why not? I'm a safe driver, remember?" He smiled. Georgia supposed that was for her benefit.

She gave him a snarky smile back.

"I would appreciate a ride," said Frida. "I don't feel so good right now, either."

Dave pointed to Georgia's bare feet. "I hate to ask, but I assume you came here wearing shoes."

She put her hand up to her forehead. "I know you think you're being totally funny and charming, but I really don't feel up to this."

"Sorry." He looked genuinely contrite, although it could have been an act. Either way Georgia didn't care. She just wanted a big glass of water and her bed. "What kind of shoes are we looking for?" he asked.

"Lime green sandals," she said, not bothering to elaborate on the description. Dave had probably never even heard of Manolo Blahnik.

She spied one of her sandals poking out beneath a card table. "I found one!" she yelled triumphantly, then instantly wished she hadn't raised her voice. It only intensified the throbbing in her head. She carefully bent over to scoop it off the floor.

Dave studied the sandal in her hand, then poked around beneath the tables and folding chairs to produce its twin. "Now these," he said, handing her the lime green silver-buckled sandal, "I can see paying seven hundred bucks for."

Georgia blinked. "Two hundred and ninety-five on eBay, only used once by the original owner."

He nodded. "Good deal." Which left her both pleased and a little speechless. Even Spencer couldn't tell the difference between a pair of Manolos and a cheap knockoff.

"And," she whispered, "I didn't pay three hundred dollars for this blouse either. I bought it at a consignment shop for forty bucks. Actually, I buy all my clothes either on consignment or on eBay. But don't tell Spencer."

Dave grinned.

Frida said her good-byes while Georgia made a point of seeking Shea out and thanking her. Tipsy or not, it was the polite thing to do.

They climbed into the front cab of Dave's truck. It was a short, quiet ride back to the Bistro. Frida wanted to sit by the window so she could roll it down and stick her head out, which forced Georgia to sit in the middle, next to Dave. She couldn't help but discreetly check him out. He wore khaki pants and a black short-sleeved polo shirt. He kept one hand on the steering wheel and the other on the stick shift. Her gaze kept drifting to the big silver watch around his wrist and to the muscles on his forearm and how they flexed a little whenever he shifted gears. The front cab wasn't overly spacious, so every once in a while Dave's arm would accidentally brush against her leg.

Georgia suddenly felt dizzy. She redirected the air-conditioning vent to hit her in the face.

He shot her a sideways glance. "You okay?"

"I'm fine," she insisted.

Dave parked his truck in the same spot it had been in this afternoon. He jumped out and opened the truck door for her and Frida, but it didn't impress Georgia. If he was trying to make up for gawking at her breasts, he was going to have to do a lot better than that.

Frida unlocked the front door to the Bistro. She threw her purse on top of the counter like it was too heavy to carry. "Thanks for the ride. Come by any time for free coffee," she mumbled dragging herself up the stairs.

Georgia was about to follow her, but before she knew it, Dave took her by the hand, pulled her against him, and kissed her.

6

She placed her hands against his chest to push him away, but the feel of hard muscle beneath his shirt brought back the dizzy rush she'd felt earlier in the truck. His bottom lip tugged gently, coaxing her to respond. Somewhere in the back of her mind she told herself to put a firm end to it. But it was just a kiss. And if Georgia were being honest, it felt sort of nice. Like being in a dream. What harm could one dreamy kiss do?

Even with her heels on, she had to stand on tiptoe to wrap her arms around his neck. She thought her enthusiastic reaction would push him into using some tongue, but it didn't. He kept it light. Just his lips over hers, the way she'd kissed in junior high—before she knew what French kissing was.

Only no eighth-grade boy had ever kissed her like this— soft and achingly slow. The tiny patch of hair beneath his lip tickled her skin. It wasn't scratchy or irritating like she'd imagined it would be.

That last thought almost made her pull away.

When had she thought of kissing Dave Hernandez?

She drew him closer.

Forget her subconscious.

Forget the eighth-grade-boy analogy.

No one had ever kissed her like *this*.

Not even Spencer, the love of her life.

Spencer.

She'd forgotten all about him!

What was she doing? She was kissing a virtual stranger! Of course, Dave had seen her breasts, so they weren't complete strangers, but still—she jerked away and broke off the kiss.

She realized about two seconds too late that she shouldn't have done that. Because her stomach didn't react well to the sudden movement. And that's when it happened.

Georgia puked all over the floor.

"Whoa!" Dave jumped back in time to avert being christened.

"Oh, God," Georgia muttered. She placed her hands on her knees and bent over, taking in large gulps of air. "I can't believe I did that. I've never done that before. I'm . . . I'm sorry." She gratefully felt him slide a chair behind her.

Dave found a glass behind the counter and filled it with tap water. "Drink this."

"Thanks." She gulped down some of the water.

"Better?"

"A little," she lied.

He threw some dishrags over the mess on the floor. She

watched, cringing, out of the corner of her eye as he cleaned it up. He tossed the rags into the kitchen sink and opened the faucet to rinse them out.

Her head wasn't spinning anymore. It was pounding. Like a blacksmith with a hammer. An evil, demented blacksmith. She thought this last part in Austin Powers speak, making her giggle. At least it kept her mind off her stomach, which surprisingly felt better now.

"Thanks for taking care of that," she said with a weak wave of her hand over the floor.

"I don't think I've ever gotten that reaction from a kiss."

"You deserved it. I'm drunk. At least, I think I'm drunk."

"I didn't think you were *that* drunk."

She cradled her head in her hands. "I don't know what was in those top-secret double-oh-seven margaritas, but I'm never going near one again."

"If you want, I could make you my grandmother's hang-over recipe," he said. "It's sort of a hodgepodge of stuff—fried eggs, sausage, bread, tomatoes—"

Georgia cut him off with a moan. So much for her stomach feeling better.

He grinned. "Maybe not."

Why had she drunk so much tonight?

She desperately tried to recall her exact conversation with Spencer. The ramifications of tonight's impromptu phone call came crashing down. Spencer wouldn't throw away five years because of one little spat. Would he? Georgia had always prided herself on thinking pragmatically, but she'd never been in this sort of situation before.

She needed some advice. Now.

"You're a man, right?"

Dave quirked a brow up. "You want some proof?"

"No! Of course you're a man." She remembered the feel of his hard chest against her palms. She'd be lying if she said it wasn't a bit of a turn-on. But she didn't want to see any part of his anatomy. Hard or not. "Yes, most definitely you're a man."

"Now that we have that out of the way," he said dryly, "what's your point?"

She bit her bottom lip. What was she going to ask him? "Oh, yeah, I remember now. I need your thoughts on something. That is, if you don't mind?"

He slid into a chair across from her and stretched his long legs out, folding his arms over his chest. "I'm all yours."

Something about the way he said that made her pause. "Okay, well, let's say you're dating this woman. A really smart, somewhat attractive—"

"Very attractive."

"All right," she said, trying not to look too pleased, "very attractive woman for five years now—"

"I wouldn't date anyone for five years."

"Why not?"

"What's the point? I'd either marry her or move on."

"Oh." She thought about it a minute. Dave didn't know all the facts. "Let me start over. Let's say, you were married before." She narrowed her eyes at him. "Are you married?" Dear God, maybe she'd just kissed a married man.

"Not married."

That was a relief. "Divorced?"

"Nope."

"Okay, let's just *pretend* you were married and divorced and your ex-wife was the spawn of Satan."

"Is that your description or his?"

"His of course, I barely know Big Leslie."

"Big Leslie? What is she, an elephant?"

"Of course not! Big Leslie is very . . . well, she's very attractive and has a very nice figure. It's just that their children are both named after them."

"Let me guess. Spencer Jr. and Little Leslie?"

"Right!"

"I bet Big Spencer didn't think Big Leslie was so awful when he married her."

"How am I supposed to ask you my question when you keep interrupting me?"

"Sorry," he said. "Go on." Only he didn't look sorry. He looked like he was thoroughly enjoying himself.

"Where was I?"

"I was divorced and my ex was Satan's spawn."

"Oh, yeah. So you're divorced and very bitter toward marriage in general, because, you know, you had all your hopes and dreams shattered, and even though this terrific person who's smart, creative, and *very* attractive comes along, you can't commit because you're afraid of risking failure again. Plus, there's children involved."

"You and Spencer have children together?"

"Of course not! He and Big Leslie have children together."

"Just checking."

She downed the rest of the water. "And these children, while being very bright and well adjusted, are in somewhat of a fragile state."

"How long have Spencer and the Spawn been divorced?"

"Seven years."

"And the kids are still in a fragile state about it?"

"They're very sensitive children."

"Uh-huh."

Georgia sniffed. "Never mind. The situation is probably impossible for you to understand."

"Oh, I understand all right. This guy has his cake and he gets to eat it too."

"I don't know what you're talking about."

"How old are you?" Dave asked.

She had to think about that. "Thirty-two."

"I take it you and Big Spencer are on intimate terms?"

"We *have* been dating for five years."

"How old is this guy? Where'd you meet him?"

"Spencer is forty. And . . ." she hesitated, knowing what his reaction to this next part would be. But there was no avoiding it. She was the one asking Dave's opinion, after all. "And he's my boss."

"You're doing your boss?"

She scowled. "That's so crude. Spencer and I are in love."

He snorted. "If you're so much in love, then why did you kiss me?"

"I didn't kiss you! You kissed me. Besides, I'm drunk. I'm not responsible for my behavior."

"Bullshit. You're not that drunk or else you wouldn't be able to carry on a conversation. Besides, I've never done anything I didn't really want to do just because I'd had a few drinks."

He was right. She hadn't initiated the kiss, but she'd liked it. And if she hadn't thrown up, who knows where it might have ended? Suddenly the whole boob-flashing scene jiggled in front of her eyes.

She shook her head miserably. "Before you, I could count the number of guys who've seen my boobs on one hand." She placed her palm in the air, displaying five fingers. "Now I have to do double appendages." She held up her second hand to add a digit. "First," she said, wiggling a finger, "there was Andy Fulton. That was back in seventh grade, but that was an accident."

At the look on his face, she explained, "I jumped off the diving board at the YMCA pool and my bathing suit top fell off. He told everyone in school he got to second base with me, but I got even. The next day in front of everyone in the lunch room I kicked him in the shin."

"Nice."

She smiled at his compliment. "Then there was Luke Bonnerman. He was my high school sweetheart. But he didn't see my boobs by accident," she said, feeling herself flush. "That was definitely on purpose."

He grinned.

She held up a third finger. "Then in college I dated this guy named Carlos Gutierra. He was from Peru and was a dead ringer for Benjamin Bratt. Very sexy. Very—"

"Yeah, let's skip him."

"Then there's my postcollege boyfriend, Jerry, who wanted to marry me, but he was in law school and I was trying to establish my career, so the timing wasn't right."

Dave nodded.

"And last, there's Spencer. And of course, now you. Oh, and your friend Steve. Only you're both sort of like Andy. An accident. So that makes seven guys."

"I'm honored to be in the club."

She made a face. "Now you're making fun of me again."

"No, I'm not. They're probably the nicest set I've ever seen." He paused. "In person."

She glanced down at her chest. "They're a B cup. On the small-to-average size, really." She couldn't help adding, "But they are kind of perky."

"Oh, they're definitely perky."

"I've always thought they were my best feature. Body-wise, that is."

His face turned mock serious. "I'd have to do a more thorough inventory before I'd go that far, but it's a strong possibility."

She frowned. "We're way off topic here. We're supposed to be talking about Spencer." She leaned forward in her chair. "So, based on your experience as a man, what do you think the odds are that Spencer will propose?"

"You're like a dog with a bone, aren't you?"

"This is my life we're talking about!"

"Okay." He sighed. "The truth?"

"Of course."

"There's not a chance in hell Spencer's ever going to propose."

"Right." She flopped back in her seat. That's what she'd wanted, wasn't it? Dave's true opinion? Of course, just because he was a man didn't make him an authority on the subject. She never blindly accepted results without questioning the validity behind it. "Have you ever asked a woman to marry you?"

He narrowed his eyes at her. "What's that got to do with anything?"

"I'm questioning your qualifications to make an informed opinion."

"What are you? Some kind of statistics freak?"

"I'm an accountant."

"Figures."

"So have you ever asked a woman to marry you?" she persisted.

He twisted his mouth like he didn't want to answer. Finally, he said, "No, I've never asked a woman to marry me."

"But you've been in love before, right?" When he didn't answer right away, she hit her forehead with the butt of her palm. "I can't believe I'm asking personal advice from a relationship moron."

"I've been in love before," he said, sounding defensive.

"When? In high school?"

"None of your business. But regardless what you think of my 'qualifications,' I can tell you this on good authority. Spencer and I are probably more alike than I want to admit. When it comes down to it, most men all want the same thing."

She cringed. "Don't say it."

"I said *men*, not boys. We aren't all that different from you, you know. Most men want to get married and have a family too."

"Then why haven't you gotten married?"

"Because I've never met the right one."

"That's such a cliché. You know what 'I just haven't met the right one' means? It means you aren't really looking."

"You know what your problem is? You overanalyze everything. It's either going to happen or it's not."

"You're telling me the reason Spencer isn't going to marry me is because I'm not the right one?"

"I'm not sure what Spencer's problem is. Maybe it's as

simple as the fact that he's already had the marriage-and-family bit and it's not for him." He softened his tone. "Sorry, babe, but from a male point of view, that's the honest-to-God's truth."

Her shoulders slumped. Dave might not have an impressive relationship résumé, but he had a point. If Spencer really wanted to marry her, what was stopping him? She mentally shuddered to think what Dave would make of Spencer's calculator gift. "How'd you get to be so smart? About women and designer shoes?"

"I told you, I have five sisters. All married."

"No brothers?"

"Nope. But I have five brothers-in-law, six nieces, and eight nephews." There was a hint of pride in his voice when he said that. "How about you? Do you come from a big family?"

"As big as they come." He looked at her expectantly. "Frida and I were raised in a commune," she blurted.

He looked taken aback. "No kidding?"

Why had she told him that? She never told anyone that. Even Spencer was a little foggy about her background. She must be tipsier than she thought. "Believe me, it's not something I'd make up."

He didn't respond. Instead he looked like he was waiting for her to elaborate. She thought about changing the subject, the way she did whenever anyone probed into her background. On the other hand, she and Dave were practically on intimate terms. He'd seen her boobs. He knew about Spencer. And did it even matter? After tonight, she was probably never going to see him again.

"You've heard of music groupies?"

He nodded.

"Well, my mom was an art groupie. She painted some, but mostly, she liked guys who painted more. There were a bunch of us kids, all with different mothers and fathers. It was very free love, that kind of thing."

A flash of recognition lit his face. "So that's where you got your name. Georgia O'Keeffe."

"I was born during my mother's vagina stage. O'Keeffe did some pretty impressive abstracts on the female anatomy." She paused, but Dave didn't appear shocked, so she went on. "My mother worshipped the Goddess."

He didn't say anything.

"You know, the Divine Feminine Being, Mother Earth, all that," she said.

He nodded slowly. "Sounds interesting. Are you two close?"

"She died a few years ago. It's just Frida and me."

"What about your dad?"

She rolled her eyes. "I told you, it was a free-love sort of commune."

For the first time, he looked uncomfortable. Was it because he felt sorry for her? She didn't like that. "So who do you worship?" she asked him.

He frowned, like he didn't get it.

"We all worship something. Or someone," she prompted.

"I guess you could say I was raised to worship the Goddess too."

At first, she was a little startled, then she remembered his last name was Hispanic. Not too hard to put two and two together. "You must mean the Virgin Mary. I take it you're Catholic?"

"Yep. I come from a big Cuban-Irish clan, all Goddess and saint worshiping. Second-generation Cuban-American on my dad's side, third-generation Irish on my mom's." There was that hint of pride again. She could picture him now, surrounded by all those nieces and nephews, like some cozy scene from a TV sitcom family. A tiny part of her couldn't help but feel jealous.

"You really believe in all that organized religion stuff?"

"I believe there's a God and that when we die we go someplace better than here."

She shook her head. "It must make your mom crazy that you aren't married yet."

"Have you been talking to her?" He grinned. "Ten years ago my mom's dream was that I'd settle down and marry a nice Catholic girl. Five years ago, she just wanted me to marry a nice girl. I think right now, she'd settle on any girl. Nice or not."

Georgia laughed. Her head wasn't throbbing so much anymore.

"What about you?" he asked. "Who do you worship?"

She thought about it a minute. No one had ever asked her that before. "I believe in things that are real. Like marriage and having kids, but I think if you wait around for some imaginary soul mate to show up, then you're going to end up waiting forever. I think you have to make goals and find someone whose goals match your own, and if everything else works out in the relationship, then that's the person you should be with."

"So you think Spencer shares your goals?" His tone edged on the sarcastic.

"Absolutely. He's successful, driven, and for the most part

he knows what he wants. As for marriage, okay, I admit, he's still on the fence where that's concerned, but nobody's perfect. I've vested five years in this relationship and I'm not going down without a fight."

"Vested? It sounds like Spencer is some sort of pension plan."

"At least I'm doing something to make my life happen. What about you? How long are you going to wait around for Ms. Right to show up?"

"As long as it takes." He shrugged. "I'll know when it's right."

She wasn't sure how to respond to his candor. For the first time tonight, the conversation between them hit a lull. She thought about excusing herself, but she wasn't ready to say good-bye to him yet. She remembered from reading his driver's license that he lived in Tampa. "So what are you doing here in Whispering Bay?"

"I'm thinking of going back into business with an old friend. You met Kitty Burke, right?"

Drew Barrymore. Georgia nodded.

"Her boyfriend, Steve Pappas, and I used to own a construction business down in Tampa. He's opening up a company here and he wants me to come along for the ride."

"Is it a good opportunity?"

He hesitated. "It's a big risk, especially in this economy. Steve's not hurting financially, so he can afford to go out on a limb. Me, not so much."

"You're right. It doesn't sound too promising."

It looked like he was about to say something more, but instead he stood. "I should call it a night."

"Already?"

He glanced at his watch. "It's almost three."

"What? It can't be!" She grabbed his wrist and checked the time for herself. "Oh." She'd had no idea they'd been talking that long. "So, thanks for the ride."

"Anytime." He smiled and she was once again reminded of Frida's description of him. Tall. Nice-looking guy. Great smile. The kind of smile that made it all the way up to his eyes—

"Hey, do you wear contact lenses?" The question jumped from her mouth before she could stop it.

"No, why?"

She cleared her throat. "Just asking."

Okay, so Frida was right. Three out of three.

But he still wasn't her type.

Plus, she was in love with Spencer. Madly and deeply in love.

"Any more questions?" he asked.

She was about to respond no, when she thought of one. "What was the kiss for?" He looked surprised. "I mean, what was the purpose behind it?"

"You don't know what a kiss is for?"

"Of course I know what a kiss is for . . ." she stammered, feeling her face go hot. "Are you making fun of me again?"

"Sorry, you just make it so easy." He smiled ruefully. "Don't overanalyze it, Georgia. Sometimes, a kiss is just a kiss."

7

IIIIII

Sometimes a kiss is just a kiss.

Had she watched an old movie last night?

Georgia woke up to the smell of fresh coffee and a strange humming noise she couldn't place. She rolled over and eyed the alarm clock on the nightstand. It was almost ten.

Shit.

She'd missed the staff meeting.

In the five years she'd worked at Moody Electronics, she'd never once missed a managers' meeting. She sat up a little too quickly. Her head was throbbing and her mouth felt stuffed with cobwebs.

And that's when she remembered she wasn't in her two-bedroom town house in Birmingham's Red Mountain district. She was in Whispering Bay, Florida, in the tiny apartment above her sister's cafe, unemployed and most certainly *not* engaged.

Last night, she'd told Spencer to fuck off. And then she'd quit her job.

What had she done?

Why had she listened to Frida's friends?

Damn those Bunco Babes or whatever silly name they called themselves.

The rest of last night's memories came flooding back. Had she really kissed Dave Hernandez? And described her own boobs as perky? She moaned aloud. It was like some weird dream, only it wasn't. It had all happened. But Dave wasn't Humphrey Bogart and she sure as hell wasn't Ingrid Bergman.

She had to fix this. *Now.*

Spencer answered on the first ring. "I hope this isn't going to be a repeat of yesterday."

"I . . . I have no excuse for my behavior."

"Give me one reason I shouldn't fire you."

Fire her? She'd quit, hadn't she?

She bit back the tiny bit of pride that wanted to remind Spencer of that particular fact. Anyway, it was a moot point. The thing was she didn't want to stop working for Moody Electronics. She'd help build the company into what it was and she wasn't about to let a spat with Spencer ruin everything she'd worked so hard for.

"Please, let me explain. I was just so . . . so disappointed. I let our personal relationship interfere with our business one. I wasn't myself last night, but I am now."

There was silence. Silence was good, right? It meant he was at least willing to listen.

She went on. "I don't think one mistake should wipe out five years of hard work."

"You're right. But I have to say, Georgia, you shocked me yesterday."

Which part? The part where she'd quit or the part where she'd told him to fuck off? She figured now wasn't the time to ask.

Maybe the best offense was some defense. "I was a little shocked too. I really hadn't counted on getting a calculator for our five-year anniversary."

"Are we going to go through that again?"

"No," she answered quickly. "I understand. I tried to rush you into something you're not ready for. I get that." Somewhere in the back of her mind she could see Dave Hernandez shaking his head. She scowled. What did Dave Hernandez know about mature love?

"I'm glad to hear you're finally being reasonable about this."

She closed her eyes and took a deep breath. Yesterday, she'd had a hissy fit. No, she'd had worse than a hissy fit. She'd "showed out" as her mother used to say. And showing out had gotten her exactly nowhere. *Keep your eye on the prize, Georgia.*

"I've been thinking about something you said," Spencer continued, "about never taking a vacation. Maybe you should take a two-week hiatus."

A hiatus? It sounded more like a probationary period. Was Spencer trying to punish her?

She could feel the muscles on the side of her face twitch. "I don't think that's a good idea. Who would do my work?"

"Like you said, Denise can fill in for you. No one is in-dispensible, Georgia. Not even you. We'll do fine for a couple of weeks without you. It'll give you time to rethink your priorities."

Rethink her priorities? She didn't want to rethink anything. She already knew what she wanted. She wanted her job back. And to marry Spencer. She just had to find a way to make it happen.

She padded her way to the bathroom, brushed her teeth, and rinsed out her mouth. The dull humming noise was getting louder. It was coming from downstairs, from the Bistro. A stab of white-hot guilt speared through her. All she'd thought about this morning was herself. Frida had to be feeling as crappy as she did, at least physically. But no doubt Frida had been working since dawn.

Georgia raided Frida's closet again and found a spotless pair of khaki shorts and a plain white T-shirt. It was uncanny how they wore the same size. She splashed water on her face, braided her shoulder-length hair (still not red), and slid into her running shoes.

The place looked busy. Ed gave her a quick hug, then went back to filling an order. Ed had always reminded Georgia of that nerdy boy in class—the proverbial Napoleon Dynamite. His frizzy blond hair and tortoiseshell glasses aided the image. He was tall and gangly, had kind eyes, and spoke with a soft voice. You couldn't help but like Ed. Georgia just wished he was more ambitious.

Frida gave Georgia a morning-after sympathy smile, then resumed taking a customer order.

Georgia poured herself some coffee, then doctored it up with cream and artificial sweetener and took a big sip.

"What can I do to help?" she asked Ed, feeling semi-human again.

Ed nodded at an empty table cluttered with dishes. "You can bus that table."

Georgia had bussed enough tables in her lifetime to be able to do it in her sleep. She'd had a full scholarship to Stanford, but she'd still had to work through school for spending money. She found a damp rag and wiped down the table, then dumped the dirty coffee mugs into a large sink filled with warm, soapy water. The next thirty minutes went by quickly. She toasted bagels, cleaned tables, and refilled the toilet paper roll in the bathroom. By eleven they were officially closed and the last of the customers had gone. The tiny kitchen area was a mess and the sink overflowed with dirty dishes.

"You need to hire some help," Georgia said. "Or at the very least use paper products."

"It's not always this busy," Frida said. "Besides, we can't afford to hire anyone. And paper products are bad for the environment."

Georgia was about to respond when the door opened. "Morning," Dave said pleasantly. He wore navy blue shorts and a collared shirt with deck shoes.

"We're closed," Georgia blurted.

"Georgia!" Frida glared at her. "Don't be rude. I promised Dave free coffee anytime." She turned and smiled at him. "What would you like?"

"Just a black coffee. Don't worry," he said to Georgia. "I'll take it to go."

"Don't be silly," Frida said. "Stay as long as you want."

Georgia could feel her face turn red. Frida was right; she

was being rude. But she couldn't help herself. Dave Hernandez was the last person she wanted to see this morning.

Dave glanced between the sisters. "I'll still take it to go," he said.

"We don't do paper products here, so unless you have a to-go mug . . ." Frida shrugged, looking a little embarrassed. "I sell them, but I'm out right now." She handed Dave a large ceramic cup full of hot coffee.

"Thanks." He pulled out his wallet and handed her a couple of dollar bills. "And I'll pay for my coffee."

Frida began to protest, but Dave stopped her. "I plan to stop by a lot for coffee. I don't want to take advantage of your offer last night."

Frida reluctantly took the bills, then introduced Dave to Ed and the two men shook hands. Georgia was bent over a table wiping it down when she overheard Dave mention he had a tee time.

She jerked up. "You play golf?"

He took a sip of his coffee. "Anything wrong with that?" he asked mildly.

"It's just . . . you don't seem the type," she said, hearing the defensive tone in her voice. What was wrong with her?

The door opened again. This time the Charlie's Angels trio came strolling in. Pilar and Kitty looked as bleary-eyed as Georgia felt. Shea wore dark sunglasses that she didn't take off. After they exchanged greetings with Dave, they hugged both her and Frida (apparently hugging was the norm greeting in Whispering Bay) and proceeded to get their own coffee.

Didn't anyone in this town know the meaning of a Closed sign?

"We're having our weekly Friends of the Rec Center meeting," Frida explained to Georgia. "Want to sit in? We're finalizing plans for Black Tie Bunco."

Why not? She was on a two-week hiatus. It wasn't like she had anything better to do. "Sure."

"Too bad you won't be in town long enough to attend," Shea said.

"Actually, it looks like I'll be in town for a while," Georgia said, feeling Dave's gaze on her.

Kitty and Shea exchanged a guilty look. "That's right," said Kitty. "You quit your job last night. I'd forgotten about that."

"You're not having second thoughts, are you?" asked Pilar. "You're a Stanford grad. Remember that."

Georgia bit back a response. It wasn't fair to blame anyone for last night. No one had forced her to drink those margaritas. Or pick up the phone and drunk dial Spencer. Not really. "I talked to Spencer this morning. I still have my job for now. I'm going to take a two-week vacation and re-think my options." She couldn't stop the bitterness that seeped into her voice.

Frida's face tightened. "What options?"

Besides slit my wrists? "Don't worry," she said, putting on a bright smile. "I have no intention of leaving Moody Electronics. It'll work out. But right now, I think I'll hang out here—get a little sun. If that's okay with you."

"Of course it is," Frida said, still looking worried.

"Maybe I'll help out with this Black Tie Bunco thing. It sounds kind of fun," Georgia said.

Shea finally took off her sunglasses. "It *will* be fun. And we're thrilled to have you on board, Georgia. We can always use an extra set of hands." Georgia understood why Shea had kept the sunglasses on until now. She looked as bad as Kitty and Pilar. Her eyes were bloodshot and the skin beneath them puffy. It appeared everyone was paying the price for last night's antics.

Shea pulled a hot pink leather folio case and a pen from her bag and laid them on the table. "All we need is Viola and we can start our meeting."

As if on cue, an older woman with salt-and-pepper chin-length hair came strolling into the restaurant. She wore a bright orange T-shirt and a cream-colored cotton wraparound skirt with sandals. She had sparkly blue eyes and her cheeks were flushed. "Hello, girls! Sorry I'm late, but I had a yoga class in Destin."

"Viola is learning to become a yoga instructor," said Kitty, tossing the older woman a proud smile.

Frida introduced Georgia to Viola Pantini. "Besides being on the Friends of the Rec Center committee, Viola is also head of the Gray Flamingos."

"The what?"

"Don't you remember? We told you about them last night," Kitty said. "The Gray Flamingos are Whispering Bay's senior citizen watch group, sort of the like the Gray Panthers but without the mean animal association."

Viola smiled at Georgia and extended her hand. Her grip was warm and steady. "Of course you're Frida's sister! You could be twins."

Dave snickered. Georgia decided to ignore him. "Um, thanks," she said.

"Shall we start?" Viola asked, taking a chair next to Shea.

Shea sat up straight, her demeanor all business. "Black

Tie Bunco is our kickoff event, so it's important we set the right tone for the rest of the fund-raisers we have planned. We all know there are factions here in town that would like to see us fail. For their own personal, selfish reasons, of course," she added.

The group nodded.

Georgia frowned. Who wanted to see them fail?

"But that's not going to happen, because Black Tie Bunco is going to make a huge splash." Shea spread her hand through the air like she was reading some invisible marquee. "Think glamour, think Hollywood, think—"

A blonde woman carrying a small dog in her arms walked into the restaurant.

"Think about locking the door next time," Pilar muttered.

"Am I late?" the woman asked breathlessly. Then before anyone could answer, she looked at Frida and smiled. "Frida, be a doll and get me some coffee, will you? On second thought, make that a latte, skinny, one Splenda."

"Sorry, Bettina, I've already cleaned the latte machine," said Ed. "But I'd be happy to pour out the last of the coffee for you." Ed held up a pot with a few inches of what were obviously the dregs.

The woman wrinkled her nose. "No, thanks." The dog in her arms began to yip. "Quiet, Tofu," she cooed to the little white dog. It looked like a poodle, only not.

"Bettina, we're in the middle of a meeting," Shea said.

"The Friends of the Rec Center meeting, right? I'm here to represent the Bunco Bunnies."

8

||||||

How she could actually say Bunco Bunnies with a straight face was beyond Georgia. This must be the infamous Bettina Bailey she'd heard about last night. Bettina was average height and slender in her white tennis shorts and form-fitting fuchsia tank top. Her skin was tan and she wore sparkly sandals. Her toenail polish matched the color of her top. Georgia sneaked a peak at her breasts. If they were any perkier they'd hit her chin.

There was a moment of uncomfortable silence before Viola said, "The Bunco Bunnies?"

"That's the name of Bettina's new Bunco group," clarified Pilar.

"We had our first game last night at my house," Bettina said, taking the last empty chair at the table. She settled Tofu onto her lap. "And can I just brag a little and say that it was a *grand* success?"

"That's great," Kitty said, catching Pilar's gaze.

"So who's in your group?" asked Shea.

Tofu began whimpering and flailing her paws in the air. The dog's nails were painted the same color as Bettina's. "Let's see. Christy Pappas for one. She's so much fun! And Laura Barnes and Felicia Morgan—"

"Those are our subs," protested Shea.

"Sub-terfurger," Pilar muttered under her breath.

Kitty sighed. "That must be Pilar's word for someone who sneaks off with our subs," she whispered to Georgia.

Bettina must not have heard them because she smiled. "Exactly, and they were thrilled that someone in this town had the gumption to start another Bunco group. Surely you can't expect them to wait around forever until one of you Babes keel over—no offense meant. But girls just want to have fun, you know!"

Tofu started to bark. Bettina glanced at Georgia. "It's about time you hired some help, Frida." She plucked Tofu off her lap and tried to hand the wiggling pooch off to Georgia. "Be an angel and take her outside for me, will you? She needs to tinkle."

Georgia's eyes narrowed. Was this woman serious?

"I'll be happy to take care of your dog," interjected Dave. He'd been sitting on a stool by the kitchen counter and had been so quiet, Georgia had almost forgotten about him. He stood and held his hands out. Tofu practically leapt into his arms. "Hey, there," Dave said, stroking Tofu's fluffy head with his long fingers. "What kind of dog is this?"

"She's a shitzpoo," said Bettina. "It's a cross between a shih-tzu and a poodle." She looked Dave up and down, her brown eyes widening appreciatively. "And who are you?"

"Dave Hernandez," he said, introducing himself.

"Dave is an old friend of Steve's," said Kitty. "And this is Georgia, Frida's sister."

After a couple more seconds of gawking at Dave, Bettina turned her attention back to Georgia. "How sweet of Frida to hire her own sister!"

Georgia grit her teeth. "I don't work for—"

"Georgia's the chief financial officer of a very prominent electronics company in Birmingham," Kitty piped in.

"And she's a Stanford grad too," said Pilar.

Bettina didn't seem impressed. "That's nice." She turned her attention back to Dave. "Are you sure you can handle Tofu? She's pretty frisky." Bettina batted her eyelashes with this last part.

Dave caught Georgia's eye. "I can handle frisky." Was that supposed to be for her benefit? She ignored him. "C'mon, girl," he said, readjusting Tofu in his arms, "let's go take care of you."

Bettina waited till Dave walked out the front door to giggle. "He can take care of me anytime," she said, using her hand to fan her face. At the silence around the table, she straightened in her chair and sniffed. "If I wasn't married, of course."

"Bettina," Pilar began, "I think it's awfully *sweet* that you want to help, but we've pretty much got the whole Black Tie Bunco thing under control, so there's no need for you to spend your valuable time here."

"But I want to help! It's practically my civic duty. And since the event involves Bunco, as head of the Bunco Bunnies, I really insist on being a part of this."

"We're down to the wire, Bettina," explained Shea. "All

the preplanning and ordering has been done. Most of the work now will involve physical labor. Cleaning up the senior center, putting up decorations, that sort of thing. We're doing as much as we can ourselves to save money."

"Shea," Bettina said in a tone meant for a child, "I've been handling decorations since I was in the cradle. And don't forget, I *am* head of the Whispering Bay Beautification Committee."

"Exactly. You have so much going on! And now with Josh off to college, you don't have anyone to help you cart around the twins," said Shea. "Aren't you always complaining how much time you're in the car shuffling them to all their after-school activities?"

Bettina sighed wistfully. "I do miss my Josh. That's my oldest son," she clarified for Georgia's benefit. "He's a freshman at Florida. That's his daddy's alma mater." Her smile suddenly went coy. "I must have forgotten to tell you, Shea, I have a nanny to help me with the twins now. You even know her." She paused dramatically. "Persephone Hall?"

Shea went rigid. "You hired Persephone? Bettina, I have to warn you. I fired Persephone yesterday after I caught her drinking on the job."

"That's what she told me, but she explained it was all a big misunderstanding. Persephone doesn't drink alcohol of any kind. She's allergic to it. Plus, I checked out her references and they're impeccable."

"Allergic? Bettina," Shea ground out, "didn't you hear me? I caught her drinking beer from Moose's hunting stash."

"She thought it was a lime cooler. Really, Shea, haven't you heard of giving people the benefit of the doubt? Besides, the twins adore her, and so do I. She was up at the crack of

dawn doing laundry. Laundry!" Bettina laughed disbeliev-
ingly. "I told her it wasn't in her job description. That's what
I have Consuelo for, after all, but Persephone said she wanted
to help around the house too."

"And that doesn't strike you as a little suspicious?" Shea
asked.

Bettina sighed. "I'm glad I'm not as cynical as you. It's
really kind of unattractive, you know?"

Shea began to sputter.

"Maybe we should just get down to business," said Kitty.

"Good idea," Viola added quickly.

Kitty handed Bettina a sheet of paper. "So here's the
menu. I think we have all the details ironed out beautifully."

Bettina cocked up an eyebrow in surprise. "You're doing
the desserts?" she asked Frida.

"Frida makes wonderful cheesecakes," said Kitty. "All the
food is being donated. The Harbor House is catering the
main dishes, Frida is doing desserts, and the liquor is being
provided by Cooper's. We're using only local vendors. Of
course, the waitstaff will be paid, but there's no getting
around that."

"Uh-huh." Bettina looked unconvinced.

"Here's the decorating scheme," said Shea, unfolding a
floor plan of the senior center.

Bettina eyed the schematic and frowned. "There aren't
enough balloons. You can never have enough balloons. And
you need something big here," she said, indicating the top of
the diagram. "Something dramatic that will catch everyone's
attention. Like a stage."

"We don't have time for that," Viola said patiently.

"If I had been consulted in the beginning, then we would

have had time," Bettina said. "It's not just the locals coming, you know. Bruce has invited the entire board of directors from the bank, as well as prominent businessmen from all over the panhandle. And of course, Ted Ferguson and some of his business associates from down south will be attending. We can't look like a bunch of yahoos."

"We're not going to look like yahoos," Pilar said, her voice rising.

"And what's this big white blob?"

Georgia craned her neck to see what Bettina was pointing to.

"That's the tent," Shea said. "The main room in the senior center only holds around a hundred and fifty people, but we're expecting at least two hundred. The band and the food will be set up in the tent and the Bunco tables are going to be in the main room. When it's time for the video presentation, we'll have to shuffle everyone out into the tent."

Bettina frowned. "What video presentation?"

Dave walked back into the Bistro with Tofu in his arms. Bettina's demeanor instantly changed. "Did my little baby-waby go tee-tee?"

Dave looked perfectly serious as he said, "She sure did."

"Come here, baby," Bettina purred, reaching out for Tofu. But Tofu only snuggled deeper against Dave's chest. "Tofu, come back to Mommy," she ordered in a firm voice.

Tofu snarled and bared her teeth.

Bettina looked taken aback. "She's never reacted like this before."

Dave shrugged. "I don't mind holding her while you conduct your meeting."

Bettina looked more miffed than hurt by Tofu's rejection.

"Go on," she said, waving her hand in a general direction to the group. "What were you saying about a video presentation?"

"Shea has prepared a short video on the history of Whispering Bay and the senior center," said Kitty.

"It's sort of a montage-homage thing," Shea said. "It's really very good, even if I say so myself."

Bettina rolled her eyes. "So, not only are you *not* going to have a stage, you're going to bore everyone to tears with a piece from the History Channel?"

Georgia could feel her hackles rising. Who was this woman? And why did they all let her just walk in and take over like she was the friggin' queen of the world?

"Personally, I think a stage will look tacky," Georgia said.

Bettina narrowed her eyes at her. "What's your name again?"

"Georgia. Like the state." She purposely avoided Dave's direction.

"Well, Geor-gia, I'm not sure what kind of experience you've had with gala functions, but this sort of thing is right up my alley."

"I think we've already decided there isn't time to make a stage. And even if there were, the main room in the senior center is too small," said Viola.

Shea nodded. "That's why we have to set up the video presentation in the tent."

"That's another thing, Shea," Bettina said. "A tent? Whose big idea was that? It's still summer, for God's sake. Do you know how hot and humid it's going to be?"

Shea looked like she was nearing the end of her patience.

"There will be an evening breeze coming off the ocean. It won't be that bad, Bettina."

"This is supposed to be a classy affair. Not a hoedown. I, for one, have no intention of going out into a hot, bug-infested tent. My hair will go flat. And you two," she gave a little laugh and pointed to Frida and Georgia, "I'd hate to see what a little humidity will do to those mops of yours."

Georgia would love to solve Bettina's hair problem. By tearing it all out. Lock by lock. "Why don't we show the video inside then?" Georgia said, keeping her voice as neutral as she could.

"Didn't you hear what Shea said? We can't fit everyone inside. The main room is too small. Face it, girls, you haven't given this whole thing enough thought—"

"So make the room bigger. Just tear down a wall," Georgia said. Where that came from, she wasn't sure. But she loved the look her suggestion put on Bettina's face.

"Tear down a wall?" Bettina mimicked. "You can't just tear down a wall."

"Sure you can," Dave replied. He leaned over the table and studied the schematic for a few seconds, then readjusted Tofu so he had a free hand to point to the diagram. "This wall right here can come down."

"Won't, like, the whole building collapse?" Bettina asked.

Georgia could see Dave struggling not to smile. "If it's not a weight-bearing wall, then it'll be no problem, and if it is, all I have to do is build a few support beams."

Viola nodded enthusiastically. "That would work. And it really doesn't matter what we do with the building. It's going to be demolished in a couple of weeks anyway."

"Can you do that?" Bettina asked Dave. "I mean, *you* personally?"

"Sure. I do construction for a living. I could use another set of hands, though." Dave glanced at Georgia. "How about it?" he asked casually.

"Me?"

"It was your idea. Plus, I heard you say you wanted to help." When she didn't say anything right away, he added, "It's not complicated."

"I'm sure it's not. I mean, you do it for a living, right?" The minute she said it, she wanted to take it back.

"Right," he said, good-naturedly, which only made her feel like shit. She'd sounded petty, which wasn't like her. It was this Bettina Bailey. She was bringing out the worst in Georgia.

"Well, that's settled," Viola said. "Everything's under control." Then, as if she remembered Bettina's presence, she added, "Maybe you can be in charge of ordering more balloons? I think you're right about that. We can never have too many balloons."

"Fine," Bettina sniffed. She glanced at her watch. "I have to get going. I have a tennis match in thirty minutes." She pursed her lips and blew a few air kisses at Tofu, snatching him out of Dave's arms. "C'mon, baby, Mama needs to go bye-bye." Then she stuffed a struggling Tofu into her bag and flew out the door. All she needed to complete the picture was a broom.

"Good Lord," Kitty muttered under her breath. "As if we didn't have enough to do, now we have to babysit Bettina Bailey and her balloons."

Shea and Pilar giggled.

"I should get going too," Dave said. He glanced at Georgia. "Project Demolition starts tomorrow morning. Seven a.m. sharp. Wear something cheap and practical. Something you can toss out if it gets ruined."

In other words, no designer clothing. Did he think she'd wear her Manolos to do construction?

"Sure." What else could she say? If she protested, she would only sound childish. He was right. It had been her idea to begin with. So what if he'd seen her boobs? So what if he'd kissed her? She could handle one day working alongside Dave Hernandez. No big deal.

He said his good-byes and left. Georgia listened half-heartedly as they talked about how many tables to set up and where exactly to place the band. She still didn't get it. Why had they let Bettina Bailey swoop in and practically take over?

"Let me get this straight," Georgia said, unable to help herself as she interrupted a discussion on napkins, "Bettina isn't really on the Friends of the Rec Center committee but she's married to Bruce Bailey, who's the vice president of the bank and is on the city council?"

"Don't forget, she's also head of the Whispering Bay Beautification Committee," Viola said, her blue eyes twinkling.

"Isn't she awful?" Pilar said. Kitty and Shea nodded in agreement. Frida just sighed and Viola smiled in sympathy.

"Why didn't you all tell her to go to hell?"

Shea let out a long-suffering sigh. "We've found it's simpler to just go along with her."

"At least with Bettina pretending to be on the committee, we won't have to worry about her bad-mouthing the event," said Kitty.

"Or trying to sabotage it," Pilar added.

"I think she should be put in her place," Georgia said. "Not humored."

This led a round of laughter as if Georgia had been making a joke.

"You don't know Bettina," said Frida. "She can be pretty vindictive if she's crossed."

They all went back to studying the menu. Case closed.

But not as far as Georgia was concerned.

Georgia had met a lot of women like Bettina in her lifetime. Going all the way back to first grade. Bettina was the girl who bullied all the other little girls into making fun of the girl who couldn't afford a new outfit or the latest lunch box—girls like she and Frida had been. But the Bettina Baileys of the world had also been useful. They might bring out the worst in Georgia, but they also brought out the best. It had been girls like Bettina who had pushed Georgia into making straight As and earning a scholarship to Stanford.

And while the Bettina Baileys of this world might not be very nice, they had it all. While the Frida Hamptons had . . . well, not much. Frida had a business she was a slave to, a husband who—while being really good-natured—didn't carry his load of the weight, a tiny apartment, no kids, and probably not much money in the bank. But then, was Georgia really any better off than her sister? Sure, she had a top-notch education and enough money saved that she didn't have to worry about finances for a while, but she was husbandless, childless, and now even her job seemed unstable.

It wasn't fair. It really wasn't.

She remembered back to her sophomore year at Stanford when she'd almost flunked out of Financial Accounting. For one crazy weekend she'd considered dropping out of school, or the very least changing her major. But she hadn't, of course. She picked herself up by the bootstraps and studied her ass off. She'd even managed to squeak by with a B in the class. It hadn't been easy. But she'd done it. She'd steadied her course and kept her eye on the goal.

Which is exactly what she needed to do now. This was no time to be feeling sorry for herself! She'd let Spencer cool down. She'd call him daily, be sweet and caring and thoughtful. She wouldn't be stupid and pressure him again. He'd realize soon enough that he needed her.

She sat back in the chair and rejoined the conversation on the napkins. Everything was going to be all right now that she had a plan.

9

|| | | ||

Seven a.m. sharp. That's what the man said and Georgia didn't intend to be late. She pulled her hair back in a pony-tail, then dressed in the blue jeans and oversized T-shirt she'd bought yesterday in Destin. Since she'd originally planned to only be in Whispering Bay for a couple of days, she hadn't packed much—just a few outfits and a couple of bathing suits. But a trip to Target had solved that.

She'd stocked up on the type of clothes she normally never wore—bargain-priced shorts and shirts. And practical underwear—the kind that came packaged in threes and she'd never get caught dead in—but the granny-style white cotton briefs provided much needed skin coverage in the cheap ill-fitting jeans she'd bought for Project Demolition.

By the time Georgia descended the stairs it was quarter to seven. There were only a couple of customers in the Bistro. She placed the two large stainless-steel coffee mugs she'd bought at Starbucks yesterday on top of the kitchen counter, then immediately thought better of it. She tried to hide the mugs from Frida, but she wasn't fast enough.

"I can't believe you went to Starbucks behind my back!"

"I was shopping and needed a pick-me-up. Besides, you're out of to-go mugs, right?"

Frida suddenly looked defeated. "Right."

Georgia thought she detected more than just a competitive envy. "What's wrong?"

A customer walked in. Frida took his order, then handed it over to Ed to fill. "Sorry," she said to Georgia. "I'm just a little sensitive. By the time Ted Ferguson finishes building his version of Condo World, businesses like mine could be extinct. The Bistro by the Beach could very well be pushed aside for a Starbucks."

Georgia had never thought of that before. She tried not to look guilty. "I think you're going to be surprised by how much business you're going to pick up from this condo project. And if a business like Starbucks does try to take you over, then you just have to fight back."

"It's Starbucks! How do I fight Starbucks?"

"By being better than them."

"Easier said than done," Frida muttered.

Georgia filled both mugs with coffee. She added cream and sweetener to one and left the other one black, then screwed on the lids. "We'll talk about this later. I promised Demolition Dave I'd meet him at exactly seven."

"Why don't you like Dave? He seems like a really great guy."

Georgia stilled. "What makes you think I don't like him?"

"I don't know. I just sort of get a strange vibe from you whenever he's around."

"I guess I still feel weird about the whole boob-flashing thing."

"He saw my boobs too, you know."

But he didn't kiss you, did he?

For a second, she thought about confiding in Frida. Not about her role in the condo deal, of course. Frida didn't seem to be in the right state of mind for that. But about the whole Dave-kissing thing.

Georgia took a sip of her coffee. Maybe it was better to let sleeping dogs lie. She needed to focus on mending her relationship with Spencer. Not dwell on some innocent-never-to-be-repeated kiss.

She picked the second mug off the counter and turned to leave when she spied a pile of mail tucked back in the corner. A letter with a registered seal lay on top. "Who'd you get a registered letter from?"

Frida averted her gaze. "The bank. It's no big deal."

A registered letter from a bank certainly *was* a big deal. Georgia picked up the letter and broke the seal.

"Hey! That's private." But Frida didn't make an attempt to take the letter away.

Georgia quickly scanned the contents. "Frida, they're going to foreclose on the Bistro!" she whispered fiercely.

Frida didn't look surprised. "I figured that's what it was. I just didn't want to read it." Frida glanced over at Ed, who was cleaning off a table. There were no customers waiting in line. "Let's go outside," she said to Georgia.

Georgia picked up the letter and the two mugs and followed Frida out to the parking lot. She clicked the door opener to her Honda Accord and placed the coffee mugs in the drink holders, then turned to face her sister. "That's the reason you don't have any to-go mugs, isn't it?"

Frida nodded. "We fell behind in the payments a few months ago. I've tried scrimping on inventory to catch up, but it hasn't helped."

"What does Ed think you should do?"

Frida didn't say anything.

"Ed doesn't know?" Georgia could hear the hysteria in her voice. She tried to calm down. "Why doesn't he know?" she demanded.

"There's nothing he can do about it. It will only screw up his mojo—"

"His mojo! I can't believe you're being so calm about this. What are you going to do if you lose your business? Where will you live? You never finished college and you don't have any experience doing anything else."

Frida shrugged. "I can wait tables. I can live in a trailer or even a tent. It doesn't matter. As long as I'm with Ed, I'll be happy."

Live in a tent?

Georgia thought she might faint.

It was like listening to their mother all over again.

"What if you get pregnant?" Georgia narrowed her eyes. "Are you going to raise your kids the same way mom raised us? Moving around all over the place without a real house or—"

"Ed and I decided a long time ago that kids weren't for

us. So you don't have to worry about that. Like I said, it's just Ed and me, and I can be happy anywhere."

Georgia scanned the letter again. Frida had ten days to come up with twelve thousand dollars or the bank was going to start foreclosure proceedings. Okay. She took a deep breath. Twelve thousand dollars was definitely doable. "I'm going down to the bank on Monday and pay this off. Then we'll figure out some sort of budget—"

"*No.*" Frida shook her head. "I'm not taking money from you."

"Then call it a loan."

"No loans either. You're not even sure you have a job anymore, Georgia."

"I do so have a job! I'm just on a two-week hiatus."

"I thought you said it was a vacation."

"Same thing."

"I might not know Spencer as well as you do, but he doesn't seem the type to forgive and forget. Do you really think he'll let you go back to work for him after you told him to fuck off?" She didn't wait for Georgia's answer. "Maybe this foreclosure thing is a sign I should give up."

"Of course Spencer will forgive and forget," Georgia said. At least she hoped so. She tried not to let Frida see her uncertainty. "This is no time to get up on your high horse and it's not time to give up. I have plenty of money lying around doing nothing but collecting interest. You're my sister. I want to help."

"That's really sweet, but I can't let you." Frida gave Georgia a peck on the cheek. "This is my problem and I'll take care of it myself. I'll go to the bank this week and talk to Bruce Bailey. He'll let me work something out."

"But—"

"No buts. Promise me you'll stay out of this."

Georgia clamped her mouth tight.

"Promise me," Frida repeated.

Georgia grit her teeth. "I promise."

10

| | | | | |

The Margaret Handy Senior Center was located a mile down the beach from the Bistro. Georgia could have walked, but then she'd have to trek back during the hottest part of the day. Plus, she had the two mugs of coffee to bring along. She pulled her car into the parking lot alongside Dave's truck.

What was Frida thinking? *Live in a tent?* Could sniffing coffee beans all day make you delusional?

The front door was open. Other than Dave, no one else was in the building.

"You're late," he said, eyeing her cheap jeans, baggy T-shirt, and sneakers. "But at least you dressed right."

He was wearing jeans too, but his fit him a whole lot better than hers did. *Tall, good-looking guy, nice smile.* Now she could add great ass to that list.

She scowled. "I'm only ten minutes late. And I brought

you coffee, you ingrate. Black, just the way you like it."
Georgia handed him the mug.

"Ah, honey, you remembered."

"I'm not your honey."

"Yeah, but you want to be."

He said it with such a straight face, that despite her
mood, she had to laugh. "How did you get inside?" She hadn't
thought to ask how to get into the building. Or think about
the fact that they would be here alone.

"I got a key from Kitty. I'm staying with her and Steve."

Georgia downed some of her coffee and nodded. She'd
heard from Frida that Kitty and her new boyfriend were living together. She thought about asking Dave if he'd given
any more consideration to Steve's job offer, but she didn't
want to make small talk. The only thing she wanted was to
get in her car, drive back to the Bistro, and shake some sense
into her sister. Georgia didn't give a rat's ass about Ed's
mojo.

Dave took a long appreciative sip of his coffee. "I've already checked out the wall. It's not weight bearing, so this is
going to be a piece of cake." He handed her a pair of safety
glasses and some work gloves.

"Now what?" she asked.

He picked up a couple of large sledgehammers and handed
her one. "Now we get to have some good, clean fun."

She surveyed the wall. There were no doors and she noticed the electrical sockets had been stripped. Dave must have
done that, she thought. She gripped the heavy sledgehammer
firmly in her hands and drove it as hard as she could into the
wall. Plaster sprayed down on top of her head. She pounded
away for a couple of minutes, then stood back and took a

deep breath. Damn, that felt good. "You're right. This *is* fun."

She heard Dave chuckle. She turned around and watched as he picked up his sledgehammer and made a huge dent in the wall causing it to vibrate. They hacked away, side by side, until there were two separate holes peeking into the other room, although Dave's hole was a lot bigger than hers. Sweat dripped from her forehead onto her nose. It probably wasn't even eight yet and it was already sweltering.

"Is the air-conditioning on?" she gasped.

Dave's brown hair was covered in white dust and the sides of his shirt were soaked with perspiration. "Kitty said the unit isn't working well. They're doctoring it up with some Freon, but they're afraid if we use the air-conditioning before the party it won't last."

He walked over to a small cooler tucked in the corner of the room, took out two bottles of water, and handed her one. "That's why we need to get an early start. We'll work during the coolest part of the day. Today we'll do the basic teardown and tomorrow we'll see what we have left to do to make it presentable enough for the party."

"Tomorrow?" She hadn't planned on spending more than a day at this. She placed the icy cold bottle of water against her forehead. "Why can't we just get it all done now?"

"Like I said, in a couple of hours it's going to be too hot to keep working. Plus, I have a tee time at noon. I'm on vacation, remember?"

Technically so was she, but not for long. Not if she had anything to do with it. She took a sip of the water and picked up the sledgehammer. She didn't bother turning to see if

Dave had resumed working. She could hear him behind her, the sound of wall smashing tempered only by an occasional male grunt. He worked on the top part of the wall, the part she couldn't reach, while she concentrated on the bottom. There was something strangely primal about the whole thing. The two of them working side by side, sweating and grunting . . .

"You looking for a job?" he shouted above their pounding. He didn't even sound winded.

Georgia turned around. "Wh-what?" She shouldn't be this out of breath. She could do an hour on the elliptical, for God's sake.

"Either you're trying to impress me with your work ethic or you're just really pissed."

"I already have a job, thanks."

"Then you must be pissed." There was a pause. "Spencer?"

"For your information Spencer and I are back together. Sort of."

"Sort of? What does that mean?"

"It means that it's none of your business."

His expression gave away exactly nothing. "If that's what you want, then I'm happy for you."

She resumed tearing into a stubborn section of wall. Her biceps ached, but she didn't care. After a couple of minutes, she turned around again. "It's Frida," she blurted. "She's the reason I'm so . . . so wound up."

Dave waited patiently while she caught her breath to continue. "The bank is going to foreclose on the Bistro and Frida won't let me help her. She's so *damn* stubborn. I have plenty of money. I just don't get it." *Or her,* Georgia wanted to add.

Dave looked at her thoughtfully. "Maybe she doesn't want your money."

Georgia blew out a lungful of air in frustration. "It's the only help I can give her. I have a job in Birmingham I have to go back to."

"Yeah, the CFO of Spencer's company."

"I *earned* that job," she shot back.

"I didn't think you hadn't."

She relaxed a little. She'd had to defend herself before on that count. "When Spencer hired me his company was in the ground. In the past five years I've nearly tripled his assets. Both his business and his personal assets," she added proudly.

"Nice."

He said it like he meant it, which prompted her to confide in him. "You know this big condo project that's coming to town?"

"I'd have to be dead not to have heard about it."

"The developer, Ted Ferguson, he's a friend of Spencer's."

Dave's eyes narrowed. "Let me guess? Spencer is an investor in the deal."

"It was my idea for Spencer to branch out into real estate. It's been pretty successful so far. You'd think a community like Whispering Bay would be grateful for the development." She shook her head, "I don't know. All Frida can predict is gloom and doom. She won't even try to look at the big picture."

They resumed their work. This time, they didn't stop until the wall lay in a pile of rubble all over the floor.

"Now what?" she asked.

He pointed to a couple of wheelbarrows poised against the opposite wall. "Now we load this stuff up and cart it outside so Steve's company truck can haul it off."

She frowned. There were at least a couple dozen or so trips that would have to be made. Probably even more. She pulled off her gloves and flung off the safety glasses. Her jeans felt heavy and wet and chafed against her inner thighs. Even her hair felt like it weighed a ton, all sweaty and matted against her head. "Can't we do that tomorrow?"

"I thought you were all gung ho to finish in one day."

"I didn't think it would be this exhausting. Or this hot," she admitted.

"I've already arranged for the truck to come today." Dave pulled off his shirt. "But if you're too tired, you can skip out. I'll finish it myself."

"I'm not skipping out. I said I'd help and I meant it," she said, trying not to stare at his chest. But it was impossible. All that hard muscle she'd felt that night when she'd pushed him away was now in plain sight. She gulped. "What . . . what are you doing?"

"You're right. It's too damn hot. I need to cool off before I keep working." He yanked off his work boots and nodded his head in the direction of the large plate-glass window overlooking the ocean. "I'm going for a swim. Want to join me?"

"I didn't bring a bathing suit."

He grinned. "Neither did I."

She watched in horrified fascination as he unbuttoned his jeans. He wasn't going to strip down to nothing, was he?

Oh, shit. He was.

11

Dave pulled off his jeans. Underneath he had on a pair of board shorts. Georgia crossed her arms over her chest. "*That's a bathing suit.*"

"You sound disappointed."

"Well, I'm not."

He gave her a look that said he didn't believe her. "Your turn."

"I'm not stripping down to my underwear."

"Suit yourself." He walked out the sliding glass doors and onto the beach.

Georgia watched, blatantly jealous as he dove into the cool blue water.

He made her feel prudish. But she wasn't a prude. There was just something . . . unnerving about him. Like she was betraying Spencer. Which was ridiculous. Dave had absolutely nothing over Spencer. Spencer was classically handsome, smooth, successful, smart, urbane, thoughtful (well, most of the time).

Dave on the other hand, was just sort of good-looking. Sure, he had a nice butt and every once in a while he could be funny, but he was like beer. It was tasty, but who wanted beer if you could have champagne? And she was definitely a champagne kind of girl.

If Dave could strip down to almost nothing, then so could she. Besides, he'd already seen her boobs. And it wasn't like she was naked. She was wearing a bra and underwear. Her bikini was a lot more revealing than—

Her fingers froze on the jeans zipper.

Shit. She'd forgotten she was wearing granny panties.

But that was good, wasn't it? It was in no way revealing. Or sexy. Or anything remotely connected to sexy.

She bit her bottom lip. What if Dave thought this was the sort of underwear she wore all the time? She craned her neck to see him floating on top of the calm water. It looked absolutely blissful.

A river of sweat ran down her back, pooling into her already-damp jeans.

The hell with it. What did she care what Dave Hernandez thought of her underwear?

She peeled off the jeans and dumped them onto the floor. Just stripping down felt good. She could only imagine how the cool ocean water would feel next to her overheated skin. She'd keep the sweaty T-shirt on till the last second. Just in case someone should come by.

She waded over the shore and dipped her toe into the ocean. Dave was still floating, oblivious to her.

"Go ahead, it feels great," he called out.

What? Did he have eyelids on the side of his head?

"Don't look!" she yelled, hastily working her way out of the T-shirt. She dumped it onto the sand, then ran into the water and dove in. It felt as delicious as she had imagined, the salty water all cold and tingly against her skin. She surfaced and planted her feet on the sandy bottom. The water was chest deep.

"What wasn't I supposed to look at?" Dave asked, coming out of his floating position. He ran his hand through his wet hair, slicking it back. It emphasized his strong cheekbones and square jaw. Her gaze drifted lower, to his mouth. She remembered how slowly he'd kissed her—

"Nothing," she said, relieved that he'd obviously not caught sight of her granny panties. She'd worry later about him seeing them when they got out of the water.

She dipped her head into the ocean and combed her hair back with her fingers like he'd done. It felt wonderful. She couldn't believe she'd almost not gone in.

"So what are you going to do about your sister?" he asked.

She shaded her eyes with her hand, trying to gauge the expression on his face. He looked sincere enough. "I already told you she won't take my money."

"I thought you were some kind of financial genius. Didn't you say you'd tripled Spencer's assets?"

She was about to make a flippant reply, then snapped her mouth shut. Dave was right. The answer was staring her in the face. Why hadn't she thought of it before?

She'd just been so freaked out by Frida's lackadaisical attitude that she hadn't been thinking straight. If she could turn around Spencer's company, then she could do the same thing for her own flesh and blood. She'd promised Frida she'd stay out of her business. But what Frida really objected to was borrowing her money.

Her brain buzzed with excitement. "I'm going to get the bank to restructure her loan. On *my* terms. And then I'm going to work up an investment plan for her so she'll never be in this situation again."

He nodded. "Now you're thinking."

She relaxed. It was going to be all right. She would make sure of it.

"Thanks," she said.

"For what?"

"For listening to me. And for taking the time to help me see things clearly." Suddenly, she wanted to help him too. "So tell me about this job Steve's offered. Maybe I can help you sort it out."

"I already told you, he's started up a new construction company here in town and he wants me to be his partner."

"What are the pros and cons?"

"The pros? That's simple. We were a good team once and he knows how to make a lot of money."

"That last part sounds good."

He went quiet for a few seconds. "I'm not taking it."

He said it with a firmness that told her the decision had been made a long time ago.

"Does Steve know that?"

He shrugged, looking uncomfortable.

"Why haven't you told him?"

"He dicked me over once; I'm not about to let that happen again. Not where my business is concerned."

"I thought your kind believed in turning the other cheek."

"I've forgiven him. I'm giving the friendship another chance, aren't I?"

Now it was her turn to be quiet. She didn't know how to respond to that.

"We should go back and clean up," he said abruptly.

Crap. This was it. There was no way she could get out of the water without him seeing her underwear. On the other hand, maybe she was making too big a deal of the whole thing. He probably wouldn't even notice.

She sloshed her way through the water till she reached the shore.

Dave started to laugh.

Okay, so he noticed.

She placed her hands on her hips, silently daring him to keep laughing.

"That gives the phrase 'putting on your big-girl panties' a whole new meaning," he said, pretending that he was trying hard to act serious.

Honestly, it wasn't that funny.

She glanced down at herself to see the white cotton underwear hanging on her hips, all wet and heavy. Like a soggy parachute. Apparently, in order to fit properly, granny panties should be sized down.

She tried not to smile. So maybe it was a tiny bit funny . . .

He shook his head. "No wonder Spencer hasn't proposed. Or maybe he's the kind of guy who gets turned on by those." His grin turned evil. "What's Spencer's mother like?"

Okay, not funny at all.

She scooped her T-shirt off the sand and made a show of calmly drawing it over her head and smoothing it down until it reached mid-thigh. "Screw you."

"Ouch. I guess I hit a sore spot."

She turned to face him, giving him a falsely sweet smile. "Spencer and his mother have a lovely, *normal* relationship, not that it's any of your business. Furthermore, Spencer isn't the sort of visually stunted, immature male who needs a pair of thong panties to get turned on. He happens to be attracted to my mind."

"Yeah, and I have some swamp land for sale in the middle of the Everglades. You forget, babe, I've seen your tits. I know exactly what Spencer is attracted to."

"*Tits?* Wow, well, I think I know exactly why you haven't found the *right one* yet. Wanted," she mimicked, "one brainless Barbie look-alike with a great rack and an endless ability to withstand bad jokes."

"I think my jokes are pretty funny, thank you."

She turned her back on him and began walking toward the building. He grabbed her by the elbow and spun her around. "Hey, what's with the attitude? I'm just kidding around."

"Attitude? I don't have an attitude."

"Sweetheart, you have a chip on your shoulder as big as Alaska. I'm not the guy who's been stringing you along for the past five years. Remember?"

It was true. Dave had been nothing but nice to her. Except of course, when he'd tried to take advantage of her during her drunken state. But then she'd puked all over the floor. So technically, they were even. After today, she didn't even feel weird around him anymore. "I'm sorry, you're right."

"I am?"

She nodded.

"That's not some kind of girl trick is it?"

She smiled. How did he always manage to pull her out of a bad mood? "It's just, I'm not usually so emotional about everything. It's like I've been on a roller coaster for the past few days," she admitted. "But it's going to be okay. I know what I have to do now to help Frida. And, as for Spencer," she hesitated, unsure exactly why she felt the need to tell him, "I'm going to do everything I can to win him back."

There was that expression again. The one where she couldn't tell what he was thinking. "Sounds like your life is back on track."

"It is. Everything's going to be perfect. I can feel it."

"That's great. I'm happy for you, Georgia."

Something about the way he said her name made her pause. Probably because it was the first time he actually said her name out loud. Or maybe it was something in the inflection, something she couldn't put her finger on that made it sound different from the way anyone else said it. But that was ridiculous.

They walked back to the senior center to find Kitty and Steve surveying the mess.

"I figured you could use some help," Steve said, nodding his head toward the huge pile of rubble on the floor. He briefly eyed their state of semi-undress. "Unless of course, we're interrupting something."

Dave discreetly gave Steve the finger.

Steve grinned and began loading up the wheelbarrow.

It was obvious the two men had a close friendship. As Dave said, he'd forgiven Steve, but he hadn't forgotten. Why had Dave confided that to her? She'd only known him a few days. Maybe it was because she'd confided all her Spencer angst to him. Probably that was it.

"We were just taking a quick swim break," Georgia told Kitty, feeling the need to explain. She retrieved her discarded jeans and tried to put them back on, but she couldn't. They were just too gross, all sweaty and heavy. The T-shirt covered more than a short dress did, so she decided to stay the way she was.

Dave, on the other hand, slipped back into his jeans and work boots and began helping Steve load the debris into the wheelbarrows.

"I guess I should give them a hand," Georgia said to Kitty.

"Don't worry about it." Kitty handed her a bottle of water from Dave's ice chest. "They've got it."

Georgia took a sip of the water. "Thanks. I'm pretty beat."

Kitty smiled at her. "This looks amazing," she said, gazing at the large open space they'd created by knocking down the wall. "You guys got a lot accomplished this morning."

"Thanks," Georgia said. She liked Kitty. She was warm and easy to talk to.

The two of them chatted and watched on as Dave and Steve worked in unison. They scooped up the debris, loaded it into the wheelbarrows, then made quick work of dumping the mess outside.

"They make a good team." Kitty said. "Steve's really hoping Dave will move here to work with him."

Georgia lowered her eyes. "They do make a good team," she agreed, knowing she didn't sound overly enthusiastic. It bothered her knowing that Dave had already made up his mind about the job. It seemed almost unfair. But then Georgia really couldn't blame him. It was a risk. Turning it down was actually the smart thing to do. Georgia waited till both men were out of the building to ask, "What exactly happened between them? They were partners once, right?"

Kitty nodded, hesitating slightly as if she was pondering what to say. "They had a construction company down in Tampa. From what Steve's told me, it was pretty successful. But Dave wanted to keep the company small and Steve wanted to expand. Then Steve met his ex-wife, Terrie. She hooked him up with this developer, Ted Ferguson," Kitty paused. "I think we mentioned him the other night at Bunco."

Georgia cleared her throat. "Yes, I think my sister referred to him as the evil land baron."

Kitty grimaced. "To be fair, I sort of helped Ted in his evil expansion."

Me too! Georgia wanted to shout. "How did you help?" she asked instead.

"I was the Realtor in the deal, but that's another story," Kitty said, rolling her eyes. "Back to Steve and Dave. Steve broke up the partnership and left Dave to form a company with Terrie and Ted. They all made a lot of money and everyone was happy. For a while."

"Everyone except Dave."

"Yeah," Kitty admitted reluctantly. "But Steve's more than ready to make it up to him. He wants to put Dave in charge of renovations at Dolphin Isles."

"Dolphin Isles?"

"It's a development of tract homes that Steve's company built here a few years ago. The workmanship is kind of spotty.

It's one of the things Steve wants to fix. He thinks it's right up Dave's alley."

Except that Georgia knew Dave had no intention of getting on board. She decided to change the subject. "So, Steve's divorced?" she asked carefully. Kitty didn't seem the type to mind a personal question.

"Three times."

"Holy shit," Georgia muttered.

Kitty looked like she was used to the reaction. "Pretty bad odds for a relationship, wouldn't you say?" Georgia followed Kitty's gaze as Steve maneuvered the empty wheelbarrow back into the center.

"But you're in love with him," Georgia said softly.

"It's that obvious, huh?"

Georgia smiled. From what she could see the feeling looked mutual. Did she look at Spencer the way Kitty looked at Steve? And just as important, did Spencer look at her the same way too?

Dave began piling debris into the wheelbarrow. He glanced over at Georgia. "Thanks for your help today. We can get the rest of this."

"You're sure?"

"Positive," he said.

"What time should I come back tomorrow?"

Dave barely looked at her. "No need. I can do the follow-up myself."

"Okay, well, I guess I'll see you around."

"Sure," he said without much conviction.

She couldn't help but feel like she'd been dismissed, which was silly. She'd only planned to spend one day on this project and tomorrow was Sunday. She needed to work up a kick-ass financial plan to restructure the loan on the Bistro so she could present it to the bank first thing Monday morning.

So really, it was just as well.

12

||||||

Monday morning came bright and early. Georgia took a quick shower, then helped Frida and Ed with the first wave of business. At eight thirty, she made a bogus excuse about running an errand, then ducked out and ran up upstairs to get ready to go mano a mano with Bruce Bailey.

Although she seriously didn't expect much of a fight. Any man married to Bettina had to be . . . well, quite frankly, a pushover, to put it nicely.

She hadn't called to schedule a meeting, primarily because there hadn't been time, but that was all right. In her experience, most times a surprise attack worked in your favor. She'd arrive the second the bank opened, ambush Bruce, then wow him with her proposal before the poor schmuck knew what hit him.

She couldn't wait to see the expression on Frida's face when she discovered that the Bistro would be safe after all.

She'd thought about discussing her loan restructure plan with her sister, but there was always the marginally slim chance that Bruce would reject her proposal, and she didn't want to get Frida's hopes up.

She dressed in the Alexander McQueen navy blue slacks and matching blouse she'd worn on the drive down from Birmingham. After slipping on a pair of pearl earrings and carefully applying makeup, she took one last look at herself in the tiny mirror above the dresser in Frida's guest room. She looked more put together than she had in days. Other than the night of the Bunco party, she'd been going native—letting her hair dry naturally and running around bare-faced. But now she looked more like her old self. Feminine, but definitely businesslike. A take-charge look that screamed "I am woman, hear me roar," yet was soft enough that it didn't rile up any of the male lions in the pride.

She tiptoed down the stairs and managed to slip out of the Bistro without either Frida or Ed noticing. At exactly 9:05 a.m. her Honda Accord was parked in the Whispering Bay Community Bank parking lot. She slipped her leather satchel under her arm and walked inside the building.

There was a counter at the rear with two tellers servicing a small line of customers, an office to the left, and one to the right. Both office doors were closed.

A woman sitting behind a desk in front of the lobby smiled at her. "Welcome to Whispering Bay Community Bank. May I help you?"

"I'd like to see Bruce Bailey, please."

"Do you have an appointment?"

Georgia didn't want to reveal too much, but on the other hand, she didn't want to be turned away either. She hesitated a moment, then pulled the business card proclaiming her as Moody Electronics's CFO from the side pocket of her leather satchel and handed it to the receptionist. "I'm afraid not, but I'm only in town a few days and I was hoping Mr. Bailey would agree to see me." It wasn't really cheating. If the receptionist thought Georgia's business had something to do with Moody Electronics, then that was her assumption.

The woman looked at the card. "Mr. Bailey is with a client right now. But if you wouldn't mind waiting?" Her gaze slid over to an empty chair.

"Of course, thank you." Georgia took a seat. Waiting wasn't so bad really. It gave her time to mentally rehearse what she would say to Bruce. Every once in a while, she glanced over to check out the activity in the bank line.

An elderly gentleman accompanied by a middle-aged woman with short, spiky, gray hair entered the lobby. The man walked slowly, using a cane. He took one look at Georgia and scowled. "I have a bone to pick with you, missy."

Georgia stilled. "Excuse me?"

The woman accompanying the man smiled apologetically at Georgia. "Earl, that's not who you think it is."

"Course it is. I'm not blind." He shrewdly eyed Georgia. "She's just gussied up, that's all." He pointed his cane at her. "DeeDee here was at your place the other day, or was it last week? Anyway, don't matter. She was in town and I asked her to pick up a dozen of them bran muffins you make. Those things are better than any damn laxative, if you know what I mean. But there was only eleven of 'em in the bag. So unless DeeDee stiffed me, you owe me one bran muffin, girlie."

This put Frida's bran muffins in a whole new light. Georgia didn't know whether to be irritated that he'd confused her with Frida or to laugh at his whole muffin-stiffing accusation. "I'm afraid you have me confused with my sister, Frida."

The old man's bushy brows came together.

"Earl, I told you, that's not Frida Hampton," insisted the woman who Georgia supposed was DeeDee. She turned her attention to Georgia and smiled. "Sorry about that, but I can see how Earl would be confused. You and your sister look a lot alike."

Earl scrutinized Georgia further. "This isn't the coffee gal?"

Georgia extended her hand. "My name is Georgia Meyer and I'm—"

"Earl!" a male voice laced with a strong southern accent boomed. "What brings you here?"

Georgia whipped around to see a man in his early forties come out of the office. This must be the schmuck—er, Bruce. He grasped Earl's hand and gave him a vigorous handshake. Behind him was another man who looked maybe a couple of years younger. While Bruce was balding and had a small potbelly, the other man looked blue-blood handsome-sleek. He wore immaculately pressed khaki slacks, a white cotton shirt with a Ralph Lauren insignia on the pocket, and Gucci loafers. "How are you this morning, Earl?" Blueblood asked in a smooth voice.

Earl growled at him. "What do you care? Already got my land, don't you?" He turned his attention back to Bruce and began a litany of complaints about having to wait in line for a teller. Georgia glanced at the bank window. There was only one person in line that she could see.

Blueblood watched the exchange between Earl and Bruce with amusement, until his gaze settled on Georgia.

"Well, hel-lo," he said, in a tone more appropriate to a singles bar than a small-town bank. "Can I help you?"

There was something about his voice that Georgia recognized. Had she met this guy before? "Not unless you're Bruce Bailey," Georgia answered in her sweetest voice. *Kill them with kindness,* she chanted to herself, or rather *kill them with sweetness,* she amended. It might be the twenty-first century, but a woman in business could still catch more flies with honey than vinegar. She'd save her claws for when it counted.

"I wish I *was* Bruce," the man said, extending his hand. "Ted Ferguson. Maybe you've heard of me?"

Georgia tried to hide her surprise. She hadn't expected to meet Ted here. "As a matter of fact I have heard of you. I'm Georgia Meyer." She shook his hand, waiting to see how long it would take him to recognize her name.

It only took a second for the telltale gleam of recognition to light up his face. "Spencer always did have an eye for talent."

Yuck. "I'm glad to finally meet face-to-face," she said.

Ted frowned. "Did Spencer send you down to check out the condo project? Because I can assure you, everything is going according to schedule."

Georgia gazed around the bank, hoping no one was within earshot. She was relieved to see Bruce had gone off to help the old gentleman with his bank transaction.

"I'm actually here on personal business," Georgia said.

"Personal, huh? By the way," he said, leaning in way too

close to confide in a low voice, "that old coot you were talk-ing to is Earl Handy. He sold us the land we're building the condos on. Don't let his sad-old-man-with-a-cane routine fool you. He owns most of this town and is richer than Midas. He's also meaner than a junkyard dog."

And apparently he has constipation issues, she wanted to add. Maybe that's what made him so mean. Only Georgia had found Earl kind of cute. In a crotchety-old-man sort of way.

Ted glanced at his watch. "I'd love to stay and talk, but I have to get going. You sure your visit here has nothing to do with the condo project?"

What? Did he think he could trick her into making some sort of admission? "Positive," she said, smiling sweetly.

"It's a pleasure to finally meet you, Georgia. And tell Spencer I'm sorry to miss the big game this weekend. Got this Black Tie Bunco shindig in town I can't pass on. Public relations and all," he said with a wink. She'd have to be blind not to notice the way he was staring at her breasts.

It was official now. She didn't care how chummy he and Spencer were. Frat brother or no, Ted Ferguson was off her wedding invitation list.

It was ten more minutes before Bruce Bailey came over to greet her. He had her business card in his hand. The re-ceptionist must have slipped it to him when Georgia wasn't looking. "Please, step into my office," he said, ushering her through the door. He pulled out her chair, a move Georgia found old-fashioned for a business situation, but it was also a little endearing too. She noticed the bald spot on Bruce's head was shiny with perspiration. Oh, dear. He was a sweater.

"It's quite a coincidence you're here this morning, Ms. Meyer. Ted Ferguson and I were just talking business." He paused. "He didn't mention you were in town."

"Actually, I only met Mr. Ferguson a few minutes ago, in your lobby."

He eyed her card again. "I was under the impression he and Mr. Moody were close acquaintances."

Georgia shifted in her chair. It did seem a little odd that Spencer had never introduced her to Ted. Come to think of it, she'd never met any of Spencer's old college friends. But then she never went to any of the Bama football games or other alumni functions Spencer was always running off to. Someone had to stay and run the ship. Moody Electronics might be open Monday through Friday, eight to five, but behind the scenes it was a twenty-four-hour endeavor. "I've spoken to Mr. Ferguson on the phone many times," she said firmly.

This seemed to satisfy Bruce. "Let me assure you, that whatever banking Moody Electronics is in the market for, Whispering Bay Community Bank can provide. With first-rate, special service, I might add."

"I'm sure Mr. Moody will be happy to hear that," she said carefully. "The thing is, Mr. Bailey, I'm not here this morning representing Moody Electronics."

"You're not?"

How should she word this? "I'm here representing another business. A client of yours actually."

Bruce didn't hide his disappointment. "What client is that?"

She cleared her throat. "The Bistro by the Beach."

Bruce blinked. "I see."

Georgia set her leather satchel on the edge of his desk. "I realize the Bistro hasn't been run as efficiently as it could be. But that's all in the past. I've put together a payment plan that will bring the loan up to speed within six months." She handed Bruce her loan restructure outline.

He skimmed the page. "Let me get this straight. Mrs. Hampton has hired you as, what? Some sort of business consultant?"

"Exactly," she said, liking the sound of that.

He glanced at the paper again. "There's one problem. You forgot to add in late penalties. And usually whenever we restructure because of past late payments, we require a good faith amount up front."

"I was hoping those could be overlooked. My—Mrs. Hampton has been a loyal customer for a long time."

"Forgive me for putting this bluntly, Ms. Meyer, but if Mrs. Hampton put her money into making her payments on time instead of hiring you, she wouldn't have a problem. I assume you don't come cheaply?"

"I'm doing this . . . pro bono," Georgia pulled out of the air. "I enjoy taking businesses that need help and turning them around." That part at least was true. Except in the past she'd been paid for it.

He placed the paper down on his desk. "Strange hobby."

"Small businesses need our help, Mr. Bailey. They're the backbone of America." She actually kind of liked the way that sounded.

"I'd like to help, really, I would. Mrs. Hampton is a lovely woman and she does make the best muffins I've ever tasted." Bruce patted his potbelly and gave her a dismissive smile. "But she's going to have to pay late charges just like every other customer. Plus, we really need a good faith payment upfront."

It was definitely time for the claws to come out. "As I was saying," Georgia said, as if Bruce hadn't just spoken, "small businesses are the backbone of America. And Moody Electronics wants to give back to America."

Dear God. She sounded like a bad infomercial. Still, the idea was intriguing. Maybe once things were back to normal she'd talk to Spencer about doing some pro bono work on the side. She kind of liked the idea of helping out the little guy—or gal, as in her sister's case.

Bruce frowned. "I thought you were doing this on your own. Are you saying Moody Electronics has an interest in the Bistro?"

"Not . . . like you think. Suffice it to say that I heavily influence all of Mr. Moody's financial decisions and of course, once this local condo project gets under way, a project I believe you're aware Mr. Moody has invested in?" The bald spot on Bruce's head was now wet. Georgia fought the urge to pluck a Kleenex off his desk and pat it down for him. "Anyway, I'm sure Mr. Moody will be looking to expand his investments here in Whispering Bay."

It was shameless, using Spencer's name to strong-arm Bruce like this, but men did it all the time. Why couldn't she? *I am woman, hear me roar . . .*

"Am I making myself clear, Mr. Bailey?"

"I understand," Bruce said, smiling weakly. "I'll tell you what, let me study this a bit, and I'll get back to you as soon as possible."

Georgia stood. "Excellent. You have my business card? You can reach me on my cell twenty-four/seven."

Bruce jumped from his chair to open the door for her. Whatever she thought of Bruce, his momma had raised him right.

Georgia dug her sunglasses out of the leather satchel and slipped them on as she stepped out into the bank parking lot. She looked up at the sun, beaming down bright and hot already. There was nothing better than successfully negotiating a business deal. It wasn't completely wrapped up yet, but she could smell success in the air. She'd go back to the Bistro, help Frida and Ed clean up, then slip on her bikini and catch some rays. Her sister's business was going to be saved. At least one part of her plan was going right.

Now to work on the other . . .

Georgia dialed Spencer's cell phone, but it went to voice mail so she tried his work number.

Crystal's crisp, professional voice answered, "Spencer Moody's office."

"Hi, Crystal, it's Georgia. Is Spencer in?"

"Georgia! I'm so glad to hear from you. Are you having loads of fun?"

"Um, sure."

There was a pause, then an envious sigh. "Only you wouldn't be absolutely thrilled to take a leave of absence and spend it at the beach."

Leave of absence? She hadn't thought what Spencer might tell the rest of the employees about her "hiatus." Leave of absence sounded like a prelude to a firing.

Georgia tried to keep her voice smooth and upbeat. "Can I talk to Spencer?"

Crystal's voice dropped to a conspiratorial whisper. "He's busy right now, Georgia. He's meeting with the people from Valley Tech. John Ambrose is here himself."

Georgia frowned. Valley Tech was one of Moody Electronics's biggest clients. And John Ambrose was Valley Tech's president. "I didn't know they were scheduled to come today," Georgia said. "And why are you whispering?"

Crystal giggled. "Sorry, you know how nervous I get whenever any bigwigs come around. They paid us a surprise visit. The whole plant is in chaos. I've already dropped one pot of coffee all over the floor."

Georgia bit her bottom lip. Damn it. She should be at work today helping Spencer get through this.

Was Valley Tech thinking of pulling their business? Or maybe they were thinking of expanding their contract. She glanced at her watch. It was only ten a.m. If she jumped in her car and didn't stop, she could be in Birmingham by three.

But maybe this was a good thing. Maybe it was just the wake-up call Spencer needed. After today, surely he'd realize how important her presence was in these sorts of negotiations. Plus, she couldn't just haul off and leave right now. She needed to follow up with Bruce Bailey. "Tell him . . . tell Spencer I said good luck and ask him to call me the minute his meeting is over, okay?"

"Sure thing," said Crystal.

13

||||||

Spencer didn't call back till ten that night. Georgia found it hard to believe that his meeting had gone on that long. Either Crystal didn't give him the right message or he was avoiding her. "How's Florida?" he asked casually.

Georgia didn't want to waste time with small talk. "Why were the people from Valley Tech at the plant?"

"Surprise visit," Spencer said.

"Bastards."

This produced a weak laugh. "They plan to be here for a few days. They're thinking of giving us another contract. A big one."

"Was Jim Harris in on the talks?" Jim was Moody Electronics's VP of Engineering. He was smart and customers liked him.

"No, should he have been?"

Spencer was a whiz at sales. When it came to wining and

dining a client, there was no one better. But John Ambrose liked hearing specific figures and projection rates, something Spencer didn't exactly excel at.

"It's just that Jim is always so on top of things. And it's good to have a second when you're with a big customer," she said trying to be diplomatic.

"I've got things under control. John Ambrose is practically eating out of my hand."

"That's . . . great." It's not that she wasn't happy for Spencer. And for the company. But it would have been nice to feel needed.

"So, you never answered my question. How's Florida? What have you been up to?"

"Florida is hot. And sunny. And humid. Just like Birmingham right now. I've been helping Frida out at the Bistro. Hanging out at the beach, that kind of stuff." She thought about the other day, when she'd torn down the wall at the senior center. But Spencer wouldn't be interested in that. "Oh, I ran into a friend of yours today. Ted Ferguson."

"Yeah?" Spencer chuckled. "Where'd you meet him?"

"At the local bank. I was there on business for Frida." She paused. "How come I've never met him before? Considering he's a business partner as well as a friend of yours it seems a little weird. You know?"

"He didn't make a pass at you, did he?"

"No," Georgia said cautiously.

"Good. The man's a dog. That's why I've never introduced you to him."

Was Spencer jealous? Georgia felt a tiny glimmer of hope.

"I expect he's keeping an eye out for our investment," he continued.

"It seems like the condo project is going according to schedule." An idea suddenly occurred to her. "As a matter of fact," she said, "there's this Black Tie Bunco function here Saturday night. It's a fund-raiser to help build a new rec center in town. The old senior center is being demolished because it's on the land the condos are going up on. Ted and the rest of the condo investors are going to be there."

"Uh-huh."

"It might be a good thing if you came down too. It would be good PR. And since it's for charity the trip would be tax-deductible."

"That's one of the things I love about you, Georgia, you're always looking out for me. But, babycakes, you know Bama's opening game is this weekend. If it was any other time . . ." He drifted off leaving her to assume that otherwise he might have considered it.

She sighed. It was no use. Nothing short of the world collapsing could keep Spencer from his precious Crimson Tide. Still, he'd called her babycakes. Not that she was particularly fond of that endearment, but it meant that Spencer still thought of them as a couple. There was still hope.

"Listen, sugar, I have to go, I'm exhausted. I'll call you tomorrow."

14

¦¦¦¦¦

Wednesday was a busy day at the Bistro, so cleanup took longer than usual. In the past few days, Georgia had gotten in the habit of helping Frida out. She took orders, bussed tables, chatted up the customers.

It wasn't so bad, really. Frida's friends came by most mornings for coffee—Pilar on her way to work, Kitty and Steve after their early morning run. Shea's husband, Moose, came by every morning and ordered the same thing—a low-fat blueberry muffin and a skinny latte. He'd pat his stomach and wink at her. "Think my beer gut is getting any smaller?" "Definitely," she'd answer. Then he'd grin and tell her he'd see her tomorrow.

Georgia recognized a few other members of Frida's Bunco group. There was Mimi, who Georgia now realized was married to Zeke Grant, Whispering Bay's chief of police. He also came in every morning, along with his two deputies, both of whom were named Rusty, so everyone just called them Rusty 1 and Rusty 2, which Georgia totally didn't get because neither of them had red hair. But since Whispering Bay appeared to be the twenty-first century version of Mayberry RFD, maybe it wasn't so weird after all.

Georgia met a lot of other locals, like Christy Pappas, who was married to Joey, who was Steve's cousin. Christy was sweet, even if she was Bettina's crony.

And then there were the Gray Flamingos.

On Wednesdays they held their weekly organizational meeting at the Bistro. They took up two long tables and ordered a lot of herbal tea and bran muffins and spoke in loud voices about things like senior citizens rights and who was due for a colonoscopy or a skin biopsy. Georgia had no idea how passionate the after-sixty-five crowd could be.

Her favorite of the bunch was Viola, who was a total sweetheart. She introduced Georgia to her boyfriend Gus Pappas, a widowed plumber who turned out to be Steve's uncle and Joey's father. Earl Handy had come to the meeting too. He'd asked for a free bran muffin, which Georgia had happily given him after apologizing yet again for his being stiffed a muffin last week. He paid for his bill in change and gave Georgia a quarter for a tip. One of the other Flamingos, a gentleman by the name of Mr. Milhouse had scoffed at Earl and pushed a couple extra dollars on Georgia, which she refused to take at first until the old guy's face turned so red Georgia had been afraid not to.

And last but not least, there was Dave. He also came in every morning. Along with the silver stainless-steel coffee mug Georgia had bought him from Starbucks. She couldn't help but be pleased that he was using it. He would order a black coffee and a lemon poppy seed muffin. While his order was being filled, he and Ed would chat for a few minutes, but he never stayed. If he caught her eye, he'd nod at her, but he didn't initiate conversation or seek her out to say hello. She itched to ask him how the party renovations were going but something always held her back. It was weird. She thought they'd become friends.

Now that she and Frida had finished the tedious chore of scrubbing down the place, Frida took advantage to catch up on her baking. The smell of muffins and pastries filled the mid-afternoon air. Ed was upstairs painting while Georgia secretly worked on her marketing plan for the Bistro. She'd asked Frida to provide her with last year's sales figures, invoices, receipts, and anything else she could use. At first, Frida had been reluctant, but Georgia had convinced her to hand them over.

Georgia stared at the papers sprawled over the table in front of her. From what she could see there wasn't any reason the Bistro shouldn't be a success. True, business could be sporadic, but Georgia would just have to show Frida ways to even out her cash flow. And there were literally dozens of areas Frida could tighten her belt or make cost adjustments. Taken individually, they weren't a big deal, but all together, they could add up to huge savings. She scooped up the invoices and receipts and sorted them into piles just in time to see Ed coming down the stairs.

"Nose to the grindstone, huh?" he said.

Georgia had to bite her tongue to keep from telling Ed what she was working on, but she'd promised her sister she wouldn't upset his mojo. Ed poured himself a cup of coffee.

Georgia noticed his T-shirt was stained with wet paint and his hair seemed wilder than usual.

"What are you painting?" she asked. Not that she really cared. But it only seemed polite.

"A landscape," he said, his blue eyes lighting up, which only made Georgia feel like a shrew. She wished she could get excited about Ed's passion. If only for Frida's sake.

"Is it on commission?"

The light in his eyes dimmed. "No. It's one of the paintings I hope to display at the Harbor House."

Maybe this was a good time to try to knock some sense into Ed. God knew he needed it. "How long have you been painting, Ed?"

"All my life."

Georgia didn't want to squash Ed. She really didn't. But her sister was drowning and instead of throwing her a life preserver Ed was pulling her down further. "Have you ever thought about doing anything else?"

He blinked. "Like what?"

Like get a real job, she wanted to say, but before she could, Frida appeared at the bottom of the stairs. "What are you up to?" she asked suspiciously, eyeing the papers on the table.

"Georgia thinks I should get a real job," Ed said mildly, taking a sip of his coffee.

Frida stared at her.

"I didn't say that," Georgia protested. *She'd only thought it.* "I was just wondering if Ed ever considered another career." She turned back to Ed. "You did go to college, after all. What was your major again?"

"Philosophy," Ed said.

Georgia tried not to cringe. "Oh, yeah, I forgot. But you could always teach, couldn't you?" she asked, feeling encouraged by her idea. "Granted, teachers don't make a lot of money, but there's the insurance plans and the retirement programs. Those are great benefits. And then you have your summers off. I bet you could get a lot of painting done then."

"Georgia, can I talk to you in private?" Frida asked.

Ed tossed Georgia an uncomfortable look. "I'll catch up with you girls later." He made a quick escape up the stairs.

Frida waited till Ed was out of earshot. "What's gotten into you?" she demanded. "Are you trying to make my husband feel like shit?"

"Of course not! I really like Ed, you know that. I'm only trying to help."

Frida glanced at the papers on the table. "So what is all that?"

Georgia didn't want to tell Frida about the loan restructure. At least not yet. But there was no reason why she couldn't share her business plan with her.

"I took the receipts and invoices you gave me and I've worked up a business plan. Basically," said Georgia, "it's figuring out ways to economize, but to also draw in more traffic and of course, increase profits." She made a pretend show of shuffling the papers so that she wouldn't have to meet Frida's gaze. "Have you gone to the bank yet? To work out the loan problem?"

She'd been worried Frida would try to do her own loan restructure, inadvertently messing up the one Georgia had presented. She hadn't counted on Bruce taking this long to make up his mind. If she didn't hear from him by tomorrow, she'd give him a call and try to force his hand.

Frida made a face. "Not yet. But I need to. I've just been so busy with Black Tie Bunco, and of course, putting it off, I can almost pretend it doesn't exist."

"My offer still stands. About the money," Georgia added hopefully.

"Yeah, thanks. But *no*, thanks."

When they handed out the stubborn gene, Frida must have knocked everyone else to the side to stand first in line. Georgia handed her the proposal. "Maybe this will get you revved up."

Frida read the marketing plan for about two seconds before she said, "Paper products? But you know I don't believe in—"

"I know you don't think they're environmentally correct," Georgia said. "But when you take into account all the hot water you have to use to wash dishes, it almost breaks even. Besides, you're losing an entire customer base. Paper works because it's convenient. And today's customer is all about making it easy."

"Since when did you become an expert on the coffee business?"

"It doesn't take a genius to figure out that if you want to compete with businesses like Starbucks, then you have to be more like them. Only better. For one thing, you need free Wi-Fi in this place. And trendy music, something that says 'drink more coffee.'"

Frida looked skeptical. "There's music that says 'drink more coffee'?"

"Subliminally, yes. There's music to make you buy all sorts of things. Like groceries. Supermarkets do it all the time."

"I thought they played music to make shopping more enjoyable."

"Supermarkets play music that has been market-tested to appeal to their customer base to make them buy more groceries. If a market test proved that playing bongo drums increased revenue, then you better believe they'd pipe that into their stereo system. It's not about making the experience more enjoyable, it's about making the customer spend more money. That's the bottom line."

Frida shook her head. "I don't know."

"You don't have to know. That's what I'm for. Think of me as a business consultant—without the exorbitant fees they charge. Besides, I'm not done with my plan yet. When I've figured it all out, I'm going to present it to you and Ed. And I guarantee, you're both going to love it."

"All right, work on your plan all you want, and I promise to give some serious thought to whatever you come up with. Just don't give Ed a hard time. Okay?"

Georgia was about to respond when a knock at the door caused both her and Frida to turn around.

Bettina Bailey pressed her nose against the glass door and waved.

Ugh.

"Tell her you're closed," Georgia said.

Frida ignored her and unlocked the door.

Bettina sailed in wearing a bikini and a Hawaiian print wraparound skirt with a big, floppy hat. The look said "just came off the beach" but Georgia noticed she was in full war paint. Tofu's head stuck out the top of Bettina's Coach bag. He raised his snout in the air and wiggled his nose.

"Tofu smells something fattening," Bettina said, a horrified expression on her face.

"Tofu can smell calories?" Georgia asked.

Bettina glanced at Georgia. "You're still here? Don't you have some big important job in Atlanta?"

"That's Birmingham. And I'm on vacation," Georgia said in a sweetly false voice.

Bettina produced a sheet of paper from her bag. "I've been thinking, Frida, while I'm sure your cheesecakes are really yummy, they're just a little too plain for what I've envisioned for Black Tie Bunco, so I've come up with this instead." She handed the sheet of paper to Frida. "They're straight out of the recipe book I'm putting together for the Whispering Bay Beautification Committee. So, what do you think? Key lime tarts! It's my own special recipe. And nothing says Florida more than key lime pie."

"I thought you were the balloon committee," Georgia said.

Frida threw Georgia a hard look, then studied the paper and cleared her throat. "This sounds really delicious, Bettina, but I've already purchased all the ingredients for the cheese-cakes."

"So purchase more ingredients! We need to make sure this fund-raiser goes off without a hitch. I suppose there's no reason we can't have *both* deserts."

Frida might have to kowtow to Bettina, but no way was Georgia going to let this woman run all over her sister. "I think key lime tarts sound absolutely scrumptious," said Georgia. "How many do you think you can make for the party?"

Bettina turned to gape at her. "Make? You mean as in *me* personally?"

"It's your recipe, isn't it?"

"But . . . but, I already have a job." She smiled and threw back her shoulders. "Like you said, I'm the head of the balloon committee."

"Yes, and I know how time-consuming that must be. But I thought you said with this new nanny of yours you have extra time on your hands. Time to devote especially to Black Tie Bunco. I, for one, am really looking forward to tasting these key lime tarts." She shouldn't egg Bettina on like this, but Georgia couldn't help herself.

Bettina seemed dumbfounded.

Unfortunately, it only lasted a few seconds.

She narrowed her eyes at Georgia. "I just came from the senior center. While the wall tearing down thing was a good idea, I'm afraid the space *still* isn't big enough to hold everyone to watch this little cinematic masterpiece of Shea's. So I'm getting Mr. Hunky to tear down the kitchen wall as well."

Mr. Hunky?

"Bettina, we need the kitchen to hold the food," Frida protested.

"I thought you said it was being catered by the Harbor House. Can't they bring one of those little portable kitchen thingies? They have portable toilets; they must have portable kitchens."

Mr. Hunky? Georgia couldn't help but feel a twinge of . . . something. Not jealousy. Because there was nothing to be jealous of. She just didn't like Bettina referring to Dave as a piece of meat.

"Bettina," Frida said patiently, "we need the kitchen to stay the way it is. Period. You had no authority to tell anyone to knock down a wall. Technically, Viola is head of the Friends of the Rec Center committee. You should have run it by her first."

Bettina's jaw twitched. "Fine. You call Mr. Hunky and tell him to stop. I only left there a few minutes ago. I doubt he's had time to get much done."

"Why don't you do it?" Georgia demanded.

"Because, as you can see, I'm on my way to a pool party," Bettina explained.

"I'll call Dave," Frida said. "I can get his number from Kitty."

The oven timer went off. Frida opened the door and gently pushed her finger over the top of one of the muffins and frowned. "These need a few more minutes."

"You take care of the muffins," Georgia said to Frida. She stuffed the marketing plan into her purse. *Wouldn't want Ed to accidentally find it and freak out.* "I'll go stop Mr. Hunky myself."

15

Georgia walked through the front door to the senior center to find Dave painting a freshly plastered section of wall that was now exposed thanks to their demolition work. To her relief, the kitchen wall was still standing.

He interrupted his painting to glance at her. "Hey."

Despite the fact that the windows were open allowing a soft Gulf breeze to drift in, it was hot inside. He wore a Tampa Bay Rays T-shirt and jeans. A leather tool belt hung around his hips. His forehead glistened with perspiration. For some reason, it bothered Georgia that he was here alone, working on a project that he really wasn't even involved in. He didn't plan to stay in Whispering Bay. What did he care about this Black Tie Bunco fund-raiser?

"What are you, a one-man team?" she asked.

"I like doing this. It's kind of relaxing." He dipped his

brush into a bucket of paint and wiped off the excess against the rim. "What are you doing here?"

"I came to make sure you didn't tear down the kitchen. It sort of helps to have one when you plan to serve food."

The corners of his mouth twitched slightly. "I figured that."

"Bettina seemed to think she'd convinced you it needed to go." She searched his face for some kind of clue. He had to know Bettina found him attractive. He was the sort of man most women would—on a primitive, elemental level. But was he the sort of man who'd take advantage of it? It bothered her to think he might have put the moves on Bettina. She didn't think he was the type who'd go after a married woman, but then Bettina was exactly the kind of woman most men would find hard to resist on that same primitive, elemental sort of level.

"I think Tofu has more sense than Bettina."

Georgia laughed a little too loudly. "She's a piece of work all right."

"You didn't really come down here thinking I'd torn down that kitchen wall." It wasn't a question. He didn't look at her. He just continued painting.

"I . . . I guess not."

Why *had* she come running down here? "I worked up a loan restructure for the Bistro. I think Bruce Bailey is going to go for it."

"That's great."

She tried to think of something else to say. "And I've come up with a marketing plan to bring the place into the twenty-first century. Maybe you could take a look at it."

He stopped what he was doing to stare at her. His eyes

seemed greener today. "Why would you want me to do that?"

"I don't know, I just thought . . ." God, she hadn't felt this stupid since freshman calculus at Stanford, when she'd realized everyone around her was as smart as she was—maybe even smarter. So she'd set out to prove she could beat them all. Is that what she wanted now? To show Dave she was smarter than Bettina Bailey? "I should go."

He laid down his brush and wiped the palms of his hands against the back of his jeans. "Do you have it with you?" he asked.

She nodded.

He unbuckled the tool belt and placed it on the floor, next to the can of paint, then led her toward a couple of lawn chairs on the back patio. "It's cooler out here," he explained.

They sat in silence while he read. Georgia tried not to watch his face, but instead of skimming the pages, like she'd thought he would, he took his time to study it. For some reason, his slow perusal was making her nervous. Which was ridiculous. It was a top-rate plan.

He finished reading. "This is your idea? To turn your sister's cafe into a Starbucks wannabe?"

Georgia felt like she'd been slapped. "This is better than Starbucks."

"If you're into overpriced coffee and elevator music, then nothing is better than Starbucks. What you need is to keep your sister's place unique." He glanced at the bottom of page one. "And the mermaid mural should stay."

"It's tacky."

"Says you. Plus, I have a feeling your sister isn't going to go for painting over it with"—he eyed the page again—"a tasteful greenish gray color."

She snatched the papers out of his hand. "I don't know why I bothered asking your opinion. Obviously you know nothing about the restaurant business."

"I know that in about six months this town is going to be overrun with new construction. Which means that outside businesses are going to start sniffing around Whispering Bay. If Starbucks decides to put down stakes, then your sister is shit out of luck. She needs to offer something different. A full breakfast instead of just those muffins and bagels she makes. And she should stay open for lunch. New construction means hungry men. There's not a decent fast-food joint for miles. She needs to serve up real food—burgers, sandwiches. Let her keep her fancy coffee and muffins, but she needs to add another customer base. One that will keep her afloat no matter who decides to move into town."

"What you're suggesting is impractical. Have you actually seen the kitchen area? It's way too small for making anything besides bagels and muffins."

"I've been in the kitchen area, remember?"

She felt her cheeks pink up as a vision of her throwing up and Dave cleaning it popped into her mind.

"This marketing plan of yours is nothing more than putting lipstick on a pig," he said. "In the long run it's not going to make much of a difference."

Her face went hot, but not because she was embarrassed. "You can't just close your eyes and wish for a bigger kitchen. Renovations are expensive and the loan is already on shaky ground. If we go for a bigger loan and the idea tanks, then my sister will lose everything."

"You'll never hit it big unless you take a risk."

"Look who's talking? You won't even think about going into business with Steve because you're afraid. Of what? That he'll dump you again?"

Dave shoved himself out of his chair. "I have to get back to work."

Georgia snapped her mouth shut. Maybe she'd gone too far. She stood and reached out to touch him on the arm, but he backed away. "I'm sorry. I shouldn't have said that."

"Why did you really come here today? And why did you ask me to read your big marketing plan if you're not going to listen to anything I say? To show me how smart you are?"

"No!" The way he was suddenly staring at her made her nervous. "Why are you looking at me like that?"

"Like what?"

"Like . . ." She shook her head, unable to say it out loud. *Like you want to kiss me.*

"I'm looking at you the exact same way you're looking at me. I'm not the only one who feels it, Georgia. I'm just the only one who's not in denial about it."

"I don't know what you're talking about."

"Okay, Ms. Stanford, then I'll spell it out for you. I think your tits are a work of art. They belong in a damn museum. And the rest of the package isn't too shabby either. So sue me. Any guy who tells you physical attraction doesn't matter is lying. But it's not just that. Despite the fact you're dumber than a doorknob when it comes to men, and that you have absolutely no sense of humor, for some reason I really like you."

"I do so have a sense of humor!"

"No, you don't, but I could probably help you find one."

He paused and met her gaze dead-on. "If you're interested in that, or anything else, let me know."

"What else would I be interested in?" She held her breath. Did he actually say her tits belonged in a museum?

"Interested in this." He reached out and pulled her against him.

The papers in her hand fell to the ground. The kiss started off slow, the way it had the other night, but he quickly deepened it. She followed her first instinct—to place her arms around his neck and kiss him back. She could practically drink in the mingled smell of aftershave and sweat off his neck. She wanted to drown in it. She wanted to drown in *him*. In the way he looked at her and talked to her and the way his mouth worked over hers. She wanted to drown in the buzzing sensation zinging through her veins.

His hands came down to cup her bottom, pulling her even closer. She moaned and leaned into him, against the hard muscles of his chest and—

Oh, God.

"Is that a hammer in your pocket or are you just happy to see me?" she croaked.

He half laughed, half grimaced. "Now *that's* funny. Maybe you do have a sense of humor after all." He turned serious. "It's not a hammer, Georgia."

Of course it wasn't.

What was she doing? This was going way beyond an innocent kiss. She wasn't as dense as Dave thought she was. She liked him too. She just hadn't wanted to admit it to him. Or to herself.

"I'm sorry," she said, pulling away. For the second time

today she felt stupid. And cheap. She'd mentally berated Bettina Bailey for openly gawking at Dave, but she was so much worse. She'd known Dave was attracted to her, yet she'd run down here anyway, anxious to see him. Anxious to see how far she could take the attraction. That was the real reason she'd come here today. She'd wanted Dave to kiss her again. But now she wanted a lot more than just a kiss. And it definitely involved his hammer.

She took a deep breath, trying to shake off the sexual haze produced by that one simple kiss. It wasn't like Spencer was a dud in the bedroom. She'd always been more than satisfied with their sex life. So why this strong need to make sure Dave found her desirable? Was it because she was feeling vulnerable where Spencer was concerned? Or was it because of some sick competition with Bettina?

She didn't love Dave. And she wasn't the kind of woman who engaged in casual sex. But maybe that was only because she'd never really been tempted before.

Not like this.

"I'm sorry," she repeated. "I just can't."

He smiled ruefully. "At least you didn't throw up this time."

She didn't know whether to be relieved or mad at him for taking it so gracefully. Or maybe she was just mad at herself. "You're being too nice."

"Yeah, but you don't know what I'm thinking."

She smiled. How did he always know the exact, most perfect thing to say to her?

"Obviously, I *am* attracted to you. But that's as far as it goes. I'm in love with Spencer. And I'm not a cheater." She scooped up her marketing plan and stuffed it back in her purse. "I'll think about what you said. About the kitchen expansion. Maybe you're right about that."

He grinned. "You don't really think that."

"I figured it was the polite thing to say. Considering you took the time to read it and all and I was kind of a shrew about it."

They laughed. It was all good. He wasn't going all testosterone overload on her.

"The next time you come into the Bistro, say hi to me."

He hesitated, then smiled again. "Sure."

Something in his eyes made her breath catch. It was a subtle change. One so small most people would probably never notice. But she did. He was never coming back to the Bistro again. And considering the way her libido seemed to take over whenever he was around, it was definitely for the best.

16

Before she'd even gotten to her car Georgia had her cell phone out of her purse. She needed to talk to Spencer. Right now. Not because she had anything super important to say. But after her near miss with Dave, she needed to hear Spencer's voice.

Crystal picked up on the first ring.

"Hey, Georgia, how's it going?"

"Is Spencer in?" she asked, not bothering with any niceties.

"Sure; he's busy signing contracts, but I'll put you through to him."

Contracts? What contracts? "Are the Valley Tech people still there?"

"Oh, no. They left this morning."

"How did it go?" Before talking to Spencer Georgia wanted

Crystal's take on the visit. As scatterbrained as Crystal was, she was good at picking up vibes.

"Okay, I guess." Crystal's voice dropped to a whisper. "Hey, can I ask you a personal question?"

"Sure."

"Are you looking for a new job?"

Georgia's heart stopped. "Why do you think that?"

"It's just weird. There's been a bunch of calls from head-hunters today asking about you. I mean, there's usually a couple here and there, but there was like, three right after lunch. And one of the guys from Valley Tech asked me where you were, like he was worried you'd left the company, you know? But I was real evasive. So they wouldn't know you were on hiatus."

I'm not on hiatus! she wanted to shout. "Crystal, let me make this clear once and for all. I'm not on leave or hiatus or anything else. The only place I want to work is Moody Electronics. I'm on vacation. Pure and simple. After this week I'll be back at my desk."

"I'm so relieved to hear that! I mean, this place just wouldn't be the same without you."

Georgia relaxed a little. Crystal could be a total ditz, but she really was sweet. "If any more headhunters come sniffing around, tell them to drop dead. Okay?"

Crystal giggled. "Sure thing."

"So, can I talk to Spencer now?"

"Of course!" Crystal put her through.

"Babycakes, I was just thinking about you," he said.

"You were?" A surge of relief washed through her. She and Spencer were going to be okay. They had to be.

"Yep. And I've been doing some more thinking. About

what you said to me that other day, about this Black Tie
Bunco shindig. I think you're right. I should go down there
and put in a personal appearance. We can get a hotel room
in Destin and make a romantic weekend out of it. What do
you say?"

What did she say? She said *yes*! Her heart began to
zoom. She could picture it all now. Romantic music playing
in the background, cold champagne, Spencer looking handsome in his tux. She hadn't brought anything fancy enough
to wear for a formal event, so she'd have to go shopping for
something new. Something sexy, but elegant. Spencer liked
elegant—

Then she remembered the Crimson Tide. "What about
the game?" she asked cautiously.

"Babycakes, I'm hurt. You're more important than a
football game."

"Since when?"

"I guess I deserve that," he said. "I've been doing a lot of
soul-searching since you've been gone, sugar, and I don't
want to make the same mistakes with you that I made with
Big Leslie. I'm a changed man, Georgia. At least, I'm trying
to be."

He'd compared their relationship to his and Big Leslie's.
Which could only mean one thing. *Spencer planned to propose.*

Georgia's heart rate doubled. Her plan had worked! And
she'd hardly had to do anything except put a little distance
between them. Who knew the old adage about the heart
growing fonder was true?

"You still there, sugar?"

"I'm here," she squeaked.

He chuckled. "Say, I know you're on vacation and all, but would you mind taking a look at these contracts John Ambrose gave me? There's a lot of dollar signs everywhere and you know how nervous those make me." He paused. "I can fax them to you, if you'd like."

"Of course," she said. She didn't have access to a fax machine, but she'd get it. "Let me drive into Destin and see where I can find a machine and I'll call you with the number."

"That'd be great." She was about to disconnect when he added, "I'm really looking forward to this weekend, babycakes."

Her mind suddenly flashed back to the kiss with Dave. She mentally put on her Manolos and stomped out the memory. Dave was a tempting distraction. Nothing more. Her life with Spencer—*that's* what was real.

She tossed her purse in the car and took off down the road. It was almost four and she had a lot of work to do. First, she'd find a copier store that had fax machine access and get those contracts from Spencer. Then she'd embark on a quest for a killer dress.

Black Tie Bunco was the perfect backdrop to the most important night of her life. The night Spencer would finally propose to her.

17

It was Thursday, and the first day since Georgia had been in Whispering Bay that Dave hadn't stopped by the Bistro. She'd been right about him not coming back. It was a relief not to have to face him after that kiss. In just two days she'd be reunited with Spencer and she'd never have to think about that kiss again. Not that she'd thought about it much. Not really. Except maybe once or twice. But that was normal. After all, she was only human.

She finished wiping down the last of the tables, then stretched out her lower back and yawned. Yesterday had been busy. After receiving the contracts from Spencer, she'd hit nearly every outlet store and designer shop in Destin until she'd found the right outfit for Black Tie Bunco—a Herve Leger sequin-overlay cocktail dress. It was the most beautiful thing Georgia had ever laid eyes on. The form-fitting rayon-nylon-spandex mixture hugged every curve in her body and gave her some extra ones she didn't even know she had. The official color was blue haze, but it looked more silver than blue. Spencer wouldn't be able to take his eyes off her. It was the first time in her life she'd paid full price for anything, but it was worth every cent of the two thousand dollars she'd spent.

After her shopping spree she'd stayed up all night looking over the contracts Spencer had faxed. She made adjustments and added some notes about the figures. It was a complex contract, one that required a huge commitment from both companies. Georgia hoped that John Ambrose would approve her changes.

"It's my turn to host Bunco tonight," Frida said. "So after we get the place cleaned up, we'll go ahead and set up." She dumped a pile of hot pink tablecloths in Georgia's hands. "Wait till you see the prizes."

"Has it been a week already?"

"I have a really cool theme planned—Cheeseburger in Paradise. Ed's going to grill burgers. We'll drink beer and listen to Jimmy Buffett's greatest hits CD. Everyone is wearing a Hawaiian shirt. I've got one for you too."

"For me?"

"Sure. You're going to play." Frida began moving tables to the side, setting up three of the smaller tables in the middle. "You can put the tablecloths on these."

"But I thought you only played with twelve. Besides, I planned to go into Destin again this afternoon. I need a mani and a pedi and shoes to go with my new dress."

"With that dress of yours you don't need shoes. No one is going to be looking at your feet."

Georgia grinned. "It *is* a great dress, isn't it?"

Frida stopped what she was doing. "I hope Spencer's worth it."

"What's that supposed to mean?"

"I just want you to be happy, that's all."

"I *am* happy. At least I will be once Spencer proposes and I can get my life started." Georgia glanced at her watch. It was already two p.m. She'd also planned to go by the bank, but of course, she couldn't tell that to Frida. She'd left Bruce Bailey a message on his phone, but he hadn't called back. It had been four days since she'd presented the loan restructure. It didn't take four days to make a decision. On the other hand, no news was good news. Still, it couldn't hurt to nudge Bruce a little.

"You can do your errands tomorrow. Ed is going to be busy this afternoon dropping off paintings at the Harbor House so I'm really counting on you to help me decorate and set up for Bunco."

"I'll help you get ready, but do I have to stay and play? I mean, don't your friends have some sort of rules about your subs?"

"All our subs now belong to Bettina's group, remember? Besides, all the Babes loved you. You and I can play as one. And I get a kick out of showing off my smart, beautiful sister."

The Babes loved her? They barely knew her.

"You did have fun last week, didn't you?" Frida asked, sensing Georgia's hesitation.

Besides getting so drunk she dialed Spencer and told him to fuck off, quit her job, and flashed her boobs? Not to mention kissing a stranger, then nearly puking on him. None of that qualified as Georgia's idea of fun. But she'd admit, up until then, it hadn't been as bad as she'd thought. "Sure, I had fun, I mean if you forget all the drama with Spencer."

"Last week was a fluke," said Frida. "I promise, normally we never get that wild." Then she added with a giggle, "Well, almost never."

"I guess I can get my nails done tomorrow afternoon. But you have to let me treat you to a mani and a pedi. We'll have some girl time. It'll be fun."

Frida's face twisted. "I really should go down to the bank tomorrow to face Bruce Bailey and try to figure out this loan thing. I don't think I can put it off any longer."

Georgia tried not to look alarmed. "You can go to the bank next week when they open again on Tuesday. It's not going to make a lot of difference in the outcome, is it?"

"I guess not," Frida conceded. She smiled and gave her a hug. "I wish you'd come down more often. It's been so nice this past week. It's helped take my mind off this foreclosure thing. And I've really appreciated all the work you've done around the place."

"So does that mean we'll do the girl thing tomorrow afternoon? It'll be our last chance. And we want to look our best for Black Tie Bunco."

"Sure," said Frida.

Georgia smiled, satisfied she'd talked her sister out of making a trip to the bank. Now she'd just have to make sure that sometime after tonight's Bunco and before her sister bonding session tomorrow afternoon, she squeezed in time to put some pressure on Bruce Bailey.

Georgia's Hawaiian shirt was bright blue with big yellow and red flowers. Frida had even gotten everyone leis.

"I thought the theme was Jimmy Buffet, not a Hawaiian luau," said Brenda, adjusting the lei around her neck. "Are these plastic? I'm sensitive to plastic next to my skin." Georgia remembered Brenda as being slightly negative. Until she'd gotten plastered with the secret frozen margaritas. Then she loosened up faster than a rusty hinge covered in WD-40.

"Technically, yes, the leis are Hawaiian," said Frida. "But it's the spirit that counts. And I'm not sure what material they're made of."

"Hawaiian shirts are tropical and so is the Jimmy Buffet theme," said Kitty in a tone meant to bring the discussion to an end. "I think the two of you did a great job."

The two of them meaning Georgia and Frida. Georgia glanced around the Bistro. She had to admit, the place *did* look good. Multicolored twinkling lights lit up the ceiling and the edges of the counters. A table with a pineapple centerpiece held condiments for the burgers Ed was grilling outside on the patio while Jimmy Buffett's "Volcano" played in the background.

"This is even better than sushi night," Pilar said. "Not that I didn't like your Japanese theme," she added quickly.

Shea took a drag of her beer. "Is everyone here?" She did a quick head count and frowned. "We're missing someone."

"Tina's MIA," said Mimi. She wore a white gardenia tucked behind an ear. It complimented her dark hair and the pale pink tropical shirt she wore. "She called me to say she was running late."

"Problems with Brett?" Liz asked.

Mimi pursed her lips and nodded. "Brett's had a relapse. Tina found out this afternoon he spent last weekend in one of the casinos in Biloxi, instead of camping like he'd told her."

The group moaned.

Georgia remembered now. Brett was Tina's husband and a gambler.

"Poor Tina," said Brenda. "How much longer is she going to have to put up with this?"

Pilar sighed. "Unfortunately Brett suffers from a really bad case of Y-chromo-loma."

Georgia frowned. "What?"

"That's Pilar's word for anything that a man does wrong," supplied Kitty.

"Women can be compulsive gamblers too," said Shea.

Pilar put her hand in the air, signaling she didn't want to hear it.

The front door opened. Tina walked in, wearing her Hawaiian shirt and a brave smile. The Babes swooped around her, hugging her and murmuring encouraging words.

Mimi put an arm around Tina. "Is there anything we can do?"

"You're doing it already," said Tina. "Just knowing I have you guys to lean on." She glanced around the room. "And knowing that I can come here and be myself and not have to pretend that everything is okay, when it isn't. It means a lot."

Georgia watched the scene with a mixture of sympathy and mild disgust. She felt for Tina, she really did. But there was no way she'd put up with a gambling husband. If Georgia were in Tina's shoes, she'd have given this Brett character his walking papers a long time ago.

"I didn't come here to bring everyone down," Tina announced. "I want the night to go as planned. Whatever else happens, Bunco must go on."

"Thatta girl!" said Lorraine.

Murmurs of encouragement echoed through the room.

Ed brought in a platter of burgers and the Babes dug in. All twelve Babes were present tonight, but Frida still insisted Georgia play. They would trade off games, Frida said.

Georgia had just taken a bite out of her cheeseburger when her cell phone went off. Earlier, she'd slid her phone inside the pocket to her shorts. Just in case Spencer called. She hadn't talked to him all day. With a sigh of relief she saw his number light up her screen.

"Hey, I've been hoping you'd call tonight."

"Georgia? Is that you? I can barely hear you. Are you at a bar?"

"We're hosting Bunco at Frida's. Hold on a sec." She slipped outside, to the back patio where it was quiet. Quiet except for the sound of croaking frogs and the ocean waves lapping against the shore. "Can you hear me now?"

"Much better," Spencer said. Then a pause. "I have some bad news."

A tingle of dread ran up Georgia's spine. "Are the kids okay?"

"Who? Oh, you mean Spencer Jr. and Little Leslie? Yes, they're both fine." Another long pause. "It's about this weekend. There's just no easy way to say this, babycakes, but I can't come down. Valley Tech is giving me the runaround on this new contract. I've tried to put them off until next week, but they're like stink on a skunk."

"Is . . . is it the changes I made?"

"Your changes were fine. It's just some petty details I need to go over with John Ambrose and his crew. You know how he is."

"The Valley Tech people are still there?" According to Crystal they'd left yesterday. Had she heard Crystal wrong?

Spencer coughed into the phone. "Bastards. They're determined to ruin my weekend." He laughed in a way meant for Georgia to laugh along with him.

Only Georgia wasn't laughing.

"You know how much this new contract could mean to the company," he continued. "I really have no choice."

"I'll . . . I'll come up and help. Between the two of us we can—"

"No need, sugar. Just because my weekend's shot doesn't mean yours has to be too. You go to this Black Tie Bunco shindig and have fun. Make sure to make a big contribution from the company. Okay?"

Georgia couldn't talk.

"Babycakes, did you hear me?"

"Sure," she said weakly.

"You are coming back to work next week. Right? Thanks for being so sweet. I promise I'll make it up to you." He hung up before she could say anything else.

The back door opened. It was Frida. "We're waiting for you," she said shuffling Georgia back inside the building and into a chair. "We're rolling for ones. You remember how to play, right?"

"Sure."

She'd been reduced to a one-word vocabulary.

"You're my partner this round," Kitty said. She studied Georgia a second then frowned. "Are you all right?"

Did she look as numb as she felt? She started to say it. The dreaded *sure*. Instead, she just nodded. She didn't say anything else the rest of the game. Not when Kitty rolled a Bunco that added mega points to their score. Not even when they won and went on to the next table and Georgia found herself partnered with Shea, who was babbling on and on about Black Tie Bunco and the hot pink cocktail dress she was planning to wear and how hard it had been to find a tux to fit Moose.

Crystal said the Valley Tech people were gone. And Spencer said they were still in Birmingham. One of them was lying. Crystal had no reason to lie. And Spencer *never* missed a Bama football game. It didn't take an IQ of 140 to figure it out. Spencer never had any intention of coming down for Black Tie Bunco. Just like he had no intention of ever asking her to marry him.

She didn't say anything when she lost, or when someone slipped another beer in her hand even though she'd never finished her first one. She half listened as Mimi spoke of the house she and Zeke were buying, and how great it was that the house was so close to Shea's, and what a bummer it would be to have Bettina Bailey for a neighbor.

All she wanted was to go upstairs and cry. To call her best friend and tell her what a lying-piece-of-shit scumbag Spencer was. Only she realized she didn't have a best friend. She didn't have any friends, really. She worked sixty hours a week for a man who would rather watch a football game than sacrifice one weekend to make her happy. Her only friend in Birmingham was Denise, and that was because she worked for Georgia. They went out to lunch sometimes, and every once in a while, they'd catch a movie, but the majority of Georgia's time was spent at work. Or with the lying-piece-of-shit scumbag she thought loved her enough to marry her.

Georgia stood and placed her hands on the card table. "I just caught Spencer in a big lie," she announced.

Playing stopped.

Why had she blurted that out? Last week she'd had the excuse of being drunk. But she'd barely had half a beer tonight.

"Isn't that the guy you told to fuck off?" asked Brenda, looking confused.

"Yeah, but they sort of got back together the next day," Pilar said.

The Babes all began to talk at once.

"What happened?" Frida asked softly.

"He told me he couldn't come down this weekend because he needs to wine and dine a client. Only I know from his secretary that the client left the plant yesterday." She didn't know why she was telling them this. She didn't want anyone feeling sorry for her or murmuring consoling platitudes. She'd scream if they started that.

"What did he say when you called him out on it?" Pilar asked.

"I didn't call him out on it."

"Why not?" Frida demanded.

"I froze up. And I guess because . . . because this time, no matter what excuse he comes up, I'm done with him."

Shea stood and wrapped an arm around her. "Sweetie, I'm so sorry."

The rest of the Babes came up one by one to hug her and offer condolences.

"You'll find someone better than him," said Mimi.

"He'll get his. What goes around comes around," said Kitty.

Even Tina, who God knew had enough problems of her own looked genuinely sympathetic when she said, "He's dog shit. No, he's not even that good. He's bird dung."

"Bird dung isn't as bad as him," quipped Lorraine, "he's lovebug gung. You know, the kind that sticks to your car?"

This last part made Georgia laugh. It didn't feel so bad. Being the object of their pity.

As a matter of fact, she kind of liked it.

"This sucks," Brenda muttered.

"What are you going to do?" asked Pilar.

"I don't know. I don't think I can go back to work for him after this."

"Of course you can't!" agreed Shea.

"I know what you're going to do," said Frida. "Saturday night, you're going to get all dolled up in that hot silver blue dress you bought and you're going to go to Black Tie Bunco and have the time of your life. And you're going to forget all about that creep."

Georgia shook her head. "I can't go to Black Tie Bunco. Not now."

"But you have to!" Kitty protested. "You worked so hard knocking down that wall. And besides, what are you going to do? Sit here all alone and mope?"

Georgia looked at their faces. They'd had the same expression earlier in the evening when they were talking about

Tina and her gambling husband. "I'm really touched by your concern. Truly I am. But this Black Tie Bunco thing doesn't mean the same to me as it does to all of you. Under the circumstances, I'd rather just stay here. Besides, I would feel weird going without a date."

"There'll be lots of people going without dates," said Kitty. "Steve's friend Dave is going and he doesn't have a date. It wouldn't be weird at all."

That was the final nail on the coffin. No way could Georgia face Dave now. Not when she'd made such a big deal of her and Spencer getting back together. It would be too humiliating.

"Honestly, I'll be okay. Please, I didn't mean to ruin the evening. You all keep playing. I'm just going to slip out and—"

"Sorry, but you don't get off that easily. If you don't play, then no one plays," said Pilar.

The Babes all nodded in agreement.

"Bunco Babe rules clearly state that if a player has to stop due to emotional overload, then the rest of us stop too. We just couldn't go on," Kitty said.

It was the stupidest thing Georgia had ever heard in her life. And probably something they'd just made up. But she had no choice. She had to keep playing. Or ruin the night for everyone else. And she knew how much Frida had been looking forward to Bunco. If Tina Navarone could play despite the fact her husband had just gone off on a gambling spree, then so could she.

"I guess I'll keep playing," Georgia said

"Then let's roll for threes," said Pilar.

And that's exactly what they did. The evening went on as planned. They played Bunco and drank beer and had cheeseburgers and listened to more Jimmy Buffet and gossiped and Georgia even managed to laugh a little.

Maybe this Bunco thing wasn't so bad after all.

18
||||||

By ten, business at the Bistro had slowed, so when Georgia asked to slip out to run errands even though they weren't officially closed, Frida told her to go ahead.

It was funny.

Not funny ha-ha, but funny strange how the two of them had fallen into a comfortable routine of working together. For the most part, the job was mindless, but there was also a certain satisfaction in it. It had helped to have something physical to do this morning to take her mind off Spencer. Frida must have been feeling sorry for her, because for the first time, she'd let Georgia make her own batch of muffins.

Frida liked to experiment with her muffin recipes, always trying new and sometimes eclectic ingredients. The eggplant muffins Georgia had made today hadn't gone over well. Rusty

1, or maybe it was Rusty 2 (Georgia still couldn't remember which was which), had been the only customer to like them. But it had been fun seeing the expressions on the customers' faces when they saw what the muffin of the day was, and despite the muffin's unpopularity it hadn't seemed to hurt business any.

Muffin of the day had been Georgia's brainchild. In the week she'd been here, she made a few other, subtler changes. Like placing fresh-cut flowers in the unisex bathroom. It was a small touch, but the customers had noticed.

Georgia was beginning to understand what the Bistro meant to Frida. Which made it all the more imperative Georgia resolve the problem at the bank. She briefly thought of the marketing plan Dave had scoffed at. Could he have been right? She frowned. Once upon a time she would have never questioned herself on anything concerning business. But this whole thing with Spencer had left her feeling shaky. Maybe her instincts weren't as sharp as she thought they were. Once she had the loan restructure taken care of, she'd present the marketing plan to Frida and Ed and let them decide for themselves.

Trying hard not to look at the Herve Leger sequin cocktail dress, Georgia carefully replaced it in the plastic garment bag and hung it up in the backseat of her car. Today was her last business day in Whispering Bay and she had a lot to accomplish. She'd still been willing to do the girl thing with Frida. If only for the simple fact that her sister deserved a little pampering. But Frida had come up with the excuse that not all the cheesecakes were done for the party tomorrow and since Georgia's heart wasn't into the mani/pedi thing anymore she didn't put up much of an argument.

The receptionist in the front lobby of the Whispering Bay Community Bank smiled pleasantly. "May I help you?"

"I'd like to see Bruce Bailey please."

"I'm sorry, you just missed him."

Crap. "When will he be back?"

"You might try in about an hour."

Georgia gave the receptionist another business card. Just in case she'd forgotten her. "Will you please tell him Georgia Meyer needs to see him today?"

"Of course."

Okay, she thought, taking a cleansing breath. No biggie. She'd just have to do her errands in reverse order.

She drove the thirty-minute drive into Destin, to the specialty boutique where she'd bought the silver cocktail dress. The shop was located in a tiny strip mall next to a shoe store. Georgia tried to ignore the huge Sale sign hanging above a display of evening footwear. She should be in there buying shoes to match her cocktail dress. Not making a return. The dress was the most beautiful thing she'd ever seen. But she could never wear it. Not now.

She walked into the boutique. The same saleswoman who'd sold her the dress was standing behind the counter. Georgia remembered her name was Carrie and she was part owner of the shop.

The dressing room door flung open. Bettina Bailey sauntered out wearing a fitted, tangerine silk, above-the-knee dress. Of all the people in all the shops to run into, she would have to be here. It was like the final insult.

"Isn't this a coincidence," Bettina purred. She eyed the garment bag hanging over Georgia's arm, then ignored her to turn to a twentysomething woman with pale skin and ebony hair pulled back into a high ponytail. "Persephone, what do you think of this dress?"

Georgia did a double take. So *this* was the infamous Persephone. She was ultra-thin and had great cheekbones. She looked more like *Project Runway* than *Mary Poppins*.

Bettina twirled around. The neckline on the dress was a tad revealing. But then Bettina's boobs *were* top rate. Georgia wondered what ol' Bruce would make of all that exposed cleavage.

Bettina's boobs might be top rate but were they a work of art? Your tits belong in a museum.

Georgia tried to shake that line out of her head. Who said stuff like that anyway?

"That dress looks awesome on you!" Persephone gushed. "Like absolutely magnificent!"

Georgia had to admit, the dress did look good on Bettina. But she wouldn't go as far as awesome and magnificent. Persephone must still be hitting the bottle.

"What's the occasion?" Georgia asked.

"Black Tie Bunco, of course."

"You waited till today to shop for a dress?"

Carrie snorted.

"*Of course* I didn't wait till today," Bettina said. "I just want to explore all my options."

Georgia's gaze wandered to a black cocktail dress hung on a rack to the side of the counter. It didn't take a genius to figure out Bettina was making an exchange. And by the expression on Carrie's face, it probably wasn't the first one she'd made either.

"I guess it's important that you look your best, especially since you had such an important role in putting together the event. Being in charge of the balloon committee and all."

"That's right," Bettina said, ignoring the sarcasm in Georgia's voice. She narrowed her eyes at the garment bag in Georgia's hand.

Georgia placed the garment bag over the counter and unzipped it. "I need to return this."

Carrie gazed at Georgia with sympathy. "I remember you now. This dress looked perfect on you. You're really going to return it?"

Georgia swallowed past the knot in her throat. It was ridiculous to get so emotional over a dress. But it wasn't the loss of the dress that had her so choked up. Not really. It was what the dress represented. "I bought it to wear for Black Tie Bunco. But I'm not going anymore."

"That's too bad," Carrie said. "My husband just bought tickets. We moved to Whispering Bay a couple of months ago. Into this new housing development. Maybe you've heard of it. Dolphin Isles?"

Georgia nodded. That was the development Steve wanted Dave to take charge of. Georgia wondered if Dave had told Steve he wasn't going to work for him yet.

"Destin is getting way too crowded," confided Carrie. "Anyway, I've been looking to join a Bunco group and all anyone talks about is the Bunco Babes. Have you heard of them?"

"My sister is a Babe."

Carrie's eyes lit up. "Really? Do you think she can get me on the sub list?"

"I'll ask," said Georgia.

"You can get on my group's sub list," Bettina jumped in. "I'm head of the Bunco Bunnies."

Carrie frowned. "I haven't heard anything about them."

"That's because we're new." She clicked her fingers at Persephone. "Give her my card."

Persephone reached inside her purse to produce a business card.

"Write your name and number on the back of that," instructed Bettina. "I'll put you down on our list. As a matter of fact, you can be our number one sub."

"Thanks," mumbled Carrie. She jotted her info on the back of the card and reluctantly handed it back to Persephone.

Bettina looked pleased. "Now, where were we? Oh, yes, let me see that dress."

"What dress?" asked Carrie.

"That silvery thing," Bettina said impatiently. "Right there on the counter."

Georgia nearly choked. "You want to try on *my* dress?"

"It's not your dress if you're returning it, is it?"

Carrie glanced nervously at Georgia. "Are you *positive* you want to return this?"

Georgia tried to compose herself. To act all cool and collected, when what she really wanted was to grab the dress off the counter and run out the store. But she didn't need the dress. And she was trying hard to remember that she didn't want it anymore either. "Yes," she said, grinding out the words. "I want to return it."

Bettina picked the dress up by the hanger. Her eyes widened slightly when she noticed the price tag. "This isn't really my color."

Carrie's chin jutted out. "It's a Herve Leger. Normally, a dress like this would have to be special ordered. But I took a chance and ordered one to display in the front window. I can assure you, I won't have any problem selling it."

"What size is it?" Bettina demanded.

"It's a medium," said Carrie. "It fits an eight to a ten, but it tends to run small, so—"

Bettina tossed the dress back on the counter. "Just my luck. I find the *one* dress that might work and it's *way* too big for me." She turned to Georgia. "I wear a four."

"Good for you," Georgia muttered.

"We could have the dress altered," Carrie offered.

"By tomorrow?" Bettina asked.

"It would be cutting it close, but I think we could manage. Of course, you'll have to pay an extra alteration fee."

"Money is no object," said Bettina. "Let me try it on."

This was too much. Georgia couldn't stay for this. She couldn't see Bettina Bailey in her dress. She just couldn't. "Can I get this return over with?" she asked Carrie.

"Of course. If I could have your receipt?"

"Oh, sure," Georgia said, sorting through the contents of her purse. She flipped open her wallet. "I know I have it here somewhere." She always kept the receipt.

She searched through every compartment, but no receipt. Maybe she'd left it on top of the dresser in Frida's guest room.

"I'm afraid without a receipt, I can only offer you an in-store credit," said Carrie.

"It's a two-thousand-dollar dress and I don't live in town. I hardly think I'll be able to use that," Georgia complained. It was just her luck. The first time she paid retail for a designer outfit and she couldn't get her money back. "Isn't there someway I can get a credit on my charge card? I know I have the receipt somewhere."

"I'm sorry. My partner is really strict about that." Carrie mulled it over a few seconds, then said, "I'll tell you what. I'll give you the store credit for now. When you find the receipt bring it in and I'll credit your card. And if you can't find it," she whispered confidentially, "I'll find a way to get around my partner and give you the refund anyway." She hesitated. "You are going to mention me to your sister, right? About being on the Babes' sub list?"

"Right," Georgia whispered back, trying to keep a serious face. Who would have thought the Babes had such power?

She took the credit slip and tried for a fast escape, but it was too late. Bettina emerged from the dressing room wearing *her* dress. Technically of course, it was no longer Georgia's dress. But it was, damn it.

Georgia's heart sank. The dress looked good on Bettina. And it didn't look like it needed to be altered either.

Carrie cocked her head to the side. "I think it fits very well," she said, coming to the same conclusion. "I'd actually recommend leaving it as is."

Bettina made a face. "Are you sure there's not a mistake on the tag? There's no way I fit into a medium."

"Oh my God," cried Persephone, suddenly coming to life. "That's it! That dress was made for you."

No, it wasn't! Georgia wanted to shout. *It was made for me.*

"Do you really think so?" Bettina gave Persephone a hug. "What did I ever do without you?" She threw Georgia a sly look. "Persephone and I have totally bonded just like sisters this past week. We stayed up all night making my key lime tarts for the party tomorrow. Did I mention it's my own secret recipe? Shea isn't the only one with secret recipes, you know. She really blew it when she falsely accused Persephone of stealing that liquor."

Persephone blanked her face.

"No disrespect meant to Persephone," Georgia said, "but I don't think Shea is the kind of person to falsely accuse anyone."

"And you've known Shea what? A whole week?" Bettina mocked.

"I might not have known her long, but I'm a pretty good judge of character. Besides, she's my sister's friend, so that's good enough for me."

Carrie cleared her throat. "Would you like me to ring that up for you?" she asked Bettina.

"Most definitely," Bettina answered. "But I still want it taken in. Right here," she said, pinching the dress in at the waistline.

"I don't think that's going to make any difference," said Carrie. "It can't be more than an eighth of inch."

"An eighth of an inch is perfect. Right now it's like a tent swallowing me up."

Georgia couldn't stand it a minute longer. It was stupid, but she felt like she was six again. When the Bettina Baileys of this world ruled her universe and there hadn't been anything she could do about it.

She turned and hightailed it out the store, got in her car, and drove straight to the bank.

"I'm sorry," said the receptionist, "but Mr. Bailey's wife, maybe you've heard of her? Bettina Bailey? Anyway, she's head of the Black Tie Bunco committee and she's hard at work doing last-minute prep work for the festivities tomorrow. You have heard of Black Tie Bunco, right? The whole town's talking about it."

Last minute prep work, my ass. "Yes," said Georgia, gritting her teeth, "I've heard of Black Tie Bunco."

"So with Mrs. Bailey off working on the event, Mr. Bailey had to stay home and watch his twins. He's a great father," she added, smiling broadly.

Did Bruce really think Bettina was in charge of the party? Or did he just go around telling people that? Either way, it was sort of pathetic.

"Do you think he'll be in later then?"

"Oh, no. He's taking the rest of the day off. Black Tie Bunco is a lot of work."

Yeah, and so is shopping. "Do you have a number where I can reach him? It's important."

"Sorry, I can't give that out. But he'll back Tuesday morning," she said cheerfully.

Georgia could feel her blood pressure rise. "All right, well, thank you."

She slammed her car door a little too forcefully. Bruce

Bailey had definitely blown her off. But why? A simple yes or no would have been sufficient. Then Georgia could have put Plan B into action.

Not that she had any idea of what Plan B would be. But she'd think of something. She had to. If there was any way she could pay off the past due amount without Frida finding out, she would. Case closed. In the end, Frida might not have a choice. Because if it came down to taking money from Georgia or losing the Bistro, Frida might have to retract her whole "I can live in a tent" speech.

19

‖‖‖‖

Frida stared at the two-thousand-dollar in-store credit slip Georgia had just handed her. "You returned your dress? Why did you do that? You loved that dress!"

"I told you. I'm not going to Black Tie Bunco, so I don't need it anymore."

"What I am supposed to do with this credit?"

"You can buy yourself a whole new wardrobe, that's what you can do." The more Georgia had thought about it, the more she'd realized she didn't want a refund. For one thing, she didn't want to obligate the Babes into having to take Carrie on as a sub. And she wanted Frida to have the credit. Frida never bought herself anything. Georgia knew now it was because money had been so tight.

"But I don't need a new wardrobe," Frida protested.

"Tough."

Frida sighed. "So if you're not going to Black Tie Bunco,

what are you going to do tomorrow night? Sit around and read the *Wall Street Journal*?"

"Actually, that's not a bad idea."

Frida gave her a hard stare.

"That was a joke." She wished Dave had been around. No way could he accuse of her of not having a sense of humor after that. "I'm going to rent an old movie. Something with some heart. Like *The Philadelphia Story* or better yet, *His Girl Friday*. Anything with Cary Grant in it. And I'm going to eat popcorn and drink lots of wine. And don't try to talk me out of it. I deserve a pity party. Even if I have to throw it myself."

Someone else in Whispering Bay must have excellent taste, because everything with Cary Grant in it was rented out. So she had to settle on *Transformers*. But that was okay. There was something a little Cary Grantish about Shia LeBoeuf, even if she was old enough to be his older, older, older sister.

It was almost six p.m.

Frida and Ed had dressed for Black Tie Bunco, then gone to a pre-party cocktail hour at Shea's house. Frida had begged her to at least go to that, but Georgia had been adamant.

It's my party and I'll cry if I want to.

The funny thing was she hadn't cried at all.

Not that that was so unusual. Georgia wasn't a crier. She never had been.

She hadn't cried the first day of school when someone had called her a "freak" for living at the commune. And she most certainly hadn't cried when she arrived at Stanford with a mere thirty dollars in her bank account only to find that her student financial aid had been delayed for two weeks. She'd lived on ramen noodles and instant macaroni and cheese and she'd done just fine, hadn't she?

The only time she remembered crying was when her mother had died. Corrine Meyer had been a free spirit. She'd taught Georgia the importance of self-sufficiency. But just because she loved her mother didn't mean she wanted to live her mother's life. Her mother had always encouraged her to find her own path. It just so happened that Georgia's path was meant to include the finer things in life. She'd worked hard for them. And she deserved them. There wasn't anything wrong with wanting the nice big house on the hill. A conventional marriage. A country club membership. A couple of kids.

And she'd almost had it. She'd come so close she could taste it.

So why wasn't she crying?

Why wasn't she starving herself and throwing things or being catatonic or any of the other things most women (or at least the ones she'd heard about) did when they had their hearts broken and their dreams smashed?

It must be the movie. How could she expect to get choked up watching *Transformers*?

She should have rented *Casablanca*.

That would have gotten the tears flowing.

Sometimes a kiss is just a kiss, Georgia.

She frowned. Why had she thought of that?

What she needed was more popcorn. The buttery, sticky-fingered kind. She had just placed a bag in the microwave when she heard the commotion downstairs. It sounded like a herd of wildebeests had invaded the Bistro.

But it wasn't a pack of wild animals.

It was the Babes. All twelve of them by the looks of it. Dressed in their glittery cocktail attire and armed with bags of all sizes.

"What's going on?" Georgia asked.

"We're here to get you ready for the party," said Kitty.

"And don't try to stop us," said Frida. She held a black plastic garment bag in her hands. Georgia held her breath. *It couldn't be.* The blue haze Herve Leger cocktail dress now belonged to Bettina. Minus one-eighth of an inch of fabric on either side.

Pilar dumped a large bag onto the coffee table and tossed out the contents. Lorraine and Mimi did the same thing. There were hot irons, rollers, hairspray, lipsticks, and more cosmetics than you could find behind the scenes at a Miss America Pageant.

"We weren't sure what sort of tools you had, so we brought an assortment," said Shea. She studied Georgia's hair and face, then turned to the Babes. "C'mon, girls, we have our work cut out for us."

Georgia found her voice. "This is really sweet of you guys, but I'm not going," she said firmly.

"You have to," Frida said. "Otherwise, when are you going to wear this?" She opened the garment bag to reveal the Herve Leger dress.

"How . . . how did you get this?" Georgia reached out to reverently touch a sequin. It wasn't a dream.

"We took the store credit you gave me and bought it back," said Frida.

"But Bettina Bailey bought this dress! She was even having it altered."

"She must have changed her mind," Kitty said.

The Babes gave each other a look.

"Say you'll go," said Pilar. "We went to a lot of trouble to pull this all together. We even got you shoes." She held up a pair of strappy silver sandals with a gorgeous four-inch stiletto heel. "Size eight. Right?"

Georgia nodded, a little dazed. "Right," she squeaked. "Okay, I'll go."

How could she not?

Within seconds, they'd grabbed her and tossed her into the bathroom.

"You have five minutes to shower and wash your hair," Shea yelled from the other side of the door.

Georgia emerged exactly five minutes later in her bathrobe with her hair dripping wet. She didn't dare take a second longer. These Babes meant business.

Mimi pushed her into a chair. She had a blow-dryer in one hand and a flat iron in the other. "I get her first."

"We'll have to do her all at once," said Shea. "It's the only way we'll her done in time."

"I don't look that bad, do I?" Georgia asked.

They ignored her.

Her feet were plunked into a large bowl of warm soapy water. Kitty grabbed one hand and Tina grabbed the other.

"What color should we do her nails?" mused Tina.

"I'm kind of partial to neutral colors," began Georgia.

"We didn't ask you," Kitty said.

"The dress is silvery blue. Maybe a French manicure?" Mimi suggested.

"Too boring," Tina said.

"Her nails should be black. It's very in right now," said Shea, who was sitting on a stool exfoliating one of the heels on Georgia's feet.

Black? Georgia was about to protest, then clamped her mouth shut. Did it matter what color they painted her nails? Or what they did with her hair? The fact was she felt like Cinderella. Only her fairy godmother was in the form of twelve Bunco Babes.

They hadn't known her long. Only a week. And they were probably only doing it for Frida's sake. Which went to show how much these women thought of her sister.

But still . . .

No. It didn't matter what she ended up looking like.

Despite the fact that her heart was breaking and her dreams were shattered, this was shaping up to be one of the best nights of her life.

20

If she was Cinderella, then this was definitely the ball. Georgia hadn't stepped foot in the senior center since four days ago when she'd come running over to make sure Dave hadn't knocked down the kitchen wall. But in that short amount of time the place had been transformed.

The main room sparkled with thousands of tiny white lights. There were tables set up for playing Bunco. The sliding glass doors opened into an adjoining tent where the sounds of an orchestra playing soft jazz filled the air. Black and white balloons filled with helium covered every square inch of the ceiling. Waiters with trays of appetizers and glasses of champagne zigzagged through the crush of women in cocktail dresses and men in black tuxedos.

It was all beautiful.

Georgia felt beautiful too.

The dress fit her perfectly. Mimi had blow-dried and flat ironed her hair until it lay sleek and shiny around her shoulders. They'd given her a manicure and a pedicure and had even done her makeup.

The Babes had truly outdone themselves. There was no way Georgia could ever reciprocate.

After they'd finished her makeover, the Babes had jumped back in their cars to meet their spouses and do their own last-minute touch-ups.

They were all here. Shea and Pilar and Kitty and the rest of them. They took turns introducing Georgia to their husbands. Georgia already knew Moose. He gave her a friendly bear hug. Steve was there with Kitty. He leaned down and kissed her on the cheek. Georgia was aware of a moment of supreme nervousness as she glanced around searching for Dave in the group. But she didn't see him.

She met Pilar's husband, Nick, who seemed as quiet as Pilar was animated. Brett Navarone hadn't been what Georgia had imagined either. But then she'd never met a compulsive gambler before. He was medium height and appeared mild-mannered in his wire-rimmed glasses.

Everyone looked wonderful.

Even Ed looked polished in his black tux. He'd gotten a haircut so his usual out-of-control curly blond hair was tamed down. Frida had on a white linen sheath. Her hair was pulled up with a faux diamond clip that Georgia recognized as belonging to their mother, and she'd even worn lipstick for the occasion.

Shea placed a flute of champagne in Georgia's hand. "It looks great, doesn't it?" she said, her blue eyes misting with tears. "All that hard work has paid off."

"How much money do you think you've raised?" Georgia asked. She took a sip of the cold champagne. It was delicious.

"At least fifty thousand," Shea said proudly. "Most of which came from corporate sponsorships. It might not sound like a ton of money, but an event like this not only helps raise capital for the project, it helps get the whole community involved, which then leads to hopefully more donations. Plus, we'll raise money tonight with Bunco. In order to play, you have to pay," she said, winking. Georgia followed her gaze to a large acrylic tumbler displayed on a table in the center of the room. Brenda appeared to be manning the table, directing people on how to play and handing out dice. The party had just started and the tumbler was already half-filled with bills, most of which looked like twenties and fifties from what Georgia could make out.

"We're charging people to play Bunco?" Mimi asked.

Zeke, her husband, who looked exceptionally yummy in his tux, shook his head. "I'm not seeing that," he said, his slight southern twang sounding more pronounced tonight. "As chief of police I have to remind you that gambling is against Whispering Bay ordinances."

Shea yanked on Zeke's tie in a playful gesture. "We're not gambling, Zeke. We're charging people to play. It's all for a good cause."

Zeke mumbled something and went off to follow a waiter with a tray of shrimp.

"There's a reporter from the *Whispering Bay Gazette* coming tonight. He's going to take pictures and do a big write-up," continued Shea. "Hopefully, it'll make the bigger papers in Destin and Panama City and generate more publicity for our cause."

A waiter refilled Georgia's champagne flute. She raised the flute to her lips to take a sip.

From across the room she locked eyes with Dave.

Her breath snagged in her throat. The expression "Mr. Hunky" didn't do him justice.

He had on the same black tux that every other man in the place wore. But he didn't look like any other man there. He'd gotten a haircut and was smooth shaven, except for that soul patch Georgia was warming up to. His broad shoulders filled more than just his tux. They seemed to fill the room. He looked dangerous and sexy and definitely interested.

In her.

Georgia could feel her face go warm.

She stood there, her feet frozen to the floor, aware that Shea and Pilar were talking but not listening to a word they said. How could she pay attention to anything when Dave was staring at her like that?

After what seemed like a long time, his gaze broke. She noticed he was looking around her, like he was trying to spot someone.

He was looking for Spencer. She was sure of it.

He didn't know Spencer wouldn't be here tonight. That she and Spencer weren't together anymore. At least not in Georgia's mind.

If you're interested in that or anything else, let me know.

It wasn't like she would be cheating on Spencer anymore. His blatant lie gave her a free pass.

Only it didn't. Not really.

It would *still* be cheating. At least in her mind. Until she confronted Spencer and made a clean break she wasn't a free woman.

But it couldn't hurt to go over and say hi to Dave.

She worked her way through the crowd and ran smack into Earl Handy. He had to grab on to his cane to keep from falling.

"Watch where you're going, missy!" Earl complained.

"I'm sorry," Georgia said, helping Earl right himself. She looked around for DeeDee. "Is your friend here?"

Earl's forehead scrunched up. "Who?"

"The lady who was with you at the bank the other day."

"DeeDee *ain't* my friend. She's my keeper."

Georgia laughed. Earl was a character, all right. But he was also sharp as a tack. She knew from Frida that Earl had been born wealthy but he'd graduated from the University of Florida and had gone on to do post graduate work at Duke University. He might have been born with a silver spoon in his mouth but he hadn't been a slacker. He'd owned several successful businesses in Whispering Bay, all of which he'd sold off at a profit when he'd retired.

"I'm glad I ran into you," he said, narrowing his eyes at her shrewdly. "I've been meaning to stop by that place of yours and make you a proposition."

Georgia sighed. He thought she was Frida. She should be used to it by now.

"Really, Mr. Handy, I'm not that type of girl," she said playfully.

Earl's eyes twinkled. "Your loss," he said.

Georgia giggled.

"It's about them bran muffins you make. I'll give you five big ones for the recipe."

Georgia stilled. "Five thousand dollars?"

"Hell no! Five dollars." He leaned on his cane and dug in his tux jacket to produce a wallet. "Cash."

"Mr. Handy, I don't think my sister is willing to sell her bran muffin recipe for a measly five dollars."

"You're the other one?" He scowled. "What's wrong with five dollars? I can probably get the recipe off the internet, you know. I have a password and everything. Then I don't have to pay her nothing."

"Go ahead," Georgia said. "But it won't be the same. Frida's bran muffins are the best."

He shoved his wallet back in his jacket. "Why do you think I'm willing to pay for it? Those things keep me regular. And they taste a hell of a lot better than milk of magnesia, that's for certain."

"I'm sure Frida would be happy to make you up a big batch. You can freeze them."

He winked at her. "I like 'em fresh. Like my women."

"Then I guess you'll just have to make a trip into the Bistro every day."

Earl playfully wagged a finger at her. "I'll get that recipe, missy. You'll see. You haven't heard the last from ol' Earl."

Viola came up and looped her arm through Earl's. "He's not causing trouble, is he?" she asked Georgia.

"We're doing business here, Viola," Earl told her.

"Really? Well, it just so happens I have some Gray Flamingo business I need to discuss with you." She smiled apologetically at Georgia. "You don't mind if I steal him away, do you?"

"Steal away," Georgia said, taking a sip of her champagne. She scanned the room, looking for Dave, but he was nowhere in sight.

Maybe he was out in the tent.

Georgia started for the sliding doors when someone grabbed her by the elbow and whirled her around.

"That's my dress!" Bettina Bailey whispered between clenched teeth.

"Obviously, it's not your dress," Georgia said, plucking her arm from Bettina's grasp. She had on the tangerine cocktail dress Georgia had seen her trying on at the boutique.

Bettina's eyes narrowed into catlike slits. "I was told my dress had been *misplaced*."

"That's—" Georgia snapped her mouth shut. Had the Babes gotten her dress under less-than-honest circumstances? She thought about how wild Carrie had been to be added to the Babes' sub list.

"I'm sorry," Georgia said, which was only partially true. She was sorry Bettina had been lied to, but she wasn't sorry the Babes had gotten her dress back. "It was probably a misunderstanding. But you know, I did have this dress first and I only returned it because I thought I wouldn't be here tonight."

"You all think you're so great, don't you?" she sneered. "Well, I have news for you. After tonight, the rest of this town is going to know exactly what you Babes are made of." Bettina grabbed a glass of champagne from a wandering waiter and downed it in one gulp, then stomped off.

Georgia's throat went dry. What had Bettina meant by that last statement? Maybe she should warn Frida.

She went into the tent. The dance floor was full of couples. She spotted Dave dancing with Kitty. She wanted to cut in. But something held her back. So instead, she found her sister and Shea and told them about Bettina's outburst.

"You bribed Carrie, didn't you?" Georgia asked.

"It was *your* dress," said Frida. "Bettina only wanted it to spite you."

"Frida! Now she's after blood."

"So what?" said Shea. "You were right, Georgia. We've been letting Bettina Bailey boss us around for years. We're tired of always tiptoeing around that ego of hers. Besides, Carrie was more than happy to help us. She'll fit in with the Babes perfectly." Shea waved to someone in the buffet line. Georgia saw that it was Carrie. Carrie's face split into a grin and she waved back.

Georgia took a deep breath. "I think what you guys did tonight was awesome. Getting my dress back and making me over. But I don't want it to come back and bite you in the ass."

Frida put her arm around Georgia. "Don't worry about it. Like Shea said, we're not afraid of Bettina. She's nothing but a big bag of wind. And we have you to thank for helping us see that. She's not going to push us around anymore." She shoved a plate in Georgia's hands and steered her over to a table. "Now eat. This is the best blackened grouper you're ever going to taste. And don't forget dessert," she added, "there's cheesecake *and* key lime tarts to sample."

Georgia grudgingly took a bite of the fish. Frida was right. The blackened grouper was delicious. Moose sat next to her and regaled her with stories from his football playing days at Florida State. The husbands took turns asking her to dance. More than likely at their wives' nudging.

She even danced with Ted Ferguson.

"That's some dress," he said, holding her a little too close while they danced to "You and I." It was one of Georgia's favorite songs. She'd always envisioned dancing to it at her wedding. If anything should make her cry, that would be it. She shut her eyes and tried to squeeze out a tear.

Nothing happened.

"Are you all right?" Ted asked.

"I was just thinking of Spencer. He's at the football game, you know." She waited to see if Ted confirmed what she already knew deep in her heart.

"You can't compete with the Crimson Tide, Georgia. Sometimes you just have to *roll* with the punches," Ted said, chuckling at his own witticism.

Georgia smiled weakly. "You're right." But the fact was she didn't want to compete with football. Or work. Or his kids or anything else. She understood she couldn't always come first in Spencer's life. But just once, she'd wanted to be the one snapping the tape at the finish line. She wanted to feel appreciated. Wanted.

Your tits belong in a museum.

Damn it. Get that out of your head!

The rest of the evening seemed to go in slow motion. She played a couple of rounds of Bunco, then went back into the tent. Dave never came near her, which made it abundantly clear to Georgia that whatever there'd been between the two of them was over. He had to have seen she was here alone.

She was about to go search for a piece of Frida's cheesecake when she spotted Bruce Bailey slipping outside. It was the first time Georgia had seen him all night. She followed him. "Mr. Bailey, may I speak to you a minute?"

He looked guilty. "Of course." He tossed his cigarette in the sand and crushed it with the toe of his shiny black shoe. "What can I do for you, Ms. Meyer?"

At least he remembered her name.

"I've tried calling you. Haven't you gotten my messages?"

It was dark outside, but the moon provided enough light for Georgia to spot the sweat dripping off Bruce's head. "I'm sorry, this has been a busy week."

"I need to know your decision about the loan restructure."

He sighed. "It's like I said, Ms. Meyer, your client, or should I say your *sister* is going to have to adhere to the terms of the loan. If she can't repay the back-due amount, then she's going to have to do the regular payback. We'll need upfront money and she'll have to pay late fees just like everyone else."

"I thought we'd come to an understanding about that."

Bruce pulled a white handkerchief out of his pocket to mop the sweat off his head. "You misrepresented yourself to me. I don't appreciate being lied to."

"I admit," Georgia began carefully, "that Frida Hampton is my sister, a fact I omitted because it has nothing to do with anything, but I never lied to you."

"You told me you worked for Spencer Moody. Even gave me some trumped-up business card proclaiming yourself CFO of his company. If that's not a lie, then what is?"

Georgia pulled back her shoulders. "I *am* the CFO of Moody Electronics." At least she was until Tuesday morning when she handed in her resignation.

"Not according to Spencer Moody's secretary. As a matter of fact, when I insisted you worked there, she told me to drop dead."

What?

"Oh, *that*!" Georgia laughed in relief. "I told Crystal to

say that if anyone called asking about me. She must have thought you were a headhunter."

"I wasn't born yesterday, Ms. Meyer. Now if you'll excuse me, I have a wife who needs some attention. This has been a very trying night for her."

Georgia tensed. "Is this because of my dress?"

He looked blank. "What does your dress have to do with anything?"

"This isn't some petty revenge thing because your wife wanted to wear my dress, is it?"

"I don't know what you're talking about. The truth is this: Your sister and her husband are four months late in their payments." He hesitated. "This isn't the first time this has happened. A couple of years ago we went through the same thing. I was more lenient then, but I can't be again. The simple fact is your sister doesn't know how to run a business. If there was another source of income to consider, we could arrange a different sort of repayment. But according to our records that husband of hers hasn't produced a penny in the last year from those paintings of his. With the Bistro as their only source of income I have no option but to either collect on the past-due amount or foreclose."

"What if I paid the past-due amount? Could we do that without my sister finding out?"

Bruce frowned. "What are you suggesting? That I lie? That I falsify documents? I believe that's your forte. Now you're more than welcome to pay whatever you like toward your sister's debt, but that's between the two of you. If you'll excuse me."

Georgia watched in stunned silence as Bruce rejoined the party.

This was awful. Bruce wasn't going to cave. And unless Frida got off her damn high horse she was going to lose the Bistro. *And learn how to cook s'mores over a campfire.*

Georgia could wring Crystal's neck. But the truth was this wasn't Crystal's fault. It wasn't even Frida's fault. She was doing the best she could.

The rising sound of music and laughter caught her attention. Someone else was coming outside.

It was Ed. "Hey." He reached inside his tux jacket to produce a pack of cigarettes.

"You shouldn't smoke. It's bad for your health."

He grinned sheepishly. "Don't tell Frida. She thinks I quit."

Georgia could feel her blood boiling.

He did a double take. "Are you mad at me or something?"

"Frustrated is more like it."

He waited for her to continue.

She shouldn't do it. She really shouldn't. But she couldn't help herself. "Ed, do you know that the bank is about to foreclose on the Bistro?"

He nearly dropped his pack of cigarettes. "What?"

"Frida is four months behind on the rent."

Ed's shoulders slumped. "I had a feeling something was wrong. But she kept saying everything was fine." He shook his head. "We had car problems a few months ago. Then the latte machine broke down. Our credit wasn't good, so we had to pay for a new one upfront." Suddenly, Ed looked angry. "She told you, but she didn't tell me?"

"That's because she wants to protect your *artistic mojo*," Georgia said, hating the sarcasm in her voice. But someone had to shake some sense into Ed. "How long are you going to keep pretending you can make a living as an artist?"

Ed's face fell.

Be strong, Georgia. "It's not that you're not talented. I know you've tried, but it's not working. Frida has been busting her butt for the past ten years and look where it's gotten her. You need to bring some money into the household. Some real money. Before Frida loses everything she loves."

"You're right," he said flatly. "I'm a failure."

Georgia wanted to scream. She needed Ed to be proactive, not wallow in self-pity. "Do you know that I asked her where the two of you would live if you lost the Bistro? She said you could live in a trailer, or a tent."

Ed didn't say anything.

"Look, I can help," she said, trying to hold on to her patience. "I have the money. I've offered it to Frida but she won't listen to me. But if you talk her into it, I know she'll take it."

"How much?" Ed asked.

"Twelve thousand."

He winced.

The tent flap opened. It was Kitty. "I've been looking everywhere for you two. Shea's movie is going to start in fifteen minutes."

"Okay," Ed said woodenly.

"I guess we should go," Georgia said after Kitty had gone back inside. "So are you going to take care of this? Are you going to convince Frida to take the money?" she pressed. She had to know this was a done deal.

"I'll take care of it," Ed snapped. He opened the tent flap for her but he didn't make a motion to follow her inside.

Georgia hesitated. The anger she'd felt when Bruce had told her he was rejecting the loan was now gone. If Ed was going to talk Frida into taking the money, then there wasn't anything to be upset about anymore. "Aren't you coming?" she asked him.

"I need a minute," he said, not looking her in the eye.

Georgia had never seen Ed like this. Maybe telling him about the foreclosure had been the wrong thing to do. If only she hadn't had that encounter with Bruce Bailey seconds before . . .

She headed for the bar. Her legs suddenly felt like rubber beneath her. She hadn't *wanted* to be the one to burst Ed's bubble. But Frida certainly was never going to do it. She'd done the right thing, telling him about the foreclosure.

So why did she feel like she'd just told a four-year-old that there was no Santa Claus?

She ordered another glass of champagne but it tasted flat. The night had started out like magic. But all she wanted now was to go home—back to Frida's place where she could take off the dress and wash off all the makeup and sleep for twenty-four hours.

But she couldn't go. Not yet. For one thing, she'd driven over with Frida and Ed. And after all the Babes had done for her it would be rude to leave early. Maybe once Shea's video montage played, she could excuse herself and walk home. She could slip off her sandals and take the beach route back to the Bistro. She hadn't really taken any time to think about her future, about what she was going to do after she quit Moody Electronics. One thing was certain. She *sucked* at business consulting.

Tears welled up behind her eyes.

Stop it! She was being a wuss.

She made a dash for the bathroom. But as usual, there was a line just to get inside the door.

So she opened the first closed door she could find.

It was a walk-in closet filled with brooms and cleaning supplies and carpentry tools. But it was darkish and quiet. She could stay in here until she pulled herself together and got over this ridiculous crying jag.

She hadn't been in the closet a full minute before the door opened and the light switch came on.

It was Dave. And he looked angry. "Whose ass do I have to kick?"

21

Georgia gulped. "Pardon me?"

"Whose ass do I have to kick for making you cry? And if you tell me it's Bettina Bailey, I'm going to be really disappointed."

Georgia smiled through her tears. "Because you don't ass kick women?"

"Because you should be able to take care of her yourself."

She laughed.

He swiped a tear from her cheek, making her skin tingle. "Why are you crying?"

"How did you know I was crying? And how did you know I was in here?"

"I've known exactly where you've been all night. Every long-drawn-out miserable second of it."

"You have?" For some reason, that made her feel better.

"You didn't know that?"

"I . . . I thought you were avoiding me."

"Where's your boyfriend? Wasn't he going to be here to-night?"

"Spencer's not my boyfriend. Not anymore. I caught him lying to me."

He waited for her to go on.

"You were right. He's never going to ask me to marry him. But at least now I know what I have to do."

His jaw twitched. "And what's that?"

"Quit my job. For real this time. I can't work for Spencer after everything that's happened between us." Everything she'd ever heard about office romances being a bad idea came whooshing through her head. The fact that Spencer was her boss made it doubly hard. She thought she'd been smart enough not to get tangled up in a bad situation. Apparently in matters of the heart she was as clueless as every other woman in America who made the mistake of sleeping with her boss. "But it's okay, I won't have any trouble getting a new job. According to Spencer's secretary the head-hunters are already sniffing around." Georgia could only hope Crystal hadn't told any *real* headhunters to drop dead.

"So that's why you were crying. Because of Spencer?"

"No." She'd tried to cry over Spencer. She just hadn't rented the right movies to get her going. "It's my sister. Actually, it's my brother-in-law, Ed."

"Ed made you cry?" Dave asked incredulously.

"I think I screwed up," she admitted, although the truth was she didn't think it, *she knew it*. She'd never forget the expression on Ed's face when she basically told him he was a failure. She cringed now just thinking about it. She should have found another way to get Frida to take her money.

"I told Ed about the foreclosure."

"He didn't know?"

Georgia shook her head. "And then I told him to man up and get a real job."

"I bet he took that well."

"It was like a lamb being led to the slaughter. He looked so . . . stunned." Georgia shook her head. She could feel the tears start up again. She angrily swiped them away.

Dave drew her into his arms. He felt so big and solid and warm. It was easy to just slide into him and forget about all the shit going on in her life. "And now you feel guilty," he said.

He rubbed his hand over her back, making tiny circles that sent shivers down her spine. "I don't know what to do," she said. "Or how to help them."

She snuggled in closer to him. The smell of his cologne was making her dizzy. It was the same kind of dizzy she'd experienced sitting next to him in his pickup truck the night he'd driven her home from Bunco. If she was being honest, she'd admit to herself what it *really* was.

"You're a good girl, Georgia."

"No, I'm not. A good girl wouldn't be thinking what I'm thinking right now."

She could feel him tense. "What are you thinking?"

"I'm thinking I want you to kiss me," she whispered.

She raised her head to look him in the eye. She couldn't tell if he was mad. Or turned on. Or both. But he definitely wasn't kissing her.

"Maybe I shouldn't have said that."

"Maybe you shouldn't have."

It wasn't the response she was expecting. But he wasn't pushing her away. In fact, it was just the opposite. His hand kept making those deliciously slow little circles over her back drawing her closer.

"Maybe I've got it all wrong. Maybe you shouldn't kiss me. Maybe I should kiss you," she said, feeling breathless.

"Maybe you should."

It was all the encouragement she needed. She grabbed the front of his shirt and pulled his head down. He let her take the lead in the kiss while he shrugged himself out of his jacket, letting it fall to the floor. She ran her hands across his broad back feeling the muscles tense and bunch beneath his crisp white-linen shirt.

He broke the kiss and lifted her onto a waist-high wooden workbench, bringing them eye-level. She wrapped her legs around his waist, drawing him in as close as possible.

He ran a finger over the front of her bodice, lazily following the sequins' pattern. Georgia could feel her nipples tighten. "Where did you get this dress?"

Georgia quickly worked off his necktie. It was a clip-on, thank God. "Do you like it?" she rasped, tearing through the buttons of his shirt at lightning speed. She was disappointed to find he was wearing a T-shirt. *Damn it*. She wanted to see some skin.

"Like it?" he muttered. "I don't know if I love it or hate it."

He reached for the zipper in the back, lowering the dress to her waist. With an efficiency she didn't want to think about he unhooked her strapless bra and drew one breast into his mouth. He sucked her soft and slow, making her restless. His tongue drew tiny circles around her nipples. *Your tits belong in a museum.* It might be the cheesiest pickup line she'd ever heard, but who cared? No man had ever made her feel this wanted before. The dress might be beautiful, but Dave was making *her* feel beautiful. Had Spencer ever done that?

Georgia grabbed on to the top of his head and threaded her fingers through his hair.

He placed one hand on her knee and snaked it up her inner thigh. She couldn't help but smile. She sure as hell wasn't wearing granny panties tonight.

"Whatever this is," he said, rubbing the lacy edges to her white silk bikini underwear, "I can say with utmost certainty that I like it."

"Why don't you find out?"

He locked gazes with her and grinned. God, he had the most gorgeous green eyes. She wiggled her hips from side to side allowing him to drag the white bikini underwear down her thighs, over her knees, then slowly down her ankles and over her sandals. He took a long, hard look at the small scrap of silk. "Definitely an improvement over last time."

Georgia laughed.

"What are we doing?" he asked suddenly.

"Don't you know?"

He shook his head. "I'm serious, Georgia. Either we stop. Now. Or I'm going to fuck you. Right here in this closet. With two hundred people on the other side of that door."

She swallowed hard. She didn't know how to respond to that. So she reached out and rubbed the palm of her hand over his erection. "You're right. It's not a hammer."

"Damn right it's not."

"I say we go for option number two," she said quickly, before she chickened out and changed her mind.

He stared at her a second, then leaned back in to kiss her. Only it wasn't like his other kisses. It was hot and wild and furious. His mouth was everywhere, on her neck, on her breasts, and somehow, and she wasn't quite sure how he got there (and she didn't care either), between her legs.

He wrapped her knees around his neck and pinned her waist with his hands. She couldn't get away if she wanted to. Not that she wanted to. She wasn't crazy. She leaned back on the rough wooden table and closed her eyes, oblivious to anything but the feel of his warm tongue lapping against her skin. Georgia had never experienced anything like this before. It was beyond crazy. Dave was going down on her in this tiny closet in the middle of a gala event and the only thing she knew was that if he stopped, she'd kill him. She had to muffle her scream when she came.

It could have been seconds or minutes or hours or days, she wasn't sure, but all of sudden she noticed the bright light above her head shining obnoxiously in her eyes.

"That was . . . that was . . ." She sat up and tried to read-just her dress while she fumbled for the right words. *"Thank you,"* she finally said. It seemed inadequate, but it was all she could muster at the moment.

"No need to thank me," he said, looking amused. "I was kind of hoping you'd reciprocate."

"Of course!" she said, suddenly feeling embarrassed. And extremely unsophisticated. She slid not so gracefully off the worktable to land on shaky legs. "Should I, um—" She searched the floor for a good spot to set up.

He turned her around and placed her hands firmly on the table, then leaned in and whispered against her ear. "I don't want you on your knees."

His warm breath sent a hot shiver down her spine. "Then how am I going to—"

"Bend over." He lifted the edge of her dress and slid it up to bunch at her waist. "And hold on."

Hold on?

She heard him rustle with his pants, heard his zipper lower, heard the sound of foil ripping.

"What are you doing?" she asked, although it was a stupid question because she knew exactly what he was doing.

"I'm a safe driver, remember?"

She laughed nervously.

She could hear him slipping on the condom.

And then he was slipping into her and she didn't laugh anymore. It didn't take her long to understand why he told her to hold on. It might not be a hammer inside her, but she was definitely being nailed. She gripped the edge of the table and held on for dear life.

It was like his kiss had been. Crazy and wild and she shouldn't have liked it as much as she did. But the truth was she loved every bone-jarring, mind-exploding second of it. It was like she was being truly fucked for the first time in her life.

She came hard and fast and so did he.

After it was all over, he gently turned her around into his arms and began nuzzling the bottom of her earlobe. "Are you all right?"

How he managed to speak was beyond her. She couldn't even catch her breath. All she could do was nod.

"This wasn't exactly how I pictured our first time to-gether," he said, right before he kissed her again. This time it was like the kisses of before. Slow and sweet and gentle.

And before she could ask him how he *had* pictured their first time together, or for that matter when he'd first even thought of it, somewhere in the back of her hazy, sated con-sciousness, she heard the closet door open and close again.

22

Her brother-in-law looked shocked.

Georgia quickly made sure her dress covered everything it needed to.

Dave on the other hand was as cool as the proverbial cucumber. "Can we do something for you, Ed?"

"I . . . I thought I heard someone scream."

"Really?" Dave asked mildly. "I didn't hear anything. Did you, Georgia?"

"*Right,*" Ed said, finally catching on. He scrambled for the door, accidentally stepping on her strapless bra in the process. He picked it off the floor like it was a lit grenade and handed it to her. "Um, this must be yours." His face was bright red.

"Thanks," Georgia muttered, too embarrassed to look Ed in the eye. If he'd been a few minutes earlier . . .

Ed turned around to give her some privacy. Georgia quickly put herself together.

"The movie is starting," Ed said. "You know, Shea's montage piece on the history of Whispering Bay? I thought I'd ditch out on it. That's why I came in here. Plus of course, there was that strange noise . . ."

Dave nodded, still looking composed. His bowtie, jacket, everything was back in place. "You ready?" he asked her.

Dave opened the door and the three of them stepped into the main room. If they were quiet and discreet, maybe no one would notice them.

It was eerie.

Except for the light given off from the video it was dark. And absolutely quiet. The crowd seemed mesmerized.

Georgia looked up at the screen.

It wasn't a montage history piece on Whispering Bay that had the crowd so enthralled.

It was the Bunco Babes.

"*I found this in Moose's hunting trunk,*" Pilar's voice blared through the room.

There she was on screen, holding up a bottle of liquor.

"*Moose keeps booze in his hunting trunk?*" It was Kitty who asked.

Frida's face popped up next. "*And you searched through it?*"

"*Desperate times call for desperate measures. Right, girls?*" Pilar pumped the liquor bottle in the air.

Oh my God.

It was the Bunco party at Shea's house. But how had it gotten taped? And who had put it on screen?

The video cut to a frame of Liz talking about Christy Pappas forming a new Bunco group. Her words were so slurred Georgia could hardly make them out. And she'd been there for the original.

"From Bettina Bailey. She's going to be in the group. And . . ." Liz paused dramatically. *"They're going to play on Thursday nights. Just like us."*

"Her husband, Bruce, is vice president of the bank and on the city council," added Kitty. *"He's a real pompous know-it-all."* Kitty hiccupped, then did a Wilma Flintstone giggle.

Georgia looked around the room. The crowd's attention was glued to the screen. People were whispering behind their hands to one another but other than that, no one was moving.

And it went on.

"Bettina probably strong-armed Christy into it. I mean, Christy is sweet and all but she'd never have the gumption to start a group on her own. Besides, she's always wanted to be a Babe!"

"I thought Christy had more self-esteem. How good could this group be? I mean, they're basically going to be Bunco-Babe-wannabes. It's sad, really."

"Do you think they'll find ten other women who want to play?"

"Oh, yeah. Everyone wants to play Bunco. But not everyone can be a Babe. Too bad for them."

This was followed by a group shot of the Babes cackling. One of them even fell out of her chair.

Several older women in the audience shook their heads in disgust.

It hadn't happened that way. Had it?

The shot of Pilar flashing her boobs was next.

The room broke out in chaos.

Dave placed his hand on her elbow, snapping Georgia out of her shocked stupor. "I'm going to put an end to this crap," he said, taking off for the back of the room.

It was Mimi's turn on screen. *"Man, I wish I could get my boobs lifted. Breastfeeding did a number on them. But we really need a new roof on the house and Zeke wouldn't go for it anyway. He's such a tightwad."*

"Roof, schmoof. What's more important? Your boobs or a few leaky tiles? Zeke Grant needs to get his priorities straight."

And then there were boobs everywhere.

And the part Georgia dreaded most.

"Fuck you, Spencer."

"I said fuck you. Oh, and fuck your job too because I quit!"

Georgia squeezed her eyes shut. This wasn't happening. Maybe she was still in the closet with Dave in the middle of some sort of psychedelic orgasm-induced hallucination she couldn't wake up from.

She peeped one eye open.

Nope. It wasn't a hallucination.

There was she was on screen, flashing her breasts for everyone to gawk at.

Suddenly, the screen froze and the lights in the room came back on. Great. It *would* have to freeze when it was her boobs on display.

The looks on people's faces ranged from amusement to shock to anger. Bruce Bailey looked like he'd poured a pitcher of water over his head he was sweating so much.

"I told you those Babes were out of control!" Bettina said loudly for everyone to hear.

"Moose Masterson has a drinking problem?" one woman asked.

"Apparently, it's so bad he keeps bottles of liquor stashed throughout the house and even in his garage," came another voice.

The murmuring became louder.

"I always knew those Babes were some sort of secret society!"

"Do you think they have orgies?"

"I hear they get a stripper for their birthdays," came a voice from the corner of the room.

Earl Handy banged his cane on the floor. "Who turned off the show?" he demanded. DeeDee tried to shush him, but that only made Earl louder. "It was the best part of the whole dang night!"

Georgia rushed to the center of the room, where the Babes were all huddled together in a tight circle. Sort of like the wagons did while they waited for the Indians to attack.

"This is awful," Pilar whispered.

"Where did they get that film?" Mimi asked, looking like she wanted to cry. "My parents are here tonight. My dad saw my boobs!"

"I know where they got that film," Shea said, narrowing her eyes. "It's from my nanny cam. I must have still had it on that night we played Bunco."

"Damn that nanny cam!" said Brenda. "I told you no good could come out of it."

From the corner of her eye Georgia spotted a familiar

face. She must still be in the throes of that hallucination, because she could have sworn it was . . .

She squeezed her eyes shut and opened them again.

No.

It couldn't be.

But it was.

There in living black-and-white tux, plus of course his perfectly coifed blond hair and sparkling blue eyes, was Spencer Moody.

He reached her in about three seconds.

"Georgia?" He looked stunned. Not that Georgia could blame him. It was fast becoming the look of the night. "Is that *you* on screen?"

Georgia looked up. Her boobs were still there, glaring down at everyone in the room. At least you couldn't see her face.

"Spencer, what are you doing here? I thought you were at the Bama game."

"The Bama game?" He sounded genuinely surprised. "Georgia, I told you I had to stay in town to seal that contract with Valley Tech. And guess what, babycakes? I did it! They gave us a five-million-dollar contract! As soon as I finished, I threw on my tux and drove straight here. I didn't call because I didn't want to get your hopes up in case they stayed longer and I couldn't make it."

"But I thought the Valley Tech people left a few days ago!"

Spencer frowned. "Who told you that?"

"Crystal," she said numbly. As soon as she said it, she knew she'd screwed up. How many times had Crystal gotten something wrong? Like the headhunter thing?

Spencer hadn't lied to her.

He'd been working, just like he'd told her.

And while he'd been driving down from Birmingham to surprise her, she'd been fucking Dave in the closet.

And loving every second of it.

Her throat began to swell.

But maybe that was a good thing. Maybe she was going into anaphylactic shock or whatever it was called and they'd have to code her. And naturally, with all the drugs they'd have to give her, she'd forget everything about the past twenty-four hours. But just when it seemed redemption was within reach, she found her voice. Which had to mean her throat wasn't really swelling up. She was panicking. And now wasn't a time to panic.

"Babycakes," Spencer said, looking at her sternly. "You know how Crystal gets everything mixed up." He shook his head. "If she wasn't my cousin . . . I don't know. Do you think I should fire her?"

"No! You can't fire Crystal," Georgia croaked. "Like you said, she's family."

Spencer ran a hand through his hair, mussing it up slightly to give him an adorable frat-boy look. "What you must have thought . . . Babycakes, you know I'd never lie to you, right?"

"Right," she squeaked.

Somehow Ted Ferguson wiggled his way into their group. "Interesting film, ladies," he said to no one in particular. He spotted Spencer. "Moody!" he cried, slapping Spencer on the back. "Why aren't you at the Bama game?"

Spencer gave Ted a good ol' boy handshake. "I couldn't

let my best girl here down," he said putting his arm around Georgia.

Ted raised a brow. "After the things she said about you on that video? Of course, with a set like hers, I guess all can be forgiven, huh?" He ogled Georgia's cleavage then pointed to the screen.

Spencer turned to Georgia, his gaze slowly following Ted's. "Georgia, that *is* you!"

The screen suddenly went blank.

Thank God!

"Darling, what's gotten into you? That bordered on the vulgar," Spencer whispered tightly.

There went her throat again. She wondered which of Freud's defense mechanisms "throat swelling" was classified under.

"I can explain," she said weakly.

"You don't have to explain anything," Dave said, coming up behind her.

No. No. No.

Moose was with him. And Steve and Nick, and from what Georgia could make out, the rest of the Babes' husbands.

Dave squeezed her shoulder. "Sorry it took so long to get that turned off. Someone rigged the extension cord so we couldn't find it."

"Who are you?" Spencer demanded.

"Um, this is—"

"Dave Hernandez," Dave said, cutting off Georgia's bumbling attempt at an introduction.

"This is none of your business, Mr. Hernandez, it's between me and my fiancé."

Georgia blinked. *"Your what?"*

Spencer grinned. "This is what I came down for, baby-cakes. To make that fifth anniversary dinner up to you."

Spencer fell to his knees.

For the second time tonight, the room went completely silent.

He slipped his hand in his tux jacket to produce a small black box and flipped it open to reveal what appeared to be—*holy shit*!

The diamond had to be at least four carats. And that was just the solitaire in the middle. It was surrounded by lots of other smaller diamonds along the band. She had to practically shield her eyes from the glare.

The crowd gasped.

Smiling confidently, Spencer took her hand and gazed up into her eyes. "Georgia Meyer," he drawled in that slow way of his that sent shivers down her spine, "Will you marry me?"

23

Oh my God.

This was it.

She'd waited five years for this day. Only not like this. Not after everything that had just happened.

"Spencer, please. Get up," she whispered frantically.

"Not till I get an answer, babycakes."

"Spencer, no—"

"*No?*" He looked more shocked now than when he'd realized it was her boobs on screen.

Dave wedged his way between them. "The lady said no."

Spencer looked taken aback. "This is none of your business, buddy." He stood up, toe to toe with Dave.

"Spencer, let's go outside," pleaded Georgia. If she could get him alone, maybe she could explain— Explain what? That she didn't want to marry him anymore? Is that what she wanted? To turn Spencer down? She didn't know. All she knew was that she couldn't give him an answer tonight. And she couldn't let him find out about Dave.

Spencer ignored her.

Georgia tried to make eye contact with Dave, but he and Spencer were locked in some sort of macho stare down to the death. "Dave, please, I need to talk to him."

"To turn down his proposal, right?"

"It's not that simple."

"Why not?" Dave demanded.

Spencer's face went red. "Georgia, who is this clown? I don't understand. I thought you'd be thrilled I was finally breaking down to propose. Does this new attitude of yours have anything to do with that . . . that *film* I just witnessed?"

"I told you, Spencer, I can explain—"

"I don't think I like your tone," Dave interjected. "As a matter of fact, I know I don't. You owe the lady an apology."

"And I think you should mind your own fucking business," Spencer said, giving Dave a hard shove to the shoulder.

Georgia wanted to squeeze her eyes shut. But she couldn't. She stood there, frozen, knowing absolutely without a doubt what was coming next.

Dave's fist flew, bringing Spencer down faster than the NASDAQ on a bad trading day.

Georgia ran to Spencer's side. "Are you all right?"

"That bastard broke my nose!" Spencer sat up and wiggled his nose back and forth with his fingers, testing it.

"I didn't touch his nose," Dave said to Georgia, shaking his head in disgust. "I hit him in the jaw."

Georgia studied Spencer's face. It was true. His nose looked perfectly fine to her.

Dave offered her his hand. "Let's get out of here."

It was tempting. She wanted nothing more than to take Dave's hand and run away with him. But she couldn't leave Spencer lying here on the floor. Surely Dave understood that.

"I can't," she said, trying to help Spencer up.

Dave looked like he wanted to punch Spencer again. Instead, he turned and walked out the door.

So much for understanding her predicament.

Someone started shouting. Then a scuffle broke out behind them.

It was Bruce Bailey and Moose.

"Your wife owes my wife an apology!" Bruce shouted.

"The hell she does," said Moose.

And then someone hit someone (Georgia couldn't tell who threw the first punch) and everyone started yelling. The reporter from the *Whispering Bay Gazette* ran by with his camera in hand.

After a few minutes of pandemonium, Zeke Grant forced everyone's attention with a mic.

"Folks! Let's settle down," Zeke said calmly. Rusty 1 and Rusty 2 were at his side, both in full uniform.

The room quieted.

"That's better," Zeke said, his firm voice lulling the crowd to attention. "I don't know how that film came into existence but it's obviously not a montage piece on the history of Whispering Bay."

"You can say that again!" someone yelled.

Zeke stared down the crowd. "But I can tell you this. No one's leaving until we find out what happened here tonight."

"I'll tell you what happened," Shea called out, "Bettina Bailey broke into my house and stole the film out of my nanny cam. I demand that you arrest her!"

"And I demand you arrest all those Babes!" Bettina shouted back. "They stole my dress!" She whipped around and pointed to Georgia. "That blue haze Herve Leger dress is mine!"

Spencer, still holding his nose, turned to Georgia. "Your dress is *stolen*?"

"Of course not! Well, not really," she amended.

Spencer looked at her like she'd grown two heads. "Georgia, what's gotten into you? And who was that guy who attacked me? I should go have him arrested." Spencer made a move toward Zeke.

Georgia clamped her hand over Spencer's arm, stopping him. "He's . . . no one. Just a friend of one of Frida's friends. He's probably had too much to drink, is all."

Spencer looked unconvinced.

"I never stole the film out of Shea Masterson's nanny cam," Bettina yelled. "Go ahead. Do a polygraph test. You'll see I'm telling the truth."

"Now, Bettina, you know the Whispering Bay Police Department doesn't have a polygraph machine," Zeke said.

"Then how am I supposed to prove my innocence when I'm being publicly attacked like this?" Bettina demanded.

A quiet rumble started from somewhere in another part of the room.

Georgia turned her attention to the commotion. Brenda was waving her hands wildly in the air. And Pilar looked like she was ready to burst a vessel.

"Now everyone, we need to be reasonable about this—"

"Boss," Rusty 1 said, interrupting Zeke. Or maybe it was Rusty 2. "I think we got something bigger than a stolen film to worry about."

Zeke sighed patiently. "What's the problem?"

"Um," Rusty (whichever one it was) looked uncomfortable with all the attention suddenly focused on him. "It looks like someone has stolen the Bunco cash, tumbler and all."

24

Zeke jotted down some notes in his steno pad. "How much money was in that tumbler?" He'd taken his tie and jacket off and rolled his sleeves up three questions ago.

"About thirteen thousand dollars," Shea said, twisting her hands. "At least, that was an estimate on last count."

"When was that?" Zeke asked.

"Around eleven. Just before the video presentation."

"Does this mean someone here is a thief?" Christy Pappas called out.

"It's pointless to try to speculate anything right now," Zeke said. "But one thing is certain, no one is leaving until you've given either me or one of my deputies a statement."

"You're not gonna strip-search us, are you?" asked Earl. He waved his cane in the air. "'Cause if anyone tries anything funny with me, I'm gonna shove this where the sun don't shine!"

"Mr. Handy, no one is going to strip-search anyone," Zeke admonished. "I'd appreciate it if you didn't rile up the crowd."

Georgia sat in a fold-out chair, along with Frida and some of the other Babes. The waitstaff had stopped serving alcohol and were passing out bottles of water. Spencer had gone to the bathroom to freshen up and Georgia hadn't seen him since.

"What are you going to do?" Frida asked.

"Tell the truth," Georgia said automatically. But if she told the truth, then Spencer would know she'd been in the closet with Dave. And of course, he'd want to know exactly what they'd been doing in that closet. *Oh, God.* What was she going to do?

Frida rolled her eyes. "I mean about Spencer's proposal. Are you going to say yes?"

She *should* say yes. It's what she'd always wanted. "I don't know what I'm going to say."

"Really?" Frida looked at her with interest. "I thought it was a no-brainer."

It *had* been a no-brainer. Until Dave had come along. But he'd stomped out of here madder than a hornet's nest. She couldn't even be sure she'd ever see him again. What was the proper protocol after a closet quickie?

It was their turn next. Zeke pulled up a chair. "Hello, Georgia, Frida," he said giving them a tired smile.

"Fire away, Zeke; we have nothing to hide," said Frida.

Spencer walked up behind Zeke. "Sheriff," he said, extending his hand. "Spencer Moody, president of Moody Electronics. This is my CFO, Georgia Meyer and her sister, Frida Hampton. Surely, you don't mean to detain *us*." Georgia thought it was telling that Spencer had introduced her as his employee instead of his girlfriend. But then after tonight's proposal debacle she supposed she couldn't blame him.

"I know who these ladies are, Mr. Moody," said Zeke. "And I'm not a sheriff, I'm the chief of police. I need to question everyone. Including you."

"You can't be serious," Spencer said.

"I'm afraid I am."

Ed appeared, putting his hand on Frida's shoulder in a protective gesture. Georgia hadn't seen him since they'd walked out of the closet. Her cheeks burned thinking about it. Ed wouldn't say anything to Frida, would he? He nodded to Zeke. Oh, no. Zeke was going to ask Ed for his alibi and Ed was going to out her. It didn't matter what she said.

Georgia froze.

"Ed, glad you can join us. Once I get a statement from you four, then you're free to leave." Zeke flipped to the next page in his notepad. "I'll start with you, Mr. Moody. Where were you between the hours of eleven and eleven fifteen p.m.?"

"How should I know? I wasn't looking at my watch. I only just got here."

"When did you arrive at the party?"

"I came in while that *movie* was being shown."

"The video started at exactly eleven p.m. Where were you prior to that?"

"I was pulling into the parking lot, I suppose."

"Is there anyone who can verify that? Anyone you spoke to, or who spoke to you?"

Spencer shook his head. "The minute I pulled up I came straight inside. I didn't stop to talk to anyone or even notice if anyone was around. I was in a bit of an excited rush, you see," he said, glancing at Georgia.

She looked away, feeling guilty.

Frida was next. She'd been with Kitty and Pilar and Shea. They'd helped Shea set up the video, then got refills on their drinks.

"Georgia, where were you? With your sister?" Zeke asked.

"Um, no, not at that time, I don't think," she said elusively. "I was outside for a bit, talking to Ed." She snuck a peek in Ed's direction. He ignored her. Georgia could feel the back of her neck tingle. "I saw Kitty. She came out to tell us the movie was going to start."

Zeke nodded. "So you came in to watch the film."

This was it. She could tell the truth and crush Spencer's feelings and give up any chance of ever marrying him. Or she could lie and hope that Ed might go along with it. It was probably too much to hope for. But she had to try.

"Um . . . could you repeat the question?"

Zeke looked at her strangely. "After Kitty told you the movie was about to start, what did you do? Come inside and watch it?"

"Not at that time. I . . . I think I went to the bathroom first."

Zeke jotted this down in his notebook. "Was there anyone in there?"

"I think so. I really can't recall." Her throat started the squeezing thing again.

Zeke looked over at Ed. "What about you, Ed? You were outside talking to Georgia?"

"Yeah, that sounds right."

"What were the two of you talking about?"

Neither Georgia nor Ed said anything.

"It's not really important," Zeke said, "but maybe it will help jog your memory about whom you might have seen, that sort of thing."

"We talked about my painting," Ed said finally.

"Anything else?" Zeke asked.

"Not that I recall."

Georgia involuntarily let out a whoosh of air. Ed had just partially lied. He hadn't told Zeke about the foreclosure notice. Maybe—

"You okay?" Zeke asked her.

"Huh? Yes, of course. Just a little thirsty, is all." She took a big swig of her bottled water.

"So Kitty can verify that she saw you two, then?" Zeke asked Ed.

Ed nodded.

"After you and Georgia came back inside, what did you do?"

Ed didn't answer right away. "Do I have to say?"

"I'm afraid so, Ed."

Georgia's knees began to shake. Ed wasn't going to lie for her. And why should he? She'd been awful to him. She deserved this. But Spencer didn't. The humiliation of knowing he'd proposed to her just minutes after she'd been with another man would kill him.

"Zeke," Georgia began weakly. "Can I talk to you in—"

Ed turned to Frida. "I'm sorry, honey, I didn't want you to find out like this, but I went back out again to smoke. I know you thought I quit, but . . ." Ed shrugged.

Georgia held her breath.

"Baby, you know that's so bad for you!" Frida said.

"I promise that was my last cigarette."

"What were you about to say, Georgia?" Zeke asked.

She tried to talk, but she was too stunned.

"Georgia, did you have something else to say?" he repeated.

"No, nothing," she squeaked.

Ed was *lying*. For her.

Zeke glanced between her and Ed and made another notation in his pad. "Anyone see you smoking, Ed?"

Ed shook his head. "I don't think so."

"After you had your cigarette, you came back inside?"

"Yeah, when I came back into the room, that video was on."

One of the Rustys came up and whispered something in Zeke's ear. Zeke stood. "Okay, I think that about covers it. You four are free to leave."

"Just don't leave town," Rusty added.

Spencer frowned. "You're kidding, right?"

Rusty's ears turned pink. "Yeah, I've just always wanted to say that."

"Good God," Spencer mumbled after Zeke and Rusty had gone on to interview another group. "It's like Andy and Barney in some sort of Mayberry nightmare."

"I think Zeke is doing a great job," Frida said.

"He can't honestly think any of us would risk prison for a measly thirteen grand," complained Spencer.

"Thirteen grand is a lot of money," Ed said quietly.

Kitty and Pilar rejoined them. "Bettina is still sticking to her story. She says she has absolutely no idea where that video came from and that she's actually sad no one is going to see Shea's montage piece on the history of Whispering Bay," Kitty said.

"That bitch! I can't believe anyone is buying that," said Pilar. "She's over there crying on Zeke's shoulder saying we 'stole' her dress!"

Georgia looked away. Despite what Georgia had said to Bettina earlier tonight, in a way the Babes *did* steal her dress.

"Now that the emphasis is on the stolen money, no one really cares about the video switch. Bettina is going to come out of this smelling like a rose," said Kitty.

"Who do you think could have stolen that money?" Frida asked.

Kitty shook her head. "Who knows? Poor Shea. She's kicking herself for not having secured it better. But who would have dreamed someone would take it?"

"I feel like this is all my fault," Georgia said. "My dress is what set Bettina off tonight."

"It's not your fault," Frida said.

Pilar nodded. "She would have found some other excuse to do the video switch. And no matter what she says, we know she did it."

Steve came up and took Kitty by the hand. "Let's go home, babe. I'm beat."

Kitty glanced around the half-empty room. "Where's Dave?"

Georgia tried not to look interested in his answer.

Steve shrugged. "He's a big boy. He can find his way to our house."

Kitty gave them all a hug good-bye.

"I should round up Nick," said Pilar. "We actually hired a babysitter for tonight and she's probably wondering where we are."

Frida and Ed began to follow Steve and Kitty out the door. Frida turned to Georgia. "Are you coming home with us?"

Spencer looked on with keen interest.

Georgia nodded. "I'll meet you by the car."

Spencer didn't bother hiding his disappointment. "I guess that means you won't be joining me tonight. I have a room in Destin. They'll hold it for us," he added hopefully.

"Not tonight, Spencer. I need time to think."

He covered his nose with his hand and wiggled it, like he was testing once again to make sure it wasn't broken. The gesture made Georgia feel like shit. Where had Dave stomped off to?

She turned and took one last look at the old senior center. The twinkling lights had been turned off, and the harsher, overhead lights now blared down on the half-empty room. Some of the balloons had lost their helium and had made a sad descent to the floor. The waitstaff kicked them out of their way as they picked up dirty glasses and dishware off the tables.

Georgia sighed. It had been one hell of a roller coaster. But for the life of her she couldn't figure out if it had been the best or the worst ride of her life.

25

Pilar thumped her fist against the scarred wooden table but no one in the noisy room paid her any attention. Looking exasperated, she pulled a big cowbell out of her purse and clanged it in the air. Georgia recognized it as the bell they used during Bunco. "This emergency meeting of the Bunco Babes is now called to order," Pilar announced.

The room went silent.

"That's better," she said, nodding her head in satisfaction.

After tossing and turning all night, Georgia had driven to Spencer's hotel in Destin and they'd had breakfast together. He hadn't pushed her about the proposal, but their conversation had been strained. If she told him about Dave, then Spencer would be devastated. He might even take back the proposal. On the other hand, if she didn't tell him about Dave, it would be like starting their marriage out with a lie.

Frida had called her at the hotel and asked her to come back to the Bistro for the meeting.

"But I'm not a Babe," Georgia had protested.

"Not technically, but this involves you too," her sister had replied. Spencer had driven back with her, but he'd promised to stay in the upstairs apartment with Ed, out of the way. Georgia hadn't had a moment alone with Ed. She wondered what he must be thinking about the whole closet thing. And she was dying to ask him why he'd covered for her with Zeke.

"So," began Pilar, "we know that Bettina had to have gotten a hold of Shea's tape—"

"I feel terrible about that tape," interrupted Shea. "I should have noticed it was gone from my nanny cam."

"There's no need to apologize to us," said Liz. "It's Bettina Bailey we're mad at. Not you."

"Maybe you won't feel so charitable when you see this." Shea pulled a newspaper out of her bag. "The *Whispering Bay Gazette* is coming out with a special Sunday evening edition. I was able to get an advanced copy."

She unfolded the paper and held it up for everyone to see. The caption read: "Bunco Babes Gone Wild." Beneath it was a photo montage. Some of the pictures appeared to be taken directly from stills of the video. A few of them were "reaction" shots from the crowd. There were no boob shots, but plenty of photos of the Babes drinking and laughing.

"Oh my God," said Mimi. She grabbed the paper from Shea's hands.

"The article is even worse," said Shea.

Mimi began to read. "Men, have you ever wondered what your wife really does at Bunco?" She paused and glanced tersely around the room. "A videotape shown during Saturday night's Black Tie Bunco Bash, the first in a series of fund-raisers hosted by the *questionable* Friends of the Rec Center committee exposes the truth behind the fast-paced dice game sweeping the nation."

Georgia cringed. The rest of the room didn't look very happy either.

"Who would have thought that a bunch of bored housewives—"

"Hey!" interjected Pilar, "some of us have careers, you know. Or at least we did."

Mimi glared at Pilar.

"Sorry," Pilar muttered. "Keep reading."

"Who would have that thought a bunch of bored housewives," Mimi continued, "would put any *Girls Gone Wild* video to shame." She slapped the paper down on the table. "This is such bullshit!"

"That was the good part," Shea muttered. "The article goes on to say that all we do is gossip and get drunk. And"—Shea paused to take a deep breath—"it quotes Bettina Bailey as saying that her new group, the Bunco Bunnies is collecting canned food for the holiday food drive."

There was silence.

"Last year at Christmas we raised money for the children's toy drive," Brenda finally said.

"And don't forget the walk we did for cancer research," Lorraine added.

"It doesn't matter what we've done," said Shea. "The fact is we looked like idiots on that tape and now the whole town thinks we're a bunch of degenerates." She gave them a pained look. "Our new sub Carrie called me this afternoon and asked that we take her off our list."

"This is my fault," said Georgia. "If I hadn't challenged Bettina Bailey—"

"We haven't done anything wrong," said Kitty. "All we're guilty of is having a good time. Okay, so maybe we *do* gossip a little too much during our games. And maybe we shouldn't have said those things about the Bunnies, but it's probably nothing compared to what Bettina runs around saying about us behind our backs. The only difference is her stuff isn't on tape. So what if we drank a little too much that night and flashed each other? We're a social club, not a charity organization. But that doesn't mean we haven't done some nice things for this community. Look at all the work we've done on Black Tie Bunco. We've raised fifty thousand dollars! What other group in town can say that?"

"Kitty's right," said Tina.

The Babes all nodded in agreement.

"Not exactly," said Shea. "I have some more bad news."

"Oh, no," said Brenda. "These emergency meetings are never good."

"A couple of our corporate sponsors called me today. They're questioning whether or not they should go through with their donations. Milt Davidson from Davidson Insurance told me his company doesn't want to be associated with pornography. They were going to donate five thousand dollars."

"Pornography?" Tina gasped.

Pilar's face turned red. "My sucky law firm was going to kick in ten grand. I was told this afternoon to be at work bright and early Tuesday morning for a meeting with the partners to discuss my *inappropriate* behavior during Breast-Fest."

The Babes shook their heads. Georgia didn't have to ask anyone to know Breast-Fest must be Pilar's word for that infamous night. Despite the somber mood, Georgia had to smile a little.

"They can't fire you, can they?" Lorraine asked.

"Let them try," Pilar said, "I'll slap them with a discrimination suit faster than they can say 'arroz con pollo.'"

Shea rolled her eyes. "Don't start getting your Cuban up. We need you to be levelheaded about this. As a matter of fact, we might need you to put some legal pressure on these companies if they don't follow through on their promises."

"Unless they've signed something, there's probably not a lot you can do about that," said Georgia. "But I just can't see a company take a risk with their reputation and not make a donation they've promised. It'll look bad for them."

"They can try to get around it by making a donation to the rec center under another fund-raiser. That way the money will still go to the cause, but it won't be associated with *us*," said Pilar.

"If that happens, we can forget ever trying to organize another charity event," concluded Kitty.

Shea sighed heavily. "It gets even worse. I got an e-mail from the manager of the Harbor House. He says they're re-thinking about donating all the food."

"It's too late for that now," said Tina.

"Not if they send us a bill," responded Shea.

"Can they do that?" asked Mimi.

"They can try," said Pilar, "but I'm going to review all the correspondence. I'm sure I can find something to hold them to their deal."

"I don't think they're actually going to send us a bill," said Shea, "but I think they're definitely going to give us a hard time about it. And I'm afraid there's more."

The Babes moaned.

"Bruce Bailey called me this morning—"

"He's got a lot of nerve," said Liz. "After the way he attacked poor Moose last night."

Georgia didn't think poor and Moose could be used in the same sentence, but she didn't say anything. It was awful, sitting here listening to what was happening to the Babes. No matter what anyone said, Georgia still felt like a big part of this was all her fault. They'd told her what Bettina was capable of. But she hadn't listened. Instead, she'd mocked Bettina to her face and encouraged the Babes to stand up to her. If it hadn't been for Georgia, they'd have gone on humoring her. They would never have blackmailed Carrie to get that dress and none of this would be happening.

"As I was saying," Shea continued, "Bruce called me this morning. He said the city council is asking that we resign from the Friends of the Rec Center committee."

"And his wife, who started all this I might add, gets off scot-free?" asked Mimi. "Tell me how that's fair."

"Bruce Bailey is just pissed because Moose beat him up last night," muttered Pilar.

"Moose did *not* beat anyone up last night," Shea said hotly. "He did get a punch in," she amended, lifting her chin up a notch, "but that was only after my honor was questioned."

"What has Zeke found out about the missing money?"

Kitty asked Mimi. "Maybe if it's found, we can still save face."

"Zeke won't tell me anything. *It's official police work,*" Mimi mimicked using a deep voice. "I'd have to be either Rusty 1 or Rusty 2 to get his attention right now," she grumbled.

"Who do you think could have stolen the money?" asked Lorraine.

"I wouldn't put it past Bettina. Just to make us look even worse," said Kitty.

"Ladies, do you mind if I interrupt?" a deep male voice asked.

All heads turned to see Spencer standing at the bottom of the stairs. What was he doing? She'd told him this was a private meeting.

"Spencer," began Georgia, trying not to sound perturbed. "I should be done here soon."

He walked to the center of the room and took up a casual stance at the head of the table. Georgia had to admit, he looked particularly handsome today, with his khaki pleated slacks and light blue oxford shirt that complimented the color of his eyes. "Let me see if I got this right, and pardon me for eavesdropping." It was the voice he used to charm clients. Or charm her whenever he wanted something.

Georgia glanced around the room. By the looks on the Babes' faces, it was working on them too.

"Um, everyone, I'd like to introduce my . . . boss, Spencer Moody."

The Babes all glanced at one another. They obviously remembered exactly who Spencer was.

"It seems that the fair people of this town have a very unforgiving nature," he drawled.

"Ha!" said Pilar.

"I couldn't help but overhear about the corporate sponsorships being withdrawn," he continued. "If it would help matters, I'd like to make it up to you. Or rather, Moody Electronics would." He nodded at her. "Georgia, did you make that donation we talked about?"

Georgia had forgotten Spencer had told her to make a donation on behalf of the company. Of course, her attention had been elsewhere most of the evening. She cleared her throat. "No, I forgot."

He smiled slowly, revealing a row of perfect white teeth. "Then on behalf of myself and my very competent CFO, Moody Electronics would like to donate ten thousand dollars to the rec center fund." He paused. "And I'd like to make my own private donation. Would forty thousand be enough?"

Shea gasped. "You're kidding!"

"I believe that's the amount of sponsorship money that's in danger of being pulled?"

Shea nodded eagerly.

"Granted, my donations are contingent that you lovely ladies remain on the fund-raising committee." Spencer gave Georgia his serious head-of-the-company look. "We can afford it, right?" He turned to the Babes with an apologetic smile. "I'm afraid I don't have much of a head for figures. I depend on Georgia for that."

He knew damn well he could afford it. Spencer was showboating. And the Babes were lapping it up like kittens with a bowl of cream.

"You can afford it," she said tightly. She was happy the Babes weren't going to lose out in donation money. And like she'd said, both Spencer and Moody Electronics could afford it. But somehow it felt wrong. Like Spencer was trying to buy her off by impressing the Babes.

"Then it's a done deal," he said.

The Babes burst into a wild round of applause.

"I can't tell you how much we appreciate this," Shea gushed.

"It's only fitting I give back to the community. After all, it's not the first time we've gotten involved here in Whispering Bay, and hopefully it won't be the last."

"What do you mean?" asked Frida.

Georgia froze. Spencer and his big, fat mouth.

"Thanks to my brilliant CFO here," Spencer said, putting his hand on Georgia's shoulder, "I was convinced to invest in the future of Whispering Bay."

"*You're* one of the investors in the condo project?" asked Kitty.

"I was more than happy to help. I know how much this community is depending on the condos to bring in jobs and boost the local economy. It was an added plus that I had my own personal ties here." He said this last part with a smile aimed at Frida.

Georgia had almost forgotten how good Spencer could be at spinning things. You'd think the condo project was a fund to feed starving children instead of a real estate deal he was hoping to cash in big on.

Georgia couldn't meet Frida's stare.

The newspaper made its way around the Babes and back to Shea. She folded it in half and stuffed it in her bag. "There's not much we can do about this article, but thanks to Mr. Moody, we don't have to worry about falling short on donation money." She gave Spencer a warm smile. "On behalf of the Friends of the Rec Center committee, I'd like to thank you for your very generous donations."

"Is there anything else we need to discuss?" asked Pilar.

Shea shook her head.

Pilar pulled out the cowbell and clanged it in the air a few times.

"I get goose bumps just hearing that cowbell," whispered Liz.

A few of the Babes giggled.

"Then I officially call this emergency meeting to an end," said Pilar. "If anyone hears anything else, use the phone chain. Hopefully, this will all die down and Zeke will find the missing Bunco money."

The Babes began to disperse.

"Bunco at my house this week, seven p.m. sharp," Kitty called out. She turned to Georgia. "Will you be in town? We'd love to have you."

"No," said Georgia. "I'll be back at work. In Birmingham."

"Too bad," said Brenda.

"Yeah, we'll miss you," said Liz.

"Thanks. I'll . . . miss you guys too." It was weird. But she really meant it.

"You should join a Bunco group in Birmingham," suggested Tina. "Or start one of your own."

"Maybe," said Georgia. Now that was an idea. She could put Denise in charge of it. Maybe even form a group from the office.

"How about we go out to dinner?" asked Spencer, touching Georgia's elbow to get her attention. "We can celebrate. We can invite Frida and Ed."

"Celebrate what?"

Spencer blinked. "Our engagement of course."

Out of the corner of her eye, Georgia saw Kitty walk out the Bistro door. "I'll be right back," she said to Spencer.

She caught up with Kitty by the side of her car. "Do you have a second?" Georgia asked, trying to keep the nervousness out of her voice.

"Sure," said Kitty. "What's up?"

"I was just wondering if Dave was around today." At the curious look on Kitty's face, she added, "I needed to ask him a question." It was lame, but what could she say?

"Dave went to Tampa this morning," said Kitty. "I'm not sure when he's coming back, Steve and I haven't had much of a chance to talk. This whole video thing has got me crazy. Do you want his cell number?"

Dave went back to Tampa?

Don't overanalyze it, Georgia. Sometimes, a fuck is just a fuck.

"No, that's okay."

Kitty cocked her head to the side. "Are you sure?"

She almost changed her mind and said yes. But if she had Dave's number, she'd call him, and then what would she say?

Georgia tried to see last night through Dave's eyes. They'd had some great, spontaneous sex. But she was still involved with Spencer. Technically, she still worked for him. And Dave wasn't staying in town. He had a life back in Tampa.

She smiled brightly. "I'm sure. Thanks, anyway."

It didn't matter that Dave was gone. It was a closet quickie. Nothing more. She had bigger things on her mind anyway. Like what she was going to do about Spencer's proposal, and how she was going to explain the condo deal to her sister.

26

Frida blasted her the second Georgia stepped back in the Bistro. "You should have told me Spencer was an investor with the condo project." It was just the two of them now. The Babes had all gone and Ed had found something to distract Spencer's attention outside.

"I thought you'd be in favor of it," said Georgia. "I thought new development would be good for the local economy. When Spencer asked my opinion on it, I looked into Ted Ferguson's track record and as Spencer's financial advisor, I told him to go for it. It wasn't like I rubbed my hands together and thought, *What can I do to screw up my sister's life today?*" She sounded semi-hysterical, but she couldn't help it. She didn't have the energy to do this now. All she wanted was to run after Kitty and beg her for Dave's cell phone number.

Frida softened her voice. "Hey, what's wrong?" She put her arm around Georgia's shoulder.

Georgia blinked hard. She wasn't going to cry, damn it. She just wasn't. She'd already done that last night and look where it had gotten her. Screwed in the closet. And more confused than she'd ever been in her entire life. This wasn't the way things were supposed to go. She had a well-thought-out life plan. She should have stuck to it. It was like she had failed the first test that had been put in her path. "I'm just a little overwhelmed by everything right now."

"It must have been a shocker to see Spencer show up last night."

"You have no idea."

"Have the two of you made up? I know his proposal took you off guard."

Georgia glanced out the back window. Spencer and Ed were sitting in the patio, drinking a beer. They appeared to be having an amicable conversation. Georgia briefly wondered what two men who had absolutely nothing in common found to talk about.

She was dying to confide in Frida about Dave. But if she did, she'd have to admit she lied to Zeke about her alibi, which would mean that Ed had lied to Zeke too.

Why had Ed lied for her? She had to find out.

"I'm really not sure if we've made up or not," Georgia said.

"That settles it. Ed and I aren't crashing your dinner. You and Spencer need some one-on-one time to figure things out."

One–on-one time with Spencer.

That's exactly what Georgia was trying to avoid.

Leave it to Spencer to find the most expensive restaurant on the coast. Georgia couldn't even pronounce the name. It had something to do with mussels. At least, she thought that was the translation. She'd taken Spanish, not French, in high school. She wondered briefly if Dave spoke Spanish, since he was part Cuban and all.

She frowned. She didn't want to think about Dave.

"There's something different about you," Spencer said. He paused and sat back to let the waiter uncork their bottle of wine. The waiter poured a small amount into a glass and offered it for Spencer's approval. Spencer took a whiff, then a tentative sip. He smiled and nodded.

The gesture always came off as pretentious to Georgia. But not when Spencer did it. It was like he'd been doing it since the cradle, it seemed so natural. Georgia wondered if Spencer's mother had done that with his formula.

The waiter poured out two half glasses and left them alone. Their table was secluded, hidden from the rest of the restaurant by a half-drawn heavy red-velvet curtain. Georgia had on the same outfit she'd worn to Shea's now-infamous Bunco party, or Breast-Fest as Pilar called it—the cream-colored slacks, lime green shirt, and Manolo Blahnik satin buckled sandals that would forever remind her of Dave.

Focus, Georgia.

"Different how?" she asked.

"I don't know," Spencer said quietly. He took a sip of his wine. "But I like it."

Georgia stilled. "Maybe it's my hair. I'm wearing it a little bit differently."

"No, that's not it. I missed you, Georgia."

She should be giddy. This had been part of her plan. That Spencer would miss her enough to come running down and propose. But she wasn't giddy at all. She felt sick to her stomach. She'd cheated on a good man. And now in some weird, twilight-zone kind of way, by having dinner with Spencer tonight, she felt like she was cheating on Dave.

She could almost laugh from the irony.

He reached across the table and took her hand. "I'm not a fool, Georgia. A man doesn't get punched in the nose by another man unless it's personal."

Punched in the jaw, she wanted to amend. She held her breath.

"I was an idiot. I drove down doing eighty-five miles an hour expecting that you'd jump at my proposal. And when you didn't, I behaved badly—"

"Spencer—"

He squeezed her hand. "Let me finish. I didn't sleep a wink last night. For the first time, I realized that I could lose you. Maybe I already have." He searched her face.

If ever there was a time to confess, this was it. "Spencer, I have something to tell you—"

"It doesn't matter, Georgia. Whatever you have to say won't change the fact that I love you and that I want to marry you. I could kick myself for giving you that calculator the night of our anniversary. If I had the chance to do it differently, I would." He paused and lowered his voice. "Haven't you ever done anything you've regretted?"

Dear God. *He knew.* And in a roundabout way, he was taking the blame for it.

"Spencer, did you know Frida and I were raised in a commune?" she blurted.

He smiled. "Yes."

Georgia let go of his hand. "You did?"

"I'm sorry, babycakes, but when you first came to work for me I had you investigated."

"What?"

"It's not what you think. The company was up for a few big defense contracts and we had to do background checks. Don't you remember?"

She nodded. She did remember. She'd just thought the information had been kept personal. "Why didn't you ever say anything?"

He shrugged. "I guess I thought you were embarrassed."

"I'm not embarrassed," she said quickly. "It's just, most people find it weird."

He nodded.

"Does it bother you?" she asked cautiously.

"Not if it doesn't bother you." The waiter came to take their orders, but Spencer sent him away. Georgia was glad. She and Spencer hadn't talked this honestly in ages.

"I can't say yes to your proposal. Not right now."

Spencer didn't seem surprised.

"And I don't want to go back to Birmingham. Not until I make a decision." She hadn't known she was going to say that. But it was the most rational way to go. If she didn't marry Spencer, she just didn't see how she could go back to work for him. Not after all they'd been through.

He didn't seem surprised by this either.

"Fair enough," he said. He picked up his wine and swirled it. His smile was slow and confident. "But just know this. I'm going to do whatever it takes to win you back. I'm not going home without you, Georgia."

27

Tuesday morning was like every other morning. Except that Georgia was still in Whispering Bay and Spencer was at his hotel room in Destin. Despite his adamant vow to stay and woo her, there was a tiny part of Georgia that had been sure he'd change his mind and go back to Birmingham. But he hadn't. He'd called Crystal and told her to cancel all his appointments. He was on vacation, he'd said. Only he wasn't really. They were stuck in some sort of limbo that Georgia couldn't seem to shake them out of.

Business was slow today. The Labor Day tourist crowd had gone home.

"Do you think you and Ed can close up?" Frida asked. She slipped off her apron and tossed it in the dirty laundry. "I need to go to the bank to talk to Bruce Bailey."

It had been three days since Black Tie Bunco. Frida hadn't

said anything about the foreclosure. Ed had told Georgia he'd take care of it. That he'd convince Frida to take Georgia's money. Obviously, he hadn't gotten around to it or there would be no reason for Frida to go to the bank.

"Why don't you wait till we close? That way I can go with you."

"That's sweet, but like I said, this is my problem. Not yours."

The door opened and a family of four came in. Georgia took their order. The mother was particularly chatty. They were staying in one of the nearby towns and scoping out the local beaches. Frida was gone before Georgia could stop her.

Shit.

Bruce Bailey was sure to say something to Frida about the loan restructure Georgia had proposed. And then Frida would know that Georgia had gone behind her back.

Two more customers came in. Georgia cleared off three tables and some baby spit off the floor. Finally, twenty minutes later the place was empty and she was able to confront Ed privately. He'd gone to the back pantry to place the day's leftover bagels inside the refrigerator.

"Why did you lie to Zeke?"

Ed looked up, then calmly went back to rearranging items to make room for the bagels. "Why do you think? You're my sister-in-law, Georgia. We're family."

"But it might get you in trouble."

"We could both get in trouble," he agreed.

"I thought you were going to convince Frida to take my money so she could pay off the bank."

"I never said that. I said I would take care of it."

Georgia wanted to give him a good hard shake. "Ed! She's at the bank right now talking to Bruce. How is that taking care of it?"

He sighed and closed the refrigerator door.

The sound of the little bell above the door signaled another customer. Georgia bit back a frustrated moan.

The Bistro officially closed in five minutes, but Ed was just going to have to make do on his own.

"I'm going to the bank," she told him.

"There's no reason to do that."

"Frida's my sister. If she's going to be blindsided by Bruce Bailey, then I want to be there to pick up the pieces."

The customer who'd just walked in was Spencer. "I thought we could go to the beach. You did bring your black bikini, right?" He wagged his eyebrows up and down suggestively, but instead of coming across as sexy, he just looked, well, sort of goofy.

Georgia tried to hide her frustration. It wasn't Spencer's fault he had the absolute worst timing in the world. "I can't go to the beach. Not right now."

Spencer glanced at his watch. "But it's almost closing time."

"We still have to clean up. And it's just Ed and me."

"Where's your sister?"

"She went to the bank," Ed supplied, wrapping up another batch of unsold bagels.

"Oh." Spencer nodded to Ed. "Need some help there?"

"I got it," Ed said without looking up.

The door opened again. Georgia was about to tell whoever it was that they were closed until she saw that it was Zeke, along with Rusty 1 and Rusty 2.

"Hi, Zeke," Georgia said. She nodded to his deputies.

"You boys are late today." She tried for a friendly smile, but the truth was if it had been anyone but Zeke she'd have left both Ed and Spencer high and dry.

Zeke rolled his head to the side to stretch out his neck. "We've been taking statements all morning from the party-goers who left before we were able to question them."

Rusty 1 (Georgia was almost positive it was Rusty 1) stuck a toothpick in his mouth. "Had to drive all the way over to Panama City to catch a couple of 'em." An image of him lassoing cattle popped into Georgia's head.

"Do you have any leads?" Ed asked.

"We can't say anything yet. Not officially," said the other Rusty. Which would make him Rusty 2. "Otherwise it might tip off the suspect that we're on to him."

"That sounds promising," prompted Georgia.

But Zeke didn't give anything away. He ordered his usual. "Where's Frida?" he asked, glancing around the room as he stirred some creamer into his coffee.

"She's on an errand," Georgia replied.

"What sort of errand?"

Georgia was surprised that he'd ask. "She's at the bank," she said, without thinking.

Zeke nodded.

"As a matter of fact, I should be heading there myself," Georgia said, trying to catch Ed's attention.

"What do you need to go to the bank for?" asked Spencer.

"Nothing. I mean, it's sort of personal." For one crazy minute Georgia thought about dragging Spencer down to the Whispering Bay Community Bank with her. That would prove to old Bruce that she was Moody Electronics' CFO. Only she didn't know if she still wanted to be CFO. She didn't know anything right now. Except that she had to make sure her sister was going to be okay.

"You seem nervous this morning," remarked Zeke.

"Who, me?" asked Georgia.

"Yeah. You okay?"

"Sure."

Of course she was nervous. Her sister was about to catch her in a lie. For that matter, so could Zeke.

Speaking of sisters, Frida chose that moment to return from the bank. Her cheeks were pink, like they were sunburned, but Georgia knew Frida hadn't been out in the sun recently.

"That was fast," Georgia said.

"I have to talk to you," Frida said to her. "Oh, wait, I forgot. I promised myself thirty minutes ago I *wasn't* talking to you. Ever again." She nodded to Zeke and his deputies, then gave Spencer a tight smile.

"I can explain," began Georgia, wishing fervently that Frida hadn't brought this up now. Not with Zeke and the Rustys looking on, anyway.

"Save it," said Frida. "How do you think I felt when I went to the bank to try to figure out a way to keep this place from foreclosure only to discover that my own sister has already been there trying to make some under-the-table deal?"

"It wasn't an under-the-table deal," protested Georgia. "The terms of a loan are always negotiable in business."

"Whatever." Frida narrowed her eyes at Ed. "Then I find out my husband has—" She stopped mid-sentence. Her blue eyes went wide.

"Your husband has what?" Zeke asked, taking a sip of his coffee.

"Nothing," mumbled Frida, reaching under the counter for her work apron. She plastered a bright smile on her face. "Do you want a muffin with that coffee, Zeke?"

Georgia shook her head in confusion. "What has Ed done, Frida?"

"I paid off the late balance on the loan," announced Ed.

"But . . . that was twelve thousand dollars," sputtered Georgia.

"Yep," said Zeke. "It sure was." The way he said it made everyone turn to stare at him.

"Zeke, exactly what are you insinuating?" demanded Frida.

"I haven't insinuated anything," said Zeke. "So, what's the muffin of the day?"

Georgia glanced from Zeke to Frida to Ed to the Rusty's. Nobody looked happy. "Hold on a second. You don't think *Ed* stole the Bunco money?"

Zeke sighed. "I don't think anything. I just came in to get coffee and a muffin."

"Don't go all *Columbo* on us, Zeke. Bruce Bailey told me Ed came in first thing this morning and paid off the back mortgage. In cash. But you already knew that, didn't you?" asked Frida.

Georgia's gaze flew to Ed. How in the world had Ed gotten twelve thousand dollars?

Rusty 1 pulled the toothpick out of his mouth. "We knew all right. We got an anonymous tip," he said.

Zeke threw Rusty 1 a pained look.

"Sorry, Boss," Rusty 1 muttered.

"You're not supposed to tell the suspect where we got our information," Rusty 2 complained.

"It's an anonymous tip. Even *we* don't know where the information came from," Rusty 1 shot back.

"This is ridiculous. Ed would never steal and you know it," said Frida.

"I agree. But I have to follow up on all leads." Zeke took a sip of his coffee. "Ed, did you go down to the bank this morning and give Bruce Bailey twelve grand in cash?"

"I did," said Ed.

"And what was that for?"

Frida's face turned redder. "I was late paying the mortgage on the Bistro. Bruce Bailey was threatening to foreclose. The twelve thousand is what it took to get our loan back on track."

Zeke took another sip of his coffee. "Ed, do you mind if I ask where you got the money from?"

"As a matter of fact, I do," said Ed.

Frida moaned.

Zeke looked like he was expecting Ed's response. "All right. I'll take that answer. For now." He studied the blackboard where Frida posted the daily menu. "No one ever told me what the muffin of the day was."

"It's cherry cobbler," said Georgia, stunned. Ed had paid off the back mortgage in cash? The coincidence was just too great. She thought about Ed's demeanor when he'd come barreling into the closet. He'd been rattled. But that had been from catching her and Dave. Besides, according to Zeke's timetable the tumbler had been stolen during the time they'd all been together in the closet. And if Ed had stolen the money (not that Georgia thought for a second he had), then he would have had to have it on him.

And then there was the problem of the tumbler. You just

couldn't walk out the door with it. The money was mostly in small bills. Whoever stole it would have to have a sack of some sort to put it in and Georgia hadn't noticed anything like that. Of course, at the time she'd been so rattled herself she hadn't focused on much of anything. Except covering up all her naked bits.

"Cherry cobbler muffin sounds good. I'll take one of those," said Zeke.

Ed pulled out a muffin from the bin with a pair of tongs and placed it in a bag. "Take it to go, Zeke. We're closed."

Georgia looked at Ed, a little startled by this new macho demeanor of his. Well, she'd wanted him to man up, hadn't she? But she hadn't wanted him to turn into a criminal. She mentally shook herself. *Ed was not a thief!*

Zeke gave Ed a resigned nod. "Let's go, boys," he said to his deputies.

The Rustys finished up their coffees and followed Zeke out the door.

"Frida, can I talk to you?" Ed said. "In private."

Georgia watched as Frida followed him to the back pantry.

Spencer waited until they were alone. "Why didn't you tell me Frida and Ed needed money?" he asked, although from the expression on his face he didn't look particularly surprised.

"There was nothing you could do about it. Frida wouldn't take money from me, so she sure as hell wasn't going to take it from—" She studied Spencer's face for any sign of something that didn't seem right. "Where do you think Ed got all that cash?"

Spencer shrugged. "I don't know. Maybe he's a good saver."

Georgia stilled. Ed said he'd take care of the loan problem. And he had. But instead of taking Georgia's money, he'd taken money from Spencer. She was sure of it. There was no other answer, really.

Georgia's stomach sank. First, Spencer had bailed out the Babes. And now he'd bailed out her sister's business. He said he'd do whatever it took to win her. And he was doing it in typical Spencer fashion. With his money.

It was like her entire life was being twisted around his in some sort of double helix.

And there was nothing she could do to stop it.

28

‖‖‖‖‖

Wednesday morning meant it was time for the Gray Flamingos' weekly meeting at the Bistro. Frida had made an extra batch of bran muffins for the occasion.

"I'm gonna find a way to get this recipe, you know," Earl said, chomping into his second muffin of the morning.

"Go for it," said Georgia, refilling his coffee. She enjoyed bantering with Earl. Ted had said he was meaner than a junkyard dog. But the truth was he was more like a grumpy old bloodhound. He could sniff out your weaknesses, but unless you were directly in his path, he wasn't going to bite.

Unfortunately, the Gray Flamingos weren't the only group using the Bistro as their meeting place.

Bettina Bailey and the Bunco Bunnies were there too. At first, Georgia had stewed about it, but as Frida had pointed out, a customer was a customer. And Frida could use customers. Even Tofu was present. His little head stuck out of

Bettina's bag watching the comings and goings in the cafe. Georgia had scooped up the crumbs from the apple cinnamon muffin bin and placed it on a plate for him. After all, Tofu couldn't help who he belonged to. The little dog had seemed appreciative of the gesture. Bettina had questioned the number of calories per crumb.

"Why does she come here if all she does is complain about the fat grams?" Georgia asked Frida.

"I think deep down she just can't stay away."

Georgia glanced around the cafe. Ed had been missing all morning. "Where's Ed?"

"He's on an errand. But don't you really mean, where did Ed get the money to pay off the bank?"

She and Frida had avoided this conversation for an entire day now, but they couldn't ignore it any longer.

"Are you still mad at me for going behind your back with Bruce Bailey?" Georgia asked, waiting for Frida to lay into her. She deserved it, she supposed, even if her intentions had been good.

Frida sighed. "I *should* be mad. But right now all I can think about is where Ed got that money from. He's still refusing to tell me. I'm assuming you're the one who told him about the foreclosure notice?"

Georgia nodded. "It just sort of . . . popped out. But I didn't give him the money," she rushed. "Although, I wanted to."

"I know you didn't give him the money. I saw the look on your face yesterday when I came charging in here demanding to know how Ed had paid the bank. You looked just as surprised as I was when Bruce told me." She sighed. "I could kick myself, you know."

"For what?"

"For basically giving Zeke Grant my husband's head on a plate. With Ed refusing to tell anyone where he got that money, it makes him public enemy number one."

"I think the Rustys are having way too much fun with this whole missing-money caper." Georgia paused. "You know, Spencer's the only person who could have given Ed the money."

She eyed Georgia. "Did he tell you that?"

"No, but it doesn't take an accounting degree from Stanford to figure that one out."

"Ed is being really stubborn about all this. If Spencer gave him the money, then why won't he tell Zeke?"

"It's a guy pride thing. He and Spencer have probably taken some secret oath." Although, Georgia wasn't sure why Spencer hadn't mentioned it to her. She should confront him on it. But if she did, then it would be out in the open and she'd be officially indebted to him.

"Speaking of Spencer, why is he still here?"

"He says he won't go back to Birmingham without me."

Frida looked surprised. "That's kind of romantic."

"I guess."

"Georgia, what's gotten into you? A week ago all you wanted was for Spencer to get down on his knees and pop the question. He's done it. He's made the grand gesture in a big way. So what are you waiting for?"

"I don't know." Which was the truth. What *was* she waiting for?

"I think I know what's wrong."

Georgia held her breath. "You do?" God, she hoped so. Maybe Frida could explain it to her.

"It's the old saying, 'be careful what you wish for.' Maybe

now that the thing you want most is within reach, you're afraid to go out and grab it."

"Maybe."

But that wasn't it. Georgia was certain. Before, she'd had the excuse the Bistro was in danger. And she wasn't about to abandon her sister in her hour of need. But the Bistro wasn't in danger anymore. At least not for a while. So why was she still hanging around town? Why wasn't she going back to her old life?

Because the truth was, she wasn't afraid to reach out and grab what she wanted. The truth was that for the very first time in her life she didn't know what it *was* she wanted. And because going back to her old life meant going back to Spencer. One hundred percent. And one hundred percent of the old Georgia Meyer didn't exist anymore. There was a part of her still stuck in that closet with Dave. Maybe it would be stuck there forever.

"Hey, whatever happened to that marketing plan you were working on for me?" Frida asked.

"You really want to see it?"

"Sure."

"Does this mean we're okay? I mean, I *have* noticed that you've been talking to me. Even though you said yesterday you were never going to talk to me again."

Frida grinned. "I know you couldn't help yourself, so yes, I forgive you for going behind my back with Bruce Bailey and spilling the beans about the foreclosure to my husband."

"Gee, thanks."

"You're welcome."

Georgia laughed. It felt good. She hadn't laughed since— No. She'd made a promise to herself that she wasn't going to think of him. But trying not to think about Dave these past few days had made her think of other things. Things she hadn't thought about in a long time.

"Now that you're talking to me again," Georgia said carefully, "can I ask you something?"

Frida began making a fresh pot of coffee. "Shoot."

"Do you ever wonder about . . . about your dad?"

"You mean *our* dad?"

Georgia's head shot up.

"It doesn't take a degree from Stanford to figure out we have the same father. Look at us. Do you really think we'd look this much alike with only half the same DNA pool? Mom wasn't as free lovin' as she wanted everyone to think."

Georgia thought about it a minute. What Frida said made sense. "So who do you think our dad was?"

"I'm pretty positive he was this dude who left the commune after you were born. I was three, so I remember him a little."

"Did you ever say anything to mom about it?"

Frida poured fresh water into the coffeemaker. It was such an ordinary thing to do while talking about something so extraordinary. At least to Georgia.

"Once, I did. She brushed me off, like she did whenever we'd ask too many questions. I always figured if he didn't care to stick around, then I didn't care to find out more about him." She looked off into space for a moment then met Georgia's gaze head on. "Does it really matter, Georgia? Who our father was? Or if we even had the same father? You're my sister in every way that counts."

"Why don't you want kids?" Georgia asked softly. "Is it because of, you know, the way we were raised?"

"I happen to think we were raised pretty damn well. So we didn't have a house that was our own. And we moved around some. But we had a mother who loved us. She never hit us or screamed at us. We always had food on the table, even though the table was sometimes a blanket on the floor. We always went to school. And we got to do some pretty cool things. Like that summer we backpacked through Europe. Remember that?"

"I vowed I'd never go camping again."

Frida snickered.

"Okay, so it *was* a good time," she admitted.

"And look at how you turned out. You're like a genius, Georgia."

"I just studied really hard."

"I studied hard too, but I didn't get straight As or a perfect SAT score. I didn't get into Stanford with a full scholarship." Frida flipped on the coffeemaker and turned to stare at her. "The reason Ed and I don't want kids isn't because I'm scarred from my unusual childhood. The simple fact is I just don't want them. This place," she waved her hand around, "this is my baby. And Ed's paintings are his."

And I'm going to do everything to make sure you don't lose it. She thought back to Dave's reaction to her marketing plan for the Bistro. Maybe she should get Spencer's opinion. "Let me look at that marketing plan again before I show it to you. Just to make sure I'm on the right track with it."

Bettina came up to the counter. "I don't want to interrupt whatever you two are talking about, but I just want you girls to know there's no hard feelings. About the dress."

"Gee, that's big of you," said Frida.

Bettina handed her a flyer. "Would you mind putting this

up in your window? It's for a good cause." The poster read: *Pre-Demolition Derby, sponsored by the Bunco Bunnies and the Whispering Bay Beautification Committee. Help build Whispering Bay's new recreation center. Own a piece of history for just twenty-five dollars.*

"What's this about?" asked Georgia.

"The senior center is being torn down first thing Monday morning so the Whispering Bay Beautification Committee, of which you might remember I'm head of? Anyhoo, the Bunnies, in unison with the Beautification Committee, have decided to help pick up the slack on fund-raising for the new rec center. We're sponsoring a party Friday evening. It's not anything fancy or *dramatic* like Black Tie Bunco, but I think we'll manage to raise a pretty good amount."

Frida studied the flyer. "You can tear down a piece of the center and take off with it?"

"Exactly," said Bettina. "Isn't that clever? I thought of it myself."

"It sounds dangerous," said Georgia, stacking up a pile of dirty coffee cups. "What are you going to do? Give everyone a sledgehammer and tell them to go for it?" The minute the words were out she wanted to bite her tongue. Hadn't she learned her lesson? Antagonizing Bettina wasn't smart.

Bettina gave her a smarmy smile. "Of course not. Steve Pappas and *Mr. Hunky* are going to do the actual work. Mr. Hunky is bringing his hammer."

Georgia nearly dropped the stack of cups in her hand. "I thought Dave left town."

"Did he? Well, he's back. And for twenty-five dollars he'll tear down your very own tiny bit of history. It'll make a great conversation piece for the living room mantel."

Georgia turned it over in her head. It was actually a pretty good idea. But she wasn't going to admit that to Bettina.

"So I can count on you to put this up in your window?" asked Bettina. "I know it's short notice so we're really trying hard to spread the word."

"Go for it." Frida handed Bettina a roll of Scotch tape.

"You want *me* to put it up in the window?"

"You could always call Persephone and have her come do it," Frida said sweetly.

Bettina swiped the tape from Frida's hand and marched over to the window.

"I guess I know where we'll be Friday night," said Frida. "Wait till I tell the Babes about this."

Georgia didn't say anything.

So Dave was in town.

Georgia didn't know which was worse. That he'd left town to begin with. Or that he was back and hadn't bothered getting in touch with her.

29

"Are you sure you don't want to go to Bunco tonight?" Frida asked for the zillionth time. She was lying on Georgia's bed in the guest room Georgia was fast starting to consider home. Her town house in Birmingham seemed like a universe away right now. "Everyone is really psyched that you're still in town."

"I'd feel like a party crasher," Georgia said. Although, strange as it seemed, she actually did want to go to Bunco tonight. She needed to unwind, have a little fun. But Bunco was at Kitty's and according to Bettina, Dave was back in town. If he hadn't bothered to try to see her, then she didn't want to see him either. "Besides, I promised Spencer we'd have dinner again tonight." Georgia paused. "I think he's getting antsy."

"I don't blame him," said Frida.

Georgia surveyed the small amount of clothes she had hanging in the closet. She'd been in Whispering Bay a full two weeks now. She'd have brought more clothes along if she'd known she was going to be here that long. She pulled out the simple black satin sheath dress she bought from Talbots this afternoon. With Spencer taking her out to dinner every night, she'd had to make a few additions to her wardrobe.

"That's pretty," said Frida.

"Thanks."

"You don't sound too enthusiastic." Her sister tossed a pillow at her. "Have you and Spencer had sex since he's been here?"

"That's none of your business."

"So?"

Georgia slipped on the dress. "The answer, Ms. Nosy, is no."

"Then I don't blame Spencer for being antsy. He's got this great room with a king-sized bed overlooking the Gulf and you haven't stayed over one single night. Why not?"

Georgia didn't say anything. The truth wasn't just hers anymore. Ed was tangled up in it too.

"I guess I'm not going to get an answer to that." Frida rolled off the bed.

"Are you leaving already? It's only six."

"I promised Kitty I'd come over early to help her set up. You're going to miss a terrific night. The theme this week is Football Fever."

"Will you tell everyone I said hello?"

"Sure. Have a good time. And don't come back until you do Spencer. You could use a little un-antsy-ing yourself."

Georgia put the finishing touches on her makeup and frowned at her reflection in the bathroom mirror.

Un-antsy Spencer.

Now there was a thought.

Maybe Frida was right. Maybe sex was exactly the thing she and Spencer needed to get them back to where they should be. It certainly couldn't hurt. And it wasn't like he hadn't tried to get her into bed. It was becoming downright awkward putting him off.

She dug through the slim pickings in her drawer to find the sexiest pair of underwear she could find. Or rather, the second sexiest. The see-through white lacy bikini number was the sexiest. But she couldn't wear it anymore. It would always remind her of Dave.

Maybe she should do a Bridget Jones and put on a pair of the granny panties. Just as a joke. She picked up a pair and smiled, remembering how they'd sagged around her hips when they got wet. Dave had been right to laugh. It had been funny. She sighed and stuffed them back in the drawer. Spencer wouldn't laugh. He'd be horrified.

She settled on a plain black cotton thong. Spencer liked black. And at this point, it probably wouldn't matter what she had on. She'd just finished dabbing some Dolce & Gabbana Light Blue cologne behind her ears when she heard a knock downstairs. It was too early for Spencer. He was supposed to pick her up at seven.

Zeke Grant and Rusty 2 were at the door. Zeke looked supremely unhappy. "Hello, Georgia. Is Ed in?"

"I'm not sure," Georgia said, glancing out the door into the parking lot. Frida and Ed only had one car and Frida had driven it to Kitty's. Ed's bicycle was in its usual spot though. "He might be in his loft, painting. I don't disturb him when he's in there."

"It's important we talk to him," said Zeke.

"Is this about the missing money at Black Tie Bunco again?"

Zeke nodded.

For a second, Georgia thought about telling Zeke that Ed was out. But Ed didn't have anything to hide. Except of course for the fact that he'd lied about his alibi. But then so had she.

"All right." Georgia showed them the way upstairs. She knocked on the door to Ed's loft. She could hear classical music playing softly in the background. "Ed? Are you in there?"

The music stopped. After a minute, the door opened. Ed's hair was standing on end and his T-shirt was smudged with traces of wet paint. He looked wild-eyed, but more than that, he looked . . . happy.

"Hey." The light in his eyes dimmed when he noticed Zeke and Rusty 2 standing in the hallway behind her. "What's up, Zeke?" he asked cautiously.

"I hate to ask, Ed, but do you mind if we take a look around the place?"

"As in, search it?"

"That's one way of putting it."

"Do you have a warrant?" Ed asked.

"This is ridiculous," said Georgia. "You don't really think Ed took that money, do you?"

Zeke looked grim. "It's my job to follow the evidence, and right now the evidence is pointing to Ed."

"Come back when you get a warrant," Ed snapped.

Zeke gave Georgia a pleading look. What would Frida do if she was here?

Georgia touched Ed's elbow. "Let them search. We both know you don't have anything to hide. Then they'll leave you alone and go after the real thief. A search warrant is going to be bad for business. And it'll upset Frida."

Ed thought about it a minute. "You're right." He opened the door all the way. "Go ahead, Zeke. Look all you want. You're not going to find anything."

"That's what I'm counting on, Ed." Zeke nodded to Rusty. "I'll stay up here and check out the family quarters. You do the downstairs."

"Sure thing, Boss," said Rusty 2. He took off like an excited puppy who had just been tossed a bone.

"I'll start with the bedrooms," said Zeke.

Now that Georgia was finally alone with Ed, she wasn't sure what to say. She'd only been in the loft a couple of times, but she'd never taken the time to look around. There were paintings everywhere, some of them completed and some of them a work in progress. These were different from the bright murals he'd done downstairs in the Bistro.

"What are you working on right now?" she asked.

Ed showed her a partially done landscape. The painting's focus was a sand dune, which was a common enough sight in the area, but there was something in the painting that held Georgia's attention. The colors were spectacular. Who would have thought there were so many variations on white?

"Ed, this is really good."

"Thanks." There was an edge of hardness in his voice when he added, "But you don't have to say that."

"I mean it," said Georgia.

"Yeah, well, that and a buck will buy me a cup of coffee." He paused. "This is one of the paintings I'm going to display at the Harbor House."

Georgia felt her throat go dry. Now was the perfect opportunity to have that conversation they needed. "Ed, I'm sorry about the other night. I shouldn't have said those things to you about getting a job. It's none of my business."

"No, you were right to tell me what was going on. Frida thinks I'm some sort of delicate artist who needs to be protected from the real world."

"Why did you lie to Zeke? About your alibi? I know you said it was because we're family, but you still didn't have to do it."

Ed raised a brow at her. "Is that how you wanted Spencer to find out? About you and Dave?"

Georgia felt her face go hot. "Of course not. But it's put you in a bad spot."

"We both know I didn't take that money. Let Zeke and the Rustys have their fun playing big-time cops. When they don't find anything they'll get bored and go away."

"I know how you got the money to pay off the bank," said Georgia.

"You do?"

"And I wish you hadn't done it. I wanted to be the one to give you that money."

He was about to say something when a tapping sound on the open door interrupted them. Zeke poked his head in. "I'm done with the rest of the apartment. I just need to take a quick look around here."

Ed nodded. "Go ahead."

"I hope you know how much I hate doing this," said Zeke.

Rusty 2 appeared at the doorway. He shuffled his weight from foot to foot and cleared his throat. "Um, Boss, can I see you a minute?"

Zeke went to talk to Rusty, which left Georgia alone with Ed again. "How do you know where I got the money?" asked Ed.

"It was a simple deduction."

Ed frowned.

Zeke finished his conversation with Rusty. He looked ready to spit. "Ed, I'm sorry, man, but I have to ask you to come down to police headquarters."

"That's ridiculous," protested Georgia. "He's already given you permission to search the place. What more do you want?"

"I found this in the Dumpster out back," said Rusty 2. He held up a large, clear acrylic tumbler. It looked identical to the one that had been used to hold the Bunco money. It was empty and banged up.

"Ed Hampton, you're under arrest," began Rusty 2. "Anything you say can and will be used against you . . ."

30

〡〡〡〡〡

Georgia's Honda Accord flew through the streets of Whispering Bay. She'd never been to Kitty's house, but it couldn't be that hard to find. Ed had given her the directions right before Rusty 2 had put him in the backseat of the cop car. They hadn't handcuffed him, and they hadn't used their sirens, but it had still been an awful sight. Georgia didn't think she'd ever forget it.

She made a right turn on Seville Street and stopped in front of the house with all the cars parked in front. Georgia's hands shook as she turned the ignition off. She ran to the front door and rang the bell. The house was an old-style Spanish Revival. The small lawn was neat and green with manicured flower beds and a hedge of bright pink hibiscus. Georgia could hear the Babes inside, laughing.

Too impatient to wait any longer, she opened the door and walked in.

"Georgia!" they cried in unison.

Frida grinned at her. "I knew you couldn't stay away."

"I'll go make you a name tag," said Kitty, already half-way out of her chair.

"Ed's been arrested," Georgia blurted.

Frida jumped from her seat. *"What?"*

"Zeke and Rusty 2 came over and searched the Bistro. They found an acrylic tumbler identical to the one stolen during Black Tie Bunco in the garbage bin out back."

"That's an illegal search," said Pilar. "I can get that tossed out in court. Did Rusty 2 read him his Miranda rights? That is, if Rusty even knows what they are."

"It was legal," said Georgia. "At least, I think it was." She cringed. "I sort of convinced Ed to give his permission to let Zeke search."

"I'm going to divorce Zeke Grant before this is all through," muttered Mimi. "He's being so awful right now!"

"Obviously, someone is framing Ed," said Shea. "I wouldn't put this past Bettina Bailey."

"You really can't think Bettina Bailey stole the Bunco money. Even she isn't that despicable," said Kitty.

Frida grabbed her purse. "I'm going to police headquarters to bail Ed out." Her eyes were moist. "I just can't believe this is happening."

"We're all going," said Kitty. "To show Ed our support."

"That's right," said the Babes. Most of them already had their purses and car keys in hand.

"There's no need for everyone to go running down to police headquarters," Georgia said. "I know how to get Ed out of jail."

"This is one time I'm not going to argue with you about borrowing money," said Frida.

"It's not the bail that can get Ed out," Georgia said. "I . . . I can clear him of the charges. I can give Ed an alibi for the time the money was stolen." Georgia felt the weight of twelve pairs of eyes on her. "I should have spoken up the night of Black Tie Bunco, when Zeke was interrogating everyone, but I never dreamed Ed would fall under suspicion."

"I thought you were in the bathroom. Did you go outside and see Ed smoking?" Frida asked hopefully.

"Ed wasn't outside smoking." She took a deep breath. "He was in the storage closet. With me."

No one said anything.

"What were you and Ed doing in the storage closet?" Frida finally asked.

Someone put a drink in Georgia's hand. It was a frozen fruity concoction with some bite. She gratefully took a big swig.

"It's called a Bunco Slushie. It's the signature drink of the night," supplied Brenda.

"It's good," said Georgia. She took another sip. Everyone was still waiting for her to explain. "I got in a fight with Ed the night of Black Tie Bunco," she confessed, glancing at Frida to gauge her reaction. "Not a fight, really, but we had words. I wanted him to convince you to take my money so you could save the Bistro."

"Save the Bistro from what?" asked one of the Babes.

Frida sighed. "I was behind in the payments. Bruce Bailey was threatening to foreclose."

"That's terrible!" cried Tina. "Why didn't you tell us?"

"Everyone has enough problems of their own. Plus, I was embarrassed."

"Don't you think I was embarrassed to admit Brett had a relapse?" said Tina. "But if I didn't tell you guys, I'd go crazy."

"Don't ever keep anything like that from us. Ever again," Kitty admonished Frida.

"Okay, you're right. I should have told you about the foreclosure." Frida nudged Georgia with a nod. "Go on with the rest of the story."

"That's when Kitty saw us. She came out to tell us that Shea's video montage was about to start. So I came inside. But I felt terrible. *I swear,*" Georgia vowed to her sister, "I'm never going to interfere in you and Ed's business. Ever again." She took another sip of her slushie. "After that, I needed to be alone. The bathroom was packed, so I found an empty closet. I didn't want anyone to see me cry."

"The women's bathroom is always packed," complained Mimi. "When was the last time you saw a line for the men's bathroom? You'd think they'd build bathrooms in ratios of two to one."

"And that's when Ed walked in on you?" asked Frida.

"Not exactly." She paused. "Dave saw me crying, and he followed me in the closet."

"That was sweet of him," said Kitty. "Did he make you feel better?"

"Oh, yeah," said Georgia, "He made me feel *a lot* better. Probably better than I've ever felt in my entire life."

Frida's jaw dropped. "*Oh my God.* You and Dave?"

Georgia nodded.

"Now everything makes sense. He's the reason you haven't said yes to Spencer."

Georgia gulped. "Before I knew what was happening we were doing the horizontal mamba, only it wasn't exactly horizontal, I was more like—"

"We don't need the details," said Brenda, her eyes wide.

"Speak for yourself," said Lorraine. "I like to hear details."

"Does Spencer know?" Frida asked.

"I was hoping he wouldn't find out. Not like this, anyway."

"So did Ed catch you in the *actual act*?" asked Pilar.

"No, thank God. We were done, although I wasn't completely clothed."

"No wonder Dave hit Spencer," Frida said. "I was kind of wondering about that." She wrinkled her forehead. "Are you in love with him?"

"With who?

"With Dave," said Frida.

"Of course not. It was . . . just sex."

"That doesn't sound like you, Georgia," said her sister.

"Then maybe it's something in the water here, because it *is* me. Only I can't let Ed cover for me any longer. I have to go clear this up with Zeke."

"What about Spencer? Won't he freak out when he finds out?" asked Shea.

"Probably. But I can't let an innocent man rot in jail because I'm a slut."

"You're not a slut just because you had sex with Dave. Even though it was in a closet. During a gala event. Surrounded by hundreds of unwitting partygoers," said Shea. She shrugged innocently. "Sometimes people have sex in strange places."

A couple of the Babes snickered.

"Yeah, you have to do something a lot crazier than that to qualify for slutdom," said Pilar. "Hey, that's a new word, isn't it?"

"No, it's not," said Shea. "I'm pretty sure slutdom is already a word in the Urban Dictionary."

"Isn't there some other way to get Ed off without you confessing?" asked Frida.

"I don't see how," said Georgia. "Not with this new evidence against him. I could kick myself for talking Ed into letting Zeke search the place."

"If you go down to police headquarters and tell Zeke the truth, then you'll probably lose Spencer," said Pilar.

"That's a chance I'll have to take."

"I know Ed's innocent," said Frida. "We'll get him off somehow, but this could really blow it for you with Spencer. You don't have to do this, Georgia. Obviously Ed thought it was important enough that he cover for you."

"I'll be honest," said Kitty, "After meeting Spencer, I don't think he's your Mr. Right. But if he's what you want, then we'll support you. What you told us tonight won't ever leave this room."

The Babes nodded.

"Thanks, but I really don't have a choice." She eyed Frida. "Are you coming with me?"

"We're all going with you," said Shea.

And that was that.

Frida's car led the caravan to the Whispering Bay Police Department. Georgia rode shotgun while the rest of the Babes followed after they'd piled into two minivans with the precision of a military squad. Georgia got the impression they'd done this sort of thing before.

The police department was a small one-story building that looked like it belonged in Disney World. It was painted peach and had baby blue trim and a front porch.

"We demand to see Ed Hampton," Pilar said to the receptionist sitting in the outer office. "I'm his attorney."

The receptionist, whose name was Cindy according to her nameplate, looked more excited than startled to see thirteen women mobbing the tiny office. "Y'all are the Bunco Babes, right?"

"I want to see him too," said Frida.

"Mr. Hampton already has someone in with him," said Cindy.

"Who?" Frida demanded.

Cindy shrugged. "I'm not sure, but it's the guy he used his one phone call on." She smiled at Pilar. "If you're his lawyer, then you can go on back."

"But I'm his wife," said Frida. "Can't I go back there too?"

Cindy made a face. "Gosh. That would make two visitors, plus his attorney. Sorry, but it would be against policy."

Mimi edged her way to Cindy's desk. "Hi there, Cindy."

"Mrs. Grant! I didn't see you back there." Cindy's voice went up an octave. "I knew it! You *are* the Bunco Babes. I read about y'all in the *Whispering Bay Gazette*. You guys are practically celebrities!"

"I'm glad someone thinks so," muttered Shea.

"So how about it, Cindy," Mimi asked. "Can Mrs. Hampton go on back too? I'm sure my husband won't mind."

"I guess I could look the other way. That is . . . I've heard it takes *years* to get on your sub list."

"What does our sub list have to do with—" Shea stopped mid-sentence after Pilar elbowed her in the ribs.

"I think it's very doable that we could put you on our sub list," said Pilar. "Probably you could even go straight to the top."

Cindy's eyes bugged out. "Really?" She immediately buzzed the door open. "Go on back. He's in the first room to the right. But if Rusty 2 asks, don't tell him it was me who let you in," she whispered fiercely.

"Our lips are sealed," said Pilar. She grabbed Frida's hand and the two of them rushed through the door before Cindy could change her mind.

This left the rest of them with nothing to do but pace around the tiny office.

"Look at this," Shea said. She ripped a flyer announcing Bettina's Pre-Demolition Derby off the community bulletin board. "They're all over town."

Lorraine rolled her eyes. "Whispering Bay Beautification Committee, my ass. That's just code for the Bunco Bunnies."

"It's Bettina's way of showing us up. That her party can raise just as much money as ours," complained Tina.

"They can't raise fifty thousand dollars chipping away pieces of the senior center. Not for twenty-five bucks a piece. There's not that much building," said Mimi.

"We have Spencer to thank for that," Shea reminded them. She smiled at Georgia. "I don't know if Spencer is the right man for you or not, but he's a hell of a nice guy."

Spencer!

Georgia pulled her cell from her little black purse. She

hadn't heard it ring because it was set to vibrate. She had four voice mails, all from Spencer. She pushed in his speed-dial number.

"Babycakes, where are you? I've been waiting at the Bistro for almost an hour now."

"Spencer, I'm so sorry." If she told Spencer about Ed's arrest, then he'd come running down to police headquarters and he'd discover the truth about the events at Black Tie Bunco. Spencer knew *something* had gone on between her and Dave, but to have it confirmed publicly, and then know that Georgia and Ed had lied to cover it up . . . She didn't want him to find out like this. But he needed to know. It would soon be public knowledge. She'd have to tell him tonight when she got to the hotel. "The Babes needed a sub for Bunco and I sort of got roped into playing. I forgot all about our dinner," she said, wincing at how thoughtless that sounded.

"Oh."

"I'm sorry."

"It's all right."

He was being so damn nice about it. Georgia almost wished he'd be an ass, then she wouldn't feel so bad.

"I should be finished here soon. How about I meet you at your hotel? We have a lot to talk about."

"Does that mean what I think it does?" he asked hopefully.

She was doing the same thing she'd accused Spencer of just a few weeks ago. It was time Georgia Meyer shit or got off the pot.

"We'll talk about it in person," she squeaked. So much for making a solid decision.

"All right," he said smoothly. "I've waited this long, I

guess another hour or two won't hurt. By the way," he added, "I read that marketing proposal you wanted me to look at. The one you worked up for the Bistro."

"And?"

"It's brilliant. As usual."

"You really think so? You don't think it sounds like I'm trying to make the Bistro into a Starbucks wannabe?"

"So what? There's no harm in emulating number one, is there?"

Spencer was the owner of a successful company. She should feel reassured that he agreed with her marketing plan. She just wished he'd backed up his agreement with something a little more solid.

"Babycakes, you still there?"

"I'm still here."

The door buzzed open. Ed and Frida came out first. The Babes all descended on them.

"Spencer, I have to go. I'll meet you in a couple of hours." She snapped her phone shut.

"Zeke hasn't officially booked Ed. Not yet," Frida said, trying to talk over all the shouting.

Ed smiled, but he looked tired. What was going on? If Zeke hadn't booked Ed, then that must mean he didn't have enough evidence. But Georgia still had to give Ed an alibi. She wasn't leaving police headquarters until she set the record straight.

Pilar came out next. She was in full-fledged bossy lawyer mode. "Okay, everyone, let's break it up. I think we ought to leave Ed and Frida alone. After all, he did spend almost ninety minutes in the slammer. I'm sure they're anxious for a little private time."

"Does this mean no more Bunco tonight?" asked Brenda. "I was winning most games. Just in case anyone is still keeping score."

"I say we go back to my house, minus Frida of course, and dole out the prizes. Plus, we have a whole lot more slushie to finish up," said Kitty.

"Good idea," said Shea.

And then the door buzzed open again and out walked Dave.

31

"What are you doing here?" asked Kitty. "I thought you were fishing with Steve."

Dave glanced around the room and his gaze settled on Georgia for a second, making her heart stop. "Ed called me."

"You were Ed's phone call?" Georgia sputtered.

The Babes went quiet. By the looks on their faces they were all thinking the same thing she was. If Dave had been Ed's one phone call it could only mean that Ed had called him to give him an alibi. And since Zeke had let Ed go, Dave must have told Zeke the truth.

It was a relief to know that her lie was finally out.

"I need to talk to Zeke. To make a statement," Georgia told Cindy.

Dave grabbed her by the elbow. "No, you don't." He whisked Georgia outside to the parking lot.

"What are you doing?" She pulled her elbow from his

grasp. "I need to corroborate your story with Zeke, so he'll know there's no way Ed stole the money."

"Your story and my story aren't going to jibe."

"What did you tell Zeke?" Georgia demanded.

"Are you engaged?" he asked.

"What does that have to do with anything?"

"It's a simple question. Are you engaged or not?"

She thought about telling him to go to hell. "No," she said instead. At least not yet.

"Good." He walked her to his truck, which was parked on the side of the building. She'd been so upset when she'd driven up with Frida that she hadn't noticed it.

"You were wrong, you know. You said Spencer was never going to propose." Why she brought that up now, she wasn't sure.

"So he's not as stupid as he looks." He shoved his hand in his jeans pocket and pulled out his keys. "Want to go for a ride?"

Georgia turned to see Frida and Ed getting in their car. The Babes were all piling back in their minivans. No one seemed to find it unusual that she'd gone off with Dave. She glanced at her watch. Spencer wouldn't be expecting her for a while.

But she shouldn't get in a car with Dave. She shouldn't be in any small cramped space with him ever again.

"Okay."

It was only the second time she'd been in his truck. The first time was the night he'd driven her and Frida home from Bunco and Frida had been in the front cab with them. They'd been so crunched that Georgia had had to practically sit on Dave's lap. But Frida wasn't with them tonight and there was plenty of room. Georgia sat as far from Dave as possible.

"So why aren't our stories going to jibe?"

He glanced at her. "What are you so mad about?"

"Me? I'm not mad. And keep your eyes on the road."

He grinned and shook his head.

She fiddled with the hem of her satin sheath. "Okay, so maybe I'm a little mad."

"I'm the one who should be mad," Dave said. "But I've forgiven you."

Georgia spun around in her seat. "You've forgiven *me*?"

"I'm generous that way."

She laughed incredulously. "I don't know if you're crazy, or you just like driving me crazy."

"Do I drive you crazy?" he asked quietly. "Because you sure as hell make me crazy."

The way he said that last part made her breath hitch.

"What exactly did you say to Zeke Grant?"

He shifted gears and turned onto a dirt road near the beach. Georgia didn't know where they were going. And she didn't care.

"I told Zeke that I saw Ed smoking during the time the money was stolen."

"You corroborated his lie? But why? I was going to tell Zeke the truth."

"Because I didn't want to screw things up for you." He looked at her. "In case you'd gotten together with Spencer."

"Oh." He pulled his truck into the driveway of a small town house. "That was nice of you."

"I didn't do it to be nice. I did it because I wanted you to have a choice."

Neither of them said anything for a minute as she absorbed that bit of information.

"Where are we?" she finally asked.

"My new place. At least until I find something more permanent."

This jolted her into saying, "You're taking the job with Steve?"

"I decided you were right. Maybe it's time I take a risk and put myself out there."

"Is that some kind of guy trick? Admitting that I'm right?"

He smiled. "Want to come inside?"

"Okay. But just so we can talk. I mean, we can't do anything else." She felt stupid adding this last part but he needed to know there were boundaries. Just because they'd had sex once didn't automatically mean they were going to do it again.

He unlocked the front door and turned on a light switch. The living room was small. There was a couch and a coffee table and a forty-inch plasma screen TV. It looked like a typical guy place. There were boxes everywhere, full of books and CDs. Georgia noticed a lot of Tom Petty and Steely Dan.

He kicked the door closed, spun her around, and kissed her. "I think talking is overrated."

"I agree," she squeaked.

He kissed her again as he unzipped the back of her dress. So much for boundaries . . .

"Does this place have a bed?" she asked, coming up for air.

"I hope so," he murmured, kissing his way down her neck.

She shimmied out of the black satin sheath dress and let it puddle on the floor. All she had on now was her underwear and bra. Neither of which were too shabby, in her opinion. "You don't know for sure?"

"I just moved in today."

"Speaking of which—" She placed her hand on his chest to hold him off. She'd forgotten she was supposed to be mad at him. "Where have you been? Kitty said you went back to Tampa."

"I thought you agreed talking was overrated." He reached out and easily unclasped her bra.

"It . . . is. But I still want to know why you left." He tossed her bra on the floor, next to her dress. "No fair, I'm almost naked and you're not."

"That's not my fault."

He was right about that. She unbuckled his belt and snapped open the front of his jeans. She glanced down, then back up to meet his gaze. "I guess you're just happy to see me, huh?"

He laughed. "Your sense of humor comes up at the damndest times." He let her slowly lower his jeans down his legs. "I went back to Tampa to square things away," he rasped.

"Why didn't you call me?"

She hooked her thumbs in his boxers and dragged them past his knees to his ankles. She didn't bother coming back up.

"I didn't call because I wanted to give you some space." His breathing was heavy now. "And . . . because when you didn't say no to Spencer right away, I turned into a jealous asshole."

"That's what I figured," she said. And then she didn't say anything else, because her mouth was otherwise occupied.

This time, he didn't tell her to get off her knees.

"I've never eaten pizza in bed before." Georgia opened the Tiny's pizza box. She remembered the Babes telling her Tiny's had the best pizza in Whispering Bay. It smelled delicious. Thank God for home delivery.

"Never?" Dave pulled off a slice and handed it to her on a napkin. There were no sheets on the bed. They hadn't taken time to rummage through the moving boxes, so they'd tossed an old comforter over the mattress.

"Never." She took a bite. The cheese was warm and stringy. "I guess that means you have? Eaten pizza while in bed?" she asked, trying not to talk with her mouth open.

"Yeah." He took a big bite out of his slice. "But it's definitely never tasted this good before."

She wiped the edge of her mouth off with a napkin. She was wearing an old T-shirt of Dave's and nothing else. He'd put his jeans back on to answer the door for the pizza delivery boy. "I take it you're a connoisseur? Of pizza, I mean."

"You could say I've had my fair share."

She paused. He'd used the same expression when he'd referred to women's breasts. "So what's different about this pizza? I mean, what makes it so good?"

He chewed on his slice while he contemplated his answer. "First, there's the crust. You have to start with a solid crust. None of this deep-dish crap either. It's too high maintenance. All that chewing, you know?"

She nodded.

"And it can't be too thin. I like the stuff you can sink your teeth into."

"You mean hand-tossed?"

"Exactly."

She leaned over the bed and pulled two beers free from the six-pack ring. She popped them open then offered him one.

"Thanks." He took a sip.

It had amused Georgia that he'd been in this place less than a day, but his refrigerator had been stocked with what Dave called the "essentials." A couple of six-packs of beer and a gallon of whole milk. She'd also found two boxes of Cap'n Crunch on the kitchen countertop.

"The toppings can make or break it too," he added, scooping an errant pepperoni back onto his slice. Georgia liked the way the muscles in his biceps bulged when he did that. It made her hungry. But not for pizza.

She took another sip of her beer. "I agree. Toppings are really important."

"Take this pepperoni," he said, popping it into his mouth. "You can't have a decent pizza without pepperoni."

"Not a vegetarian, huh?"

"Nah. I'm definitely a meat eater. But even the toppings can't save a pizza if the sauce isn't right. That's what makes the difference." He looked her in the eye. "You could go your whole life looking for a pizza with the right sauce."

Georgia laid her slice back in the box. She cleared her throat. "What makes this sauce so good?"

He set his slice next to hers and placed the box and their beers on the nightstand. Then he dragged her beneath him.

"The combination of oregano and basil is brilliant."

"What?" she asked, helping him free her of the T-shirt.

"The sauce," he said, swirling his tongue over her nipples. They instantly hardened.

"Oh."

"You can actually taste the tomatoes. Sweet, and not too salty."

Georgia gulped.

"I'd say this sauce is perfect."

"You would?" She worked her hand between them to palm his growing erection.

"Yeah," he grunted. She stroked him until he was hard again. "Why don't you move here?"

"To Whispering Bay?" She thought about it a minute. "But there's no industry. No Fortune 500 companies. What would I do?"

"I don't know. Do you have to work for a Fortune 500 company?"

"No, but I couldn't make the kind of salary I'm used to unless there's a business big enough to support it." She suddenly grew restless. "Do we have to talk about this right now?"

He didn't answer her. Instead, he concentrated on getting them both naked again. He entered her slowly, kissing her neck and breasts the entire time without missing a beat.

"Do you really think I'm perfect?" she whispered.

He lapped his tongue around her nipple. "Did I say that?"

She stilled. "I thought—"

She could feel him smile against her breast. "I thought I was talking about the sauce."

"Oh."

He stopped everything. Stopped moving inside her, stopped nibbling on her breast. He gazed down at her, more serious than she'd ever seen him before. "But, if I was talking about you, then yeah, I'd say you're pretty perfect too. Right up there with Tiny's pepperoni pizza."

32

If she was pepperoni pizza, then she'd been sliced, slurped, eaten, and thoroughly digested. And she'd loved every second of it. Last night hadn't been a closet quickie. But it had been just as exciting. Georgia stretched her arms above her head. She glanced at Dave, who was still asleep. She needed to get up and shower. Fridays could be busy at the Bistro. Georgia wondered what the muffin of the day was. Working at the Bistro was so different than her typical Fridays at Moody Electronics, where the only thing really going on was the weekly managers' meeting.

Moody Electronics . . .

Holy shit!

She'd completely forgotten about Spencer. *Again.*

She jumped from the bed and ran into the living room. Her black dress lay crumpled in a heap. She tossed her clothes on as quickly as she could and began combing the floor for her stilettos.

How could she have been so careless? So cruel? What must Spencer be thinking?

"Looking for these?" Dave asked, holding up her shoes. He stood in the living room doorway, wearing nothing but his boxers. His hair was messed up and his right cheek had a red mark where he'd laid his head on the pillow. He looked absolutely adorable and sexy and . . .

Georgia would love to stay and appreciate the view, but she was in a hurry. She grabbed the stilettos out of his hand. "Thanks!"

"I guess this means you aren't staying for lunch?"

"Lunch! What time is it?"

He scratched his chest and yawned. "Eleven thirty."

"What?"

She found her purse and pulled out her cell phone to check the time. She'd slept half the day away! "This can't be right. I've never slept this long before."

Dave grinned. "I guess that's my fault. I did keep you up kind of late. But then, you kept me up kind of late too."

She rolled her eyes. "That's not funny."

"Yes, it is." He shook his head and sighed. "I thought we were making a breakthrough on that sense of humor of yours."

She ignored him and checked the settings on her phone. Crap! She'd forgotten to take it off vibrate. She had five missed calls from Spencer and two from Frida. She punched in Spencer's number but it immediately rolled over to voice mail.

"I was supposed to meet Spencer at his hotel last night."

She pulled on her heels and ran her fingers through her hair. "He must be frantic."

Dave raised a brow at her.

"Do you think I'm awful?" she asked. "Forget it," she said before he had a chance to answer. "I need a favor. Can you drive me to Kitty's? That's where I left my car last night."

"So you can run over to see Spencer?"

"I can't leave things like this between us."

"So text him."

She gave him a dirty look.

He shook his head. "Okay, give me a minute." He went back in the bedroom and emerged dressed in his jeans and a polo shirt. "Let's go."

While Dave was driving her to Kitty's, Georgia called Frida.

"Spencer was ready to bust a lung last night," her sister said before Georgia could get a word in.

"Oh, God, I'm so sorry. What did you say to him?"

"What *could* I say?"

"I was at Dave's," Georgia admitted. She glanced at Dave. He didn't seem happy. What did he expect her to do? Go out for a leisurely brunch? Forget the fact that she'd left her almost-fiancé, not to mention boss of five years, waiting all night without so much as a phone call or explanation?

"I knew you were with Dave," said Frida, "so I wasn't worried about you. But I did have to convince Spencer not to call the police or go searching the local hospitals."

Georgia felt the blood drain from her face. This was awful. What in the world was she going to say to Spencer?

Sorry, I forgot our date. I was having some terrific sex with a guy who thinks my tits belong in a museum and that I rank up there with pepperoni pizza.

Somehow, she didn't think that would fly.

She promised Frida she'd call her later.

Dave pulled his truck alongside her car. "Am I going to see you tonight? At the Pre-Demolition party?"

"How did you get roped into that?"

"It's for a good cause. And the PR won't hurt our new company."

"I'll be there. I sort of promised Frida and the Babes I'd come to lend moral support." There were a million questions she wanted to ask him right now. About the company. About his future plans. And most important, about last night. What did it mean, if anything?

It suddenly felt awkward between them. She wished she could think of something clever to say. Something that would make him laugh.

He killed the ignition and opened the door for her.

She was almost in her car when he called out to her, "Um, Georgia?"

"Yes?"

"I'm sorry to tell you this, darlin', and maybe it's not what you want to hear right now, but after last night, I don't think there's any doubt about it."

Her heart stopped. "About what?"

He smiled. And his smile made her forget everything, except him. "You're *definitely* a redhead."

She sighed. "I know."

"I'm sorry but we don't have a guest by that name." The clerk behind the front desk gave her a terse smile. "Is there anything else I can help you with?" she asked, openly gawking at Georgia's rumpled dress and messy hair. Georgia hadn't bothered to look in a mirror and scope out her morning-after makeup. She probably had the raccoon-eyes thing going on.

"Check again. Please. I know he's here. Spencer Moody." She spelled it out, just in case.

The clerk hit a few keys on the computer. "Oh. It says here he checked out this morning."

"That can't be right."

"I'm sorry, miss, but he's no longer a guest."

She thanked the clerk then tried Spencer's cell again. Once more, it rolled over to voice mail. If he was trying to get even with her for last night, then it was working. He'd probably had enough and decided to return to Birmingham. Not that Georgia blamed him.

But this wasn't the way she wanted to end their relationship. *And she did want to end it.* It had nothing to do with sleeping with Dave again. Not really. If she could fall into bed so easily with someone else, then she couldn't be in love with Spencer. Could she?

She decided to try Crystal. Surely Spencer had been in touch with her.

"Moody Electronics, Mr. Moody's office."

"Crystal, have you talked to Spencer today? I need to reach him."

Crystal lowered her voice. "I'm not supposed to talk to you, Georgia."

"What? Why?"

"Spencer said that," Crystal paused, "wait, let me think exactly how he put it. He said that if I didn't keep my big mouth shut, he was going to fire me, even if I was his cousin and that would probably make his mother mad." Crystal said this like she was reading it off a card.

"Is this about the confusion over Valley Tech?"

"Exactly!" Crystal said in relief. "That was really screwy of me. You know?" Crystal laughed nervously. "But that's me, goofy Crystal."

"Crystal, how many headhunters did you tell to drop dead?"

"A few. But you told me to say that, right?"

Georgia sighed. "Right."

"I did feel weird, but I have to admit, I actually liked saying it. Some of them were so persistent! Like this guy who called from Florida. Said he worked for a bank."

"Yeah."

"And there was this guy who said he was friends with John Ambrose. Although he was actually kind of nice—"

"John Ambrose from Valley Tech?"

"Isn't that weird? I didn't realize how common a name it was. I told him to drop dead too, but that was before Spencer found out you gave me permission to tell people that. He was pretty angry."

"Who was angry? The headhunter or Spencer?"

"Spencer." There was a moment of silence. "I'm not sure if that was all part of the stuff I wasn't supposed to tell you."

"It doesn't matter. Spencer is pretty angry at me too right now. And he has good reason to be." Georgia glanced at her watch. It was almost one. She could drive back to Birmingham, but then she'd miss Pre-Demolition Derby and she wanted to lend the Babes her support. Plus, she'd told Dave she would be there. "If you hear from Spencer, tell him I'll be in the office first thing Monday morning."

"You're coming back from your hiatus?" Crystal asked eagerly.

"Not exactly." She paused. "Crystal, if any more headhunters call, just give them my cell phone number. Do you think you could do that for me? I know it's a conflict of interest but I'd really appreciate it."

"Oh, Georgia! You're not looking for another job, are you?"

Crystal was the last person Georgia should be confiding in. She was the company big mouth. But in a couple of days everyone at Moody Electronics would know she was leaving anyway.

"I'm afraid so."

"I'm so bummed to hear that!" Crystal moaned. "I knew this bogus hiatus thing would end in no good. This company just won't be the same without you."

"Thanks, Crystal, but I really think it's for the best. Besides, the company will do just fine without me. I'm really happy about the big contract Spencer got from Valley Tech."

"That went through?" She sounded surprised.

Georgia smiled. Crystal was either the first or the last to know what was going on. "Yeah, it did. Spencer is really psyched."

"I'm so glad! He was really worried, you know."

"All's well that ends well," Georgia said, trying to be philosophical. She said good-bye and began her drive back to Whispering Bay.

It felt good to admit to Crystal that she was quitting. It

was the only decision, really. After last night she'd burned her bridges with Spencer. She couldn't go back to work for him.

And as tempting as Dave's suggestion to stay in Whispering Bay was, there was nothing for her here either. She had Frida of course. But she'd always have her sister. This visit had solidified their relationship way beyond even the sister bond.

And the thing with Dave—that was great sex and lots of fun, but it wasn't love. There was no doubt she liked him a lot. More than a lot. Okay, a *super* lot. He got her in ways that Spencer never did. He made her laugh and he challenged her. But a real relationship took time. A real relationship was based on common goals, sacrifice, and mutual respect. You couldn't develop all that in just two weeks. Maybe if she and Dave had more time . . .

But she couldn't keep pretending her life was this idyllic routine of working at the Bistro, going to the beach, and hanging out with the Babes. It was fun. But that too wasn't real. Real life meant a real job with a real income and real responsibilities. It meant a husband and children and a house and a mortgage. She wouldn't have it with Spencer. And she may or may not find it with Dave.

But somehow, she'd have it.

33

|||||||

The old senior center looked different than it had the night
of Black Tie Bunco. For one thing, there was no tent. And no
one was playing Bunco. But there was a band, a buffet table,
and a cash bar.

And plenty of balloons.

There were also lots of people.

Georgia was surprised to find that she was able to recognize most of the partygoers. The Gray Flamingos were here,
led by Viola. There were members of the city council in at-
tendance as well as Bruce Bailey and the rest of the board of
directors from the bank. Ted Ferguson was hanging out at
the bar schmoozing with a waitress half his age. Zeke and
the Rustys were combing through the crowd, although the
Rustys were in uniform so Georgia guessed that they were
here in some sort of official capacity.

Georgia found out from Mimi that they still hadn't gotten statements from all the guests who'd attended Black Tie Bunco.

"You'd be shocked how many people left that night without giving an alibi," said Mimi, sipping on a gin and tonic.

"Can you believe this?" said Pilar, waving her hand around the room. "It's been barely a week since our party. Bettina just couldn't wait to show us up."

Bettina Bailey and her Whispering Bay Beautification Committee, aka the Bunco Bunnies, all had on matching hot pink polo shirts with their own special insignia. They were working the event hard, from greeting people at the door to even lending a hand to the waitstaff from time to time. Georgia noticed that most of the staff here had worked Black Tie Bunco as well.

Dave and Steve were also in "costume." They wore blue jeans with hard hats and their new company shirt with the Pappas-Hernandez Construction logo on it. If it had been anyone other than them, they might have looked ridiculous. But the women of Whispering Bay were eating it up. The line to get a personally chipped piece of the senior center extended all the way around the room. Georgia had waved to Dave, and he'd nodded back, but he'd been too busy to talk to her.

All the Babes were here too, along with their husbands. Tina and Lorraine and Brenda and Liz and the rest of them. Georgia knew all their names now, and their husbands' names and even the names and ages of their children.

"Aren't those Bunnies helpful?" said Shea, glaring at Bettina behind her drink, "hopping around picking up the slack."

"You have to admit," said Kitty, "this was a pretty good idea. Steve just couldn't say no. It's for such a good cause."

"Yeah," conceded Pilar. "I hate to say it, but you're right. I think they're going to raise a lot of money tonight for the new rec center."

Shea sighed. "I know. And I shouldn't be petty. But I'll bet my next BOTOX injection that it was Bettina Bailey who swiped our videotape and ruined our party."

Brenda blinked. "You've had BOTOX?"

"Not yet," said Shea. "But I have a connection ready when I need it."

Kitty giggled.

"If it hadn't been for Bettina, Black Tie Bunco would have been the social event of the year and our names wouldn't be mud right now," continued Shea. "And she did a lot more than just try to ruin our reputation. If those videos hadn't been switched, then the thief wouldn't have had the distraction he needed to steal that money. Let's face it, we're a lot more interesting than a history piece on Whispering Bay." She took a sip of her drink.

"Do you think Zeke will ever find the culprit?" asked Georgia.

"Maybe we'll be featured on one of those whodunit shows," said Brenda. "You know, the ones where they never solve the crime and they reenact it for TV?"

"I wonder who would play me?" mused Liz.

Bettina fluttered up to their circle. "Isn't this great?" she gushed. "We've already raised over two thousand dollars, plus a couple thousand more in donations and the party has just started. I think people are feeling extra generous tonight. On account of the missing money debacle."

"You're taking cash?" asked Pilar.

"Oh, yes," said Bettina. "And we're displaying it too. I

think it really invigorates the whole atmosphere to have people actually *see* their money. It encourages others to chip in. Of course, we're going to be a lot more careful with our cash than you girls were."

Georgia could practically see the steam coming out of Shea's ears.

Pilar craned her neck to look above the crowd. "Where do you have it? I hope it's well guarded."

"Don't worry," said Bettina. "I have Persephone on the job. And there's no one I trust more."

Georgia glanced over to a table set up against a wall. Persephone had a hot pink Bunco Bunnies polo shirt on too. A large rectangle aquarium bowl stuffed with bills sat in front of her.

"If Persephone is here who's taking care of the kiddos?" asked Shea.

"Bruce's mother is watching the twins," said Bettina. "Normally, I give Persephone Friday nights off, but she insisted on coming to help. That's what I call *loyalty*. But then, I don't go around falsely accusing my employees."

Bettina sauntered off to hobnob with another group.

"That bitch," muttered Shea. "I know she was responsible for switching videos at our party. And I'm going to prove it." She discreetly separated the edges of her bag to reveal a small camera inside. "I've figured it out. It had to be Persephone who stole those videos out of my house. She didn't want evidence of her drinking on tape. If I can catch her drinking here tonight, the way I think I will, then maybe I can blackmail her into confessing that she stole the tapes and gave them to Bettina."

Pilar rolled her eyes. "You've got to be kidding."

"Actually, I think it's a good plan," said Georgia.

"You do?" said Shea. She straightened back her shoulders and smiled at Pilar. "See, Georgia thinks it's a good idea, and Georgia's brilliant, so that settles it."

"Hey!" whispered Kitty, "look over there." She pointed in the direction of the table. A waiter placed a drink in front of Persephone. He talked to her a few minutes, then left. Persephone glanced around and when she thought no one was looking, she drained the glass.

"I knew it! Allergic to alcohol, my ass! That nanny's a lush and I have the nanny cam to prove it," Shea said.

"How are you going to get the nanny cam on her without her knowing it?" asked Tina.

"Easy. If Persephone is going to be sitting at that table all night, then all I have to do is place my bag in a strategic area, like that ledge." She pointed to a small shelf near the wall. "I guarantee you, that's not the only drink we're going to see her chug down." Shea was almost gleeful.

"But your camera is so small, are you sure it'll get what you need?" asked Mimi.

Shea patted her bag. "It might be small, but it's the best money can buy. Believe me, that drunk and her bitch employer are going down."

Georgia shook her head. "Remind me never to get on your bad side."

Shea gave her a strange look. "You don't have to worry about that. You're one of us now."

"One of what?" asked Georgia, taking a sip of her drink.

"A Babe," said Kitty. "At least an honorary one. If you lived here in town, you'd have complete Babe status."

Georgia stilled. "You mean you'd put me on top of the sub list?"

Pilar and Kitty exchanged a smile.

"For ten years now," Shea explained, "the three of us have reigned over the Bunco Babes. We started the group, so we've been in charge of who gets in or not. And it has to be unanimous, which it rarely is, because *someone* always ruins the vote." She said this part while looking at Pilar. "But this time, it was a complete no-brainer. You're definitely full Babe material."

"Because I'm Frida's sister?"

"Hell no," said Pilar. "I'd never let my sister near one of our Bunco parties." She leaned in conspiratorially, "she's got a real stick up her ass."

"You're a full-fledged Babe all on your own. We all knew the night of Frida's Cheeseburger in Paradise Bunco party," said Shea.

Kitty nodded. "When you were so upset, because you'd caught Spencer in that lie. Or at least you thought it was a lie at the time. Your life was pretty much at a low point."

"But you didn't let that stop you from playing Bunco," said Pilar.

"Bunco Babe rule number three: The game must go on," said Shea.

"You're kidding, right?" Georgia asked.

"Absolutely not," said Pilar.

The Charlie's Angels trio all laughed. Only this time Georgia laughed with them. As ridiculous as all that sounded, Georgia totally got it.

"What's going on?" asked Frida. She and Ed must have

just arrived to the party. Ed smiled at Georgia. He seemed less tense than the last time she'd seen him. Of course, that had been on his way out of jail.

"Watch my back, girls," said Shea. "This is it." She clutched her bag and serpentined her way through the crowd.

Frida sent Ed off to the bar with a drink order. "What's Shea up to?" she asked.

Kitty and Pilar filled her in on Shea's plan.

Frida looked unconvinced. "I just hope the whole thing doesn't backfire on us somehow."

Georgia mingled with the Babes for a few minutes, then tried to get in Dave's line so he could chip away her own personal piece of the center. But according to Persephone there was a thirty-to-forty-minute wait. She tried to catch a whiff of Persephone's breath, to see if she could pick up any alcohol fumes, but she couldn't.

"Try coming back in about an hour," suggested Persephone. "Maybe the line will be shorter by then."

"Thanks. I'll do that," said Georgia.

The same waiter who'd brought Persephone a drink earlier strolled by carrying a tray with white wine. Georgia bought a glass from him. She watched to see if he left a glass for Persephone, but he didn't.

Her stomach growled something fierce. It just occurred to her the last thing she'd eaten was the pizza at Dave's. Georgia dropped a donation in the fish tank and went to stand in the buffet line.

Earl came up behind her. "Smell those hush puppies?" he asked, wiggling his nose in appreciation.

Georgia smiled. "The Harbor House's finest."

Earl nodded in approval. "You've only been here a few weeks and you already know the best place to eat."

"So you know I'm the other one?" Georgia said, enjoying their banter.

"Sure," he said, "I could tell you and your sister apart after that first day. I just liked having fun with you, is all."

"The Harbor House does make the best hush puppies," Georgia admitted.

"And the best fried grouper and the best fish sandwich in town too," said Earl. "Course they don't have much competition."

They advanced a little in the buffet line. She thought about her marketing plan for the Bistro and how Spencer had thought it was top notch. And then she thought of Dave's reaction to it. "If a person wanted to get a quick bite to eat, say a sandwich at lunchtime, where would they go?" she asked.

Earl thought about it a minute. "The Harbor House has the best food in town, no doubt about it. But there's no such thing as a 'quick' bite there. It's a sit-down place and if you don't get in before the tourist crowds, then you're gonna wait in line a while. There's Sherry's Deli and they make pretty good BLTs, but they put too much mayo on everything. Gives a person a bad stomach, you know?"

Georgia nodded.

"Plus, she's a snowbird. Her place is only open November through May. Spends the rest of the year in one of them cold states."

"And that's it? There must be more places in town to eat."

"There's that pizza place everyone's crazy about—"

"Tiny's," Georgia supplied. "I hear they make great sauce." She felt her cheeks go warm at that last part. Out of the corner of her eye she saw Dave. He caught her gaze and smiled. A tingle of anticipation ran through her. They still had two nights before she had to go back to Birmingham. After that, who knew where she'd end up? Maybe she could get a job close by.

"I-talian place," said Earl, nodding. "There's also a little ice-cream stand by the beach. They do tacos, stuff like that. But they taste like rubber. Ted Ferguson keeps promising a bunch of new business when he builds those condos of his. I don't know." Earl shrugged. "I'd kind of like to see what we already got here in town do good. You know?"

Georgia's heart began to race. "Mr. Handy, who takes care of your investments?"

"My son-in-law used to. He's the one who made that condo deal with Ferguson. But I've taken over since then. No one really knows what they're doing nowadays. Buying, selling, then buying again—all faster than they can go up and down a bunch of stairs. It takes real finesse to know how to do business."

Georgia looped her arm through Earl's and led him away from the line. "Mr. Handy, just how badly do you want my sister's bran muffin recipe?"

Dave got his first break at ten p.m.

"I can't believe how hard they're working you," Georgia complained. "I've hardly gotten to talk to you tonight."

"Jealous?" he asked, playfully flicking the side of her nose with his finger.

"As a matter of fact, I am."

He looked surprised by her response. She was kind of surprised too.

"What are you doing later tonight?" he asked.

"I thought I'd try on your hard hat and maybe play around with some of your tools. There's one in particular that really stands out for me."

Dave half groaned, half laughed. "I've created a monster."

"You're the one who said you could help me with my sense of humor."

"So did you to talk to Spencer?" he asked.

"He checked out of his hotel before I got there. And he won't return any of my voice mails. I think he's had it with me and I don't blame him. I have to go to Birmingham Monday to sort this all out. I'm quitting my job, but I'll have to stay until Spencer gets a replacement. I owe him that."

"Then what?"

She took a deep breath and tried for a bright smile. "Then I look for another job. According to Spencer's secretary a few headhunters have been sniffing around asking about me. I guess I should be grateful, what with the economy sucking right now." She studied his face to gauge his reaction to this next part. "Maybe I can get a job nearby. Atlanta is only six hours away and Tallahassee and Pensacola aren't too far a drive."

He didn't say anything.

Maybe she was taking too much for granted. For all she knew Dave hadn't even considered taking their relationship past this weekend. The thought of never seeing him again made her throat swell up. Just like it had the night of Black Tie Bunco when she'd been in a near-panic state. Oh, God. She could feel herself hyperventilating.

Dave reached out and touched her elbow. "Georgia—"

"I'm okay," she blurted. "I'm going to be okay. Just forget everything I said and—"

"Georgia," he interrupted firmly. "Turn around."

Something in Dave's voice made her freeze. But somehow she still managed to shuffle her feet in the right direction to come face-to-face with Spencer.

It was official. She must be allergic to Spencer showing up unexpectedly at parties. Because the anaphylactic shock thing hit her full force. She could barely squeeze a breath in.

"Georgia, before you say anything, I want you to listen to me."

"Spencer," she wheezed, "I'm so sorry about last night."

A strained look came over his face. She could see how he struggled to keep his emotions in check. "I admit, I was upset. I left town in a snit and drove all the way back home to Birmingham before I realized what I'd done. But I forgive you, Georgia." He looked past her and narrowed his eyes at Dave. "For whatever it is you've done twice now."

Once in the closet and then two times last night, so it was actually three times, to be exact. But she didn't think Spencer would appreciate her correcting him.

"I realize it's my fault," he continued. "I've strung you along for five years and you're just giving me back some of what I deserve."

She shook her head. "No, that's not it."

"Please, babycakes, this isn't easy for me." He got down on his knees.

The band picked this exact moment to stop playing. *Great.* Now the whole room was staring at her. *Again.*

"Is this fella a glutton for punishment or what?" Earl asked.

Someone shushed Earl. Probably DeeDee.

Spencer pulled the little black box Georgia recognized from the other night and opened it to reveal that giant-ass engagement ring. Somehow, it looked even bigger than before. Must be the lighting, she thought wildly.

He reached out and plucked her hand in his. "Georgia Meyer," he said in that smooth voice of his that sent shivers down her spine. "Will you do me the honor of becoming my wife?"

It was the worst déjà vu Georgia had ever experienced. Only it was real. She glanced nervously around the room. Dave was standing less than two feet away. The expression on his face said he wasn't going anywhere this time.

"Spencer," she began gently. "I don't know what to say."

"Say yes," he said, "and make me the happiest man in the world."

For one crazy second, she actually thought about it. How could she not? She'd spent five years waiting for this moment. A tiny part of her whispered, *go for it!*

With Spencer she'd have everything she ever wanted. Marriage, financial stability, the big brick house on top of the hill. It was all here. Just waiting for her to reach out and grab . . .

A high-pitched scream caused the crowd to swing their attention. Persephone stood in the middle of the room with a panicked look on her face. "Someone stole the fishbowl with all the money!" she cried.

34

||||||

"Not again," grumbled Earl. "Don't we have any security in this town?"

"Everyone calm down," said Zeke, taking command of the room.

"Bettina, I'm so sorry I let you down!" Persephone wrung her hands together. "I tried so hard to keep my eye on the money. But there was that whole proposal thing going on and I just couldn't look away."

"There, there," said Bettina, stroking Persephone's hair. "It's not your fault." She turned to Georgia. "If your fiancé-slash-boss hadn't made a spectacle of himself, none of this would have happened!"

"You can't blame Georgia," said Pilar.

"Yeah!" chimed in the rest of the Babes.

"Persephone, when was the last time you saw the money?" asked Zeke.

Persephone began to sniffle. Bettina gave her a hand-kerchief so she could dry her eyes. "I was sitting at the table collecting money, and then that guy"—she pointed to Spencer—"got down on his knees and proposed. Everyone was so riveted. I was trying my hardest to see what was going on, but I had to stand on a chair to see above the crowd. I must have gotten careless and taken my eyes off the money for a few seconds. I was just so *engrossed* in what was happening." She stopped to sniffle some more. "The next thing I knew the money was gone!"

Rusty 1 whispered something in Zeke's ear. Zeke sighed and shook his head. "I'm afraid no one can leave here tonight until they make a statement."

Ted Ferguson elbowed his way to the front of the crowd. "Sheriff, I have a private plane in Panama City waiting to take me to Knoxville. My pilot just called and said we need to leave now before it gets too foggy. It's the only way I can make the Alabama-Tennessee football game tomorrow."

Spencer jumped off his knees. "You have a plane leaving tonight for Knoxville?"

"You can come along if you want. I have room for you—for both of you," he said nodding at Georgia.

Spencer turned and gave her a beseeching look. "What do you say, babycakes? We can celebrate our engagement by watching the Crimson Tide beat up on Tennessee. You've always wanted to meet my college friends."

"Sorry," said Zeke. "But no one can leave until we get an official statement. And I'm not sheriff. I'm the chief of police."

"Whatever, *Andy*," mocked Spencer. "Do you know how

hard it is to get tickets to the Alabama-Tennessee game?" he roared.

"Not as hard as it is to get tickets for the Florida-FSU game," Moose chimed in.

"This is ridiculous," said Bettina. "Can't everyone see this theft is some sort of scheme to make our fund-raiser look bad? It's obvious that the same person who stole the cash at Black Tie Bunco has done it again. And we all know who it is." She turned and pointed a finger into the crowd. "Ed Hampton is your thief! Ask my husband. Frida Hampton owed the bank twelve thousand dollars and just a couple of days after Black Tie Bunco, Ed walked into the bank and paid it all off. In cash!"

Everyone began talking and shouting at once.

Zeke stuck his fingers in his mouth and produced a blood-curdling whistle. "Pipe down!" He frowned at Bruce Bailey. "Bruce, isn't there some sort of Hippocratic oath or something you bankers take? Or do you discuss all the bank's business with your wife?"

"It's called HIPAA," supplied Earl.

"No, it's not. HIPAA is what protects patients' rights," DeeDee told Earl.

"Then they ought to have the same thing for bankers. I sure as hell hope you're not running around telling everyone *my* business, Bruce Bailey." Earl raised his cane and waved it at the sweating banker.

It was time to put a stop to all this nonsense. Georgia tried to catch Spencer's eye. He didn't seem overly upset that his proposal had been interrupted. As a matter of fact, he looked downright gleeful. He'd looked that way ever since Ted had announced he had a plane waiting to take him to tomorrow's football game. She hadn't wanted to do it like this. But there was no choice.

"Ed couldn't have taken the money the night of Black Tie Bunco," Georgia blurted.

"You know that for a fact, Georgia?" Zeke asked.

Georgia sought Dave out in the crowd. Unlike Spencer, she couldn't tell anything from the expression on Dave's face. "I lied to you, Zeke. I wasn't in the bathroom when the video started. I was in a storage closet with Dave Hernandez and Ed found us in there."

"What were you and Dave doing in the closet?" Zeke asked.

Georgia steeled herself for the reaction to come. "We were—"

"Dancing," Dave answered for her.

Zeke blinked. "Dancing?"

"Yeah," said Dave. "You know, it's something two people do together."

"Except you need music for that," someone yelled.

A few people in the crowd laughed.

Georgia felt her cheeks go warm. She glanced at Spencer to see how he'd taken her confession. He seemed more angry than upset.

"Is that what they were doing, Ed?" Zeke asked.

Ed nodded. "Yeah, that's what they were doing."

"Okay," said Zeke. "That's good enough for me."

"That's *it*?" screeched Bettina. "Aren't you going to ask him about the money?"

Rusty 2 made a harrumphing sound to get everyone's attention. "There's also the tumbler we found in the Dumpster behind the Bistro. Don't forget that."

"I don't know how the tumbler got there," said Georgia, "but the money can easily be explained. Spencer loaned it to Ed. Didn't you, Spencer?"

"No, I did *not*," he proclaimed hotly.

Georgia stilled. "If you didn't loan Ed the money, who did?"

"I earned the money," said Ed.

Frida's face lit up. "Baby, you sold a painting for twelve thousand dollars! Why didn't you tell me?"

Ed looked grim. "I didn't sell a painting, Frida. I got the money as an advance. I'm going to be working for Pappas-Hernandez Construction."

Everyone turned to look at Dave and Steve.

"As part of my new job, I'm taking over the renovations at Dolphin Isles," Dave explained quietly. "Ed's going to do some painting for us out there."

"You're going to be painting *houses*? At Dolphin Isles?" asked Frida. "When are you going to find time to do your own painting?"

"Maybe it's time I gave up on that for a while. I need to bring in some money, Frida."

Frida looked like she was about to cry.

"That settles that," said Zeke. "Ed has an alibi and no motive. Doesn't make sense that he'd steal the money."

"What about the tumbler?" persisted Rusty 2.

"Obviously, someone is trying to frame Ed," said Pilar, narrowing her eyes at Bettina.

"Don't look at me," said Bettina. "If it wasn't Ed Hampton, then it's another one of those Babes' husbands." She crossed her arms over her chest. "Check out Brett Navarone's alibi. He's a compulsive gambler. I bet he stole the money."

The room went still.

Tina covered her mouth with her hand. Brett had a horrified expression on his face. And the Babes looked ready to kill.

"How do you know that, Bettina?" demanded Shea. "The only people who know about Brett's gambling problem are his contacts through Gamblers Anonymous and the Babes."

Bettina started to sputter. "I ... I must have heard it around town."

"Bullshit!" said Pilar. "No one but Tina and Brett and *us* know that secret."

"The only way you could have known about Brett's gambling problem is if *you* go to Gamblers Anonymous," accused Kitty.

Bettina stomped her foot. "I do *not* go to Gamblers Anonymous! Or anything else Anonymous!" she added.

No one in the crowd looked happy with Bettina right now.

"Are you going to start accusing everyone of stealing the money, Bettina?" someone yelled.

"I go to AA," one woman said, "I'm not ashamed of it either. Do you think I took the money?"

"Of course not," Bettina, said, wild-eyed. "It's those Babes! They're responsible for all this! Didn't you see their video? How they laughed at all of us?"

"We saw them laughing at *you*," someone said.

A few of the Babes started to look uncomfortable.

"And we apologize for that," Kitty said. "We didn't mean to hurt anyone."

"Oh, hell," said Christy Pappas, "Bettina said a lot worse things about you guys at our first Bunco party. It just wasn't caught on tape."

"There's only one way you could know about Brett's gambling problem," Shea said, pointing a finger at Bettina. "You heard it on my nanny cam tapes! We talked about it on the night of Breast-Fest but that part of the tape wasn't shown at Black Tie Bunco." She looked around the crowd. "By the way, Breast-Fest is Pilar's word, not mine."

Everyone turned to look at Bettina.

"Why would I steal your nanny cam tapes?" She glanced around the room, searching out support.

"You didn't steal them. Persephone did. To keep everyone from knowing she's a lush," Shea said.

Persephone crossed her arms over her chest. "Prove it," she dared.

"All right," said Shea. She stomped across the room to the ledge where she'd stashed her bag and pulled out her camera. "This purse has another nanny cam in it. It's been aimed at Persephone and that table all night. I bet she's guzzled down enough gin and tonics to float away."

"If you got a nanny cam set on that table, then that tape can show us who the thief is," said Zeke.

Rusty 2's eyes popped out in excitement.

Zeke calmly took the camera from Shea's hands. "Let me have a look at that." He fiddled with the dials, then studied the playback. Everyone in the room held their breath, waiting for Zeke to say something.

A loud crash made Georgia turn her head. It sounded like someone had dropped an armful of dishes. One of the waiters busted through the kitchen door and took off running for the entrance. Georgia recognized him as the same waiter who'd brought Persephone her drink.

"I got him, Boss!" yelled Rusty 1.

"No, I got him!" Rusty 2 cried over his shoulder.

The crowd parted as the two deputies took off after the running waiter. After a short scuffle, Rusty 1 handcuffed him while Rusty 2 read him his Miranda rights. Funny, when had she started being able to tell Rusty 1 and Rusty 2 apart?

"You stupid cow!" the waiter screamed. "I told you this was a dumb idea."

The crowd followed his gaze to see exactly who the stupid cow was. Zeke already had Persephone handcuffed.

"I'm sorry, Alex, I couldn't help myself," Persephone sniffed.

"You had to get greedy, didn't you?" Alex sneered. "You couldn't be happy with the thirteen grand from the other night!"

"What part of 'anything you say can and will be used against you' don't these people understand?" Pilar asked.

Bettina threw herself on Persephone. "This is all a mistake," she cried. "Persephone, tell them you didn't steal the money!"

Zeke gently pried Bettina off Persephone. "Sorry, Bettina, but it's all on Shea's nanny cam. While Georgia was being proposed to, this one," he nodded his head toward Persephone, "was handing off the fish bowl to her waiter-boyfriend. They even snuck in a little kiss."

Bettina's jaw dropped. "Persephone, how could you?"

Persephone rolled her eyes in the air. "Give me a break."

"Zeke, can I take a look at my nanny cam?" asked Shea.

Zeke hesitated. "Just for a minute. I'm going to need it for evidence."

Shea fast-forwarded through most of the tape. "I knew it!" she cried triumphantly. "She's had at least five drinks that I can count. And there's probably even more!"

Zeke took the tape back from Shea.

"Persephone, you can plead temporary insanity," Bettina said. "The twins could drive anyone crazy! I'll get you the best lawyer money can buy. Don't worry, I'll have you out of jail and back with me in no time."

Persephone looked horrified. "Why do you think I stole the money? I *hate* working for you. I'd rather go to jail than spend one more day as your nanny!"

Poor Bettina, thought Georgia. She looked like she'd been run over.

"And another thing," Persephone yelled to the crowd before Zeke hauled her out the door, "I made those key lime tarts, not her! She made me stay up until four in the morning finishing them. And it's not some secret family recipe either. She got it off the friggin' internet!"

Bettina threw herself in Bruce's arms. "I need Tofu," she whimpered.

"I didn't know Bettina was one of them vegetarians," said Earl. "Seems like a strange time to be hungry to me."

"Oh my God," said Kitty. "This is awful."

"Yeah, not even Bettina deserves this," Pilar said.

Shea frowned but she didn't say anything.

Bruce disengaged himself from Bettina. "I think my wife has something to tell you." He nudged her on with a stern look. "Go on. Tell them what you told me last night."

"Do I have to?" she pleaded.

"You do if you want your credit cards back."

Bettina swallowed hard. "Okay," she said to Shea, "you

were right about Persephone stealing your nanny cam tapes. Consuelo found them in her room while she was cleaning. I got to thinking about what you said, about her drinking while on the job, so I played them. She must have gotten rid of the ones that showed her drinking, because all the tapes had on them was ... was that awful night you all got drunk." She took a big breath. "You said some really mean things about me on that tape," she ended on a shaky note.

The Babes all looked at one another guiltily.

Shea let out a long-suffering sigh like she knew she'd been beat. "You're right. We did say some mean things about you. I guess ... I guess that makes us mean girls?"

Bettina half smiled. "I guess that's right." Her expression became somber again. "Then the night of Black Tie Bunco when I saw Georgia with my dress ..." She shook her head. "It was the last straw. I wanted to bring you all down a few pegs. So I had Persephone bring over the tape and substituted it for your montage piece on Whispering Bay." She paused. "Which by the way, you should totally thank me for, because really, Shea, I've tried to watch it twice now and it's put me to sleep both times."

Georgia could see Shea struggle to keep her mouth shut.

"I'm really sorry about the dress," Georgia said. "But I loved it so much and ... well, the Babes knew how much it meant to me."

"I know you can't help yourselves," Bettina said. "You Babes all stick together."

"Bettina and I didn't mean to steal all your subs," Christy Pappas chimed in with a confession of her own. "We just wanted to start our own group."

Laura Barnes, another ex-Babe sub nodded. "I was tired

of waiting around for a phone call hoping you'd ask me to play."

"We just want to play Bunco," said Christy.

"Well, we certainly understand *that*," said Pilar.

One of the waitstaff tapped Bettina on the shoulder. "Sorry to interrupt, but we have a crisis on our hands," he said. "Now that Alex has been hauled off we're short on help. And we've run out of ice."

Christy looked alarmed.

"Don't worry," Bettina said, throwing back her shoulders. "I've got it under control." She clapped her hands. "Bunnies!" she yelled. "Come with me."

A troop of pink-clad women flocked behind their leader and marched toward the kitchen.

"I guess we should help too," said Shea. "After all, this is a fund-raiser for the new rec center and we're still on the Friends of the Rec Center committee."

"That Bettina *really* is a good organizer," said Kitty.

"*Ay, caramba,*" said Pilar, "I hate to admit it, but you're right."

"C'mon, girls," said Shea, following Bettina and the Bunnies. "We Bunco broads *all* have to stick together."

35
||||||

The Babes followed Shea into the kitchen. Except Frida. She turned to Ed, her hands on her hips. "I want you to give Dave and Steve their money back. Tell them you can't go to work for them. I don't care about the Bistro. Not enough to have you give up your dream for it."

Georgia's gaze flew to Ed. There was a stubborn gleam in his eyes she was fast coming to recognize. "You can't tell me what to do here, Frida. The fact is your sister is right. I need to man up and get a job. At least for a while, until we get back on our feet financially."

"But, baby, when will you find time to paint?"

"I can work it around my schedule," he said, not looking totally convinced. He shook his head. "It doesn't matter. I've given it my shot. Maybe it's time I got a job just like everyone else has to do." He took Frida's hands in his. "I don't want you to lose the Bistro. You've worked too hard and too long for that to happen."

If Frida looked like she was going to cry earlier, now it looked like she was on the verge of sobbing.

Georgia had vowed never to interfere in her sister's business again, but now wasn't the time to keep that promise. "If you'll let me help, I think I have an idea."

"We're *not* taking your money," Frida and Ed both said in unison.

Georgia put her hands in the air. "Okay, okay, I get it. But this idea doesn't involve me giving you money."

They stared at her, unconvinced.

"Remember that marketing plan I wrote up for you?"

"The one you never showed me?" Frida said.

Georgia glanced at Dave, who was watching her with an intensity that almost made her knees buckle. "I never showed it to you because it sucked." She stole another glance at Spencer, who merely raised his brows at that. "I thought that turning the Bistro into a Starbucks wannabe was the answer to your problem. But you're right, you can't compete with Starbucks. So you have to be different than them."

"I am different from them," Frida said proudly.

"Right. But in this economy you have to be even better. You have to fill a gap that's missing. And what's missing is a really good lunch place. A place where you can get a quick sandwich or a burger, a place where you can sit down or phone your order in ahead of time and have it ready it go."

"But I can't do that! My place is barely big enough for what I serve now. And I don't think Bruce Bailey is going to give me a loan to expand."

Georgia couldn't help but grin. "I have an investor lined

up for you. He'll put up the money in exchange for a percentage of your profits. You can even hire someone to help you. That way you don't have to count on Ed." She turned to Ed. "I was thinking, instead of working at Dolphin Isles full time, maybe you can arrange to work off your advance part time? It'll take longer, but it'll give you time in the day to do your real painting. That is"—she glanced at Dave—"if your employer is willing."

"We could arrange that," Dave said.

"Georgia," began Frida, "this all sounds great. But who would be dumb enough to make that sort of investment in the Bistro? It could take years for them to get their money back. We don't even know if the new idea will take off."

"Oh, it'll take off all right. I may not be very smart when it comes to men, but I know a good business opportunity when I see one."

Earl came shuffling up. "Did I hear someone mention me? I thought I heard someone use the word smart."

"I was just telling my sister about our proposal."

"Don't forget," warned Earl, "The bran muffin recipe is included in the deal. Without that, it's a no-go!"

Frida looked stupefied. "You want my bran muffin recipe in exchange for putting up the money for the expansion?"

Earl narrowed an eye at her. "That gonna be a problem?"

"No, no problem," Frida said quickly. "As a matter of fact, you can have any recipe you want."

"I'm not greedy. Just the bran one will do," Earl said congenially.

"Then we have a deal," Frida said. Ed put his arm around her and pulled her against him. Frida looked happier than Georgia had ever seen her.

And why shouldn't she be? Frida had everything in life that mattered. A husband who loved her. Friends who supported her.

Georgia had been wrong.

It was the Frida Hamptons of the world who really had it all.

Zeke stepped up to the mic. "I have an announcement. Rusty 1 found the fishbowl with the money in the kitchen. We have both Persephone and Alex in custody. We're hoping they'll confess and tell us where the cash from Black Tie Bunco is stashed so we can put this whole caper behind us." He signaled the band. "As far as the Whispering Bay police are concerned, everyone's free to go back to partying."

"Does this mean we can leave town?" Ted asked.

"Sure," said Zeke.

"Thank God," said Spencer. "Georgia? Are you coming?"

"Spencer, after everything that's happened, I can't believe you still want to marry me."

"Of course I do, babycakes. So, what's it going to be?"

Georgia glanced around the room. It seemed that once more everyone was holding their breath. She looked at her sister, who was clutching Ed's hand like she was going to squeeze it off. Ed looked like he didn't mind though.

And then she stole a glance at Dave. He was standing on the edge of the crowd, perfectly still.

"Spencer, can I ask you a question?"

"Go for it, babycakes."

"What do you think of my boobs?"

"Your boobs?" He said "boobs" it like it was a four-letter word.

"Yeah, you know, my tits?"

Someone in the crowd giggled.

He cleared his throat. "Is this a real question?"

"Of course it is."

"Well," he began cautiously, "I think they're very nice."

"Just nice?"

He laughed nervously and lowered his voice a notch. "Georgia, if you want a breast augmentation, just say so. I'll be happy to pay for it. Big Leslie got one. As a matter of fact, she got one before we were married, then she got a lift after Little Leslie was born. I know a top-rate plastic surgeon at UAB."

She took a deep breath. "Spencer, I'm really honored by your proposal. The fact that you've asked me twice, especially considering, well, all that's happened recently, I can't tell you how much it means to me. But the truth is I don't think we'd be happy together. As a matter of fact, I know it. The only place I could be happy with you is in the big brick house on the hill."

Spencer looked confused. "Where else would we live, babycakes?"

Georgia winced. Did he not get it? "Spencer, I'm sorry, but I don't love you. I thought I did, but I was wrong. And the thing is, you don't love me either. Well, maybe you love my mind, but that's about it. I want to be loved for all of me." She stole a glance at Dave, who grinned at her. He also looked like he wanted to kiss her, which was really very distracting.

Spencer's face turned red. "I don't know what you think you've found here in this godforsaken town, but it's time to get back to reality. You have a job, Georgia. We have a company to run." He paused. "Is that it? Do you want a share of Moody Electronics? I'll go as high as twenty-five percent, but not a lick more."

"You've got to be kidding."

"Are you trying to rob Spencer Jr. and Little Leslie of their inheritance?"

"*What?* I'm not trying to rob anyone of anything. I just don't want to marry you, Spencer."

"Okay, okay." He shoved his hand through his hair. "But this doesn't change anything else. Does it? You're still my CFO, right?"

Georgia sighed. "Spencer, I really don't see how I can go back to work for you. Not after everything that's happened."

"Why not?" His voice bordered on the hysterical.

"Because I've let our personal relationship interfere with our business one and it will never be the same. Besides, I need a change from Moody Electronics."

"It's that damn John Ambrose, isn't it? What's he offering you?"

"He hasn't offered me anything. I haven't even spoken to him," said Georgia. She narrowed her eyes at him. "Wait a minute. Did you get that contract from Valley Tech or not?"

"I'm going to fire that idiot Crystal. What has she told you now?"

"You didn't get the contract, did you?" she demanded.

"Not yet," he said, sounding like a little lost boy. "But I will. Once Valley Tech sees that you're back on the team. For some reason John Ambrose thinks the company is unstable without you."

For someone with an IQ of 140 she really was the world's biggest dummy. "You lied to me."

"Stay strong, Georgia!" someone in the crowd yelled. Georgia glanced over at the Babes and gave them a shaky smile.

"I didn't lie to you," he said, looking around the crowd for the first time. "Let's discuss this in private," he hissed.

"Sorry, Spencer, but you proposed in public, so we're going to do this in public."

He didn't look happy, but he realized he had no choice. "I didn't lie to you," he whispered fiercely, "not exactly. I was embarrassed that I couldn't get the Valley Tech contract on my own. There, are you happy now?"

"Of course I'm not happy. Why didn't you just tell me that to begin with? I would have gone back to Birmingham to meet with them." He didn't say anything. It suddenly dawned on her that Crystal hadn't gotten anything messed up. Well, maybe a little messed up, but she'd been right when she'd told Georgia that the people from Valley Tech had left midweek. "That story about John Ambrose staying in Birmingham over the weekend was all a hoax, wasn't it? You always had every intention of going to the Alabama football game. What happened? Did Crystal tell you she spilled the beans? Is that why you came running down here with an engagement ring? To fix the collateral damage?"

"Sugar," he pleaded. "Have a heart. I haven't missed a Bama game since I got out of diapers. Big Leslie understood that. That's why we got married in February. After the season was over."

Georgia covered her face with her hands. She started to shake.

"Babycakes, don't cry."

"Cry? Spencer, I'm laughing at what a total idiot I've been!"

The blood drained from his face. "Does this mean you're not coming back to work for me?"

"No, Spencer, I'm not. Wait, make that a *hell no*, I'm not. Not now. Not ever."

He looked incredulous. "I gave up last week's football game for you!"

Ted Ferguson piped up. "There's still tomorrow's game."

"See, Spencer, life isn't all bad," Georgia quipped.

"Isn't there anything I can say to convince you to keep working for me?" He braced himself as if expecting a set down.

She thought about it a minute.

"Are you still going to donate all that money you promised to the rec center fund?" she asked.

He visibly gulped. "Of course."

She pulled a business card from her purse and scratched out the Moody Electronics line and her title. Beneath it she wrote, *Georgia Meyer. Independent Business Consultant.* She handed the card to Spencer.

He read it and frowned. "What's this supposed to be?"

"Exactly what it says. I'm going into business for myself. I'll be happy to consult from time to time for Moody Electronics. My fees are a bit steep, but since we have some history together, I could probably cut you a special deal." She smiled. "As a matter of fact, I'll give you a free piece of advice right now."

He leaned in eagerly.

"Don't call your next girlfriend babycakes."

Spencer looked speechless.

Ted tugged him on the elbow. "C'mon, Moody, if we don't go now we'll miss the plane!"

This was enough to jolt Spencer out of his stupor. He and Ted practically knocked each other down to get out the door.

"Are you really going to start your own business?" Frida asked Georgia.

"Yup," Georgia said. "I just decided tonight. What do you think?"

Her sister gave her a big hug. "I think it's great!"

"It's a risk. But this way, I can be my own boss. Set my own hours. Live where ever I want."

Frida stilled. "Does this mean you might stay here? In Whispering Bay?"

She smiled at Dave. "I'd say there's a pretty good chance of that happening."

Georgia couldn't help herself. She gave Frida a hug. And then she gave Ed an even bigger one. "Thank you," she whispered in his ear.

"For what?"

"For showing me what's really important in life and for being there for my sister when she needed you. I don't think I could have picked a better husband for her."

Ed looked like he didn't know what to say.

Pilar's voice boomed over the mic. "Will Dave Hernandez please report back to duty? We have walls we need chipped down!"

"I think that's my cue," said Dave.

"Hold on," said Georgia. "I have something to say to you

too." Her throat began to spasm. Damn it. This wasn't the time to start going into pseudo–anaphylactic shock again.

She cleared her throat. "I don't know if you heard, but I'm planning to stay in town."

"I heard."

"That's partially because of you. I mean, I do have my sister here, and that's a big reason to stay. But you're also a big reason."

He started to say something, but she interrupted him. "But I'm not going to make the same mistake twice. I waited five years for Spencer to propose. In the end, it was for the best, because, after all, he wasn't the right one."

Georgia glanced nervously around. All eyes were on her again. She hadn't meant to make this public, but then, all the people she cared about in the world were here. Why shouldn't they be a part of this too? If she tanked, she'd need them to pick her up again.

"You told me that you'd know when you met the right one. And . . . if you don't think I'm the right one, then I want to know now, so that I don't waste any time. But if I am the right one, well—"

"Georgia, is this your crazy way of telling me you're in love with me?"

She gulped. "I know I've only known you two weeks and that isn't enough time to really know someone well, but, remember when I told Spencer I could only be happy with him living in a big brick house on the hill?"

Dave nodded.

"That's when I knew you were the one for me. Because I could be happy living with you anywhere. Even in a trailer. Or a tent. And I have to tell you, Dave, I'm just not a tent kind of girl. But if that's the only place we could be together, I could make it work."

He smiled. And it nearly knocked the breath out of her because it was the most beautiful thing Georgia had ever seen. And then he did something else that knocked the breath out of her.

He got down on his knees. "I didn't plan to do this tonight, but what the hell."

"Oh my God," Frida whispered.

Oh my God was right.

"I went back to Tampa to square away my business, but I went back for something else too. To ask my mother for this." He reached inside the front pocket of his jeans and pulled out a ring. It was a diamond. It wasn't four carats. It probably wasn't even one. She mentally took back what she'd just thought about Dave's smile. *This ring* was the most beautiful thing she'd ever seen.

"How many times is this gal gonna get proposed to?" Earl asked.

Everyone shushed him up.

She thought about doing the universal choke sign, but she was afraid someone might actually do the Heimlich on her and she wanted to hear every single last word of this.

"This was my grandmother's ring. I promised my mom a long time ago I'd only ask her for it once."

Georgia could feel the tears spill down her cheeks. Which was odd, because she really wasn't a crier.

"I knew the second you aimed your cell phone at me you were the right one. Georgia, will you marry me?"

She brushed the tears off her face. "I guess this means you love me too?"

"I knew somewhere deep down you had to be smart." He slipped the ring on her finger. It was a perfect fit. She pulled him off his knees and kissed him hard in front of everyone.

The room broke out in wild applause.

"Ahem!" Pilar's voice came back over the mic. "Are you two finished? Can we go back to the party now?"

Georgia laughed. Dave grabbed her to kiss her again. "Hold that thought," she said. "I'll be right back."

"Where are you going?"

"To tell the Babes all about my proposal."

He grinned. "Georgia, we've just gotten engaged in front of half the town. Don't you think they were watching?"

"Well, yeah, but they're going to want all the details," she said, blowing him a kiss as she ran off.

Because it is a truth universally acknowledged that when a woman gets a diamond engagement ring, she must show it off to her closest friends.

Dear Readers,

I'd like to introduce you to six real live Bunco groups. They've been kind enough to share some of their recipes and Bunco tips with me. Bunco groups vary in age, geographical location, number of members, and even the way they play the game. But one thing I've discovered is that all Bunco players have a few things in common. They love to eat, they love to laugh, and they love to get together with their fellow friends.

LOUISVILLE BUNCO MOMMAS
LOUISVILLE, KENTUCKY

Rae's Chicken Enchilada Salad

Put this on a salad, sandwich, in a crescent ring
if you want to get fancy, or pasta. Yum!

2 cups cooked and chopped chicken
¼ cup black olives, chopped
1 cup shredded cheddar cheese
1 can (14 ounces) chopped green chiles, undrained
½ cup mayonnaise
1 tablespoon Pampered Chef Pantry Southwestern Seasoning
    Mix (or other Mexican seasoning)

Dash of lime juice
½ cup salsa
¼ cup sour cream
Crushed tortilla chips

Mix all well. Add to whatever you like and enjoy!

LOUISVILLE BUNCO MOMMAS TIPS

Our bottom line is Bunco is an excuse to get together. We throw some dice around, indulge in fabulous food, imbibe fine wines or other adult concoctions, talk our ears off, and call it Bunco!

Do not take Bunco or life too seriously! You can learn a lot from Bunco, and the most important life lesson is to roll with the dice, but always make it fun!

DIVAS WITH DICE!
JACKSONVILLE, FLORIDA

Jell-O Shots

*Jell-O shots are the mascot of our group
and are there 90 percent of the time.
We all love them and they are easy to make.*

1 large (6 ounce) box of Jell-O
16 ounces boiling water
6 ounces cold water
10 ounces vodka

Mix the Jell-O with the boiling water until it is fully dissolved. Add the cold water and vodka. Pour the mixture into either shot glasses or paper cups. Place in the refrigerator to cool for at least 3 hours.

Please remember to drink responsibly!

These go great with tortellini pasta and dips.

Pesto Dip

1 (8 ounce) tub whipped cream cheese (see note below)
1 (8 ounce) container sour cream
4 ounces prepared pesto

Mix all the ingredients together and chill.

Note: You can use 1(8 ounce) block of cream cheese but the whipped is easier to mix.

Tomato Bruschetta Dip

1 (8 ounce) tub whipped cream cheese (see note above)
1 (8 ounce) container sour cream
4 ounces of your favorite bruschetta sauce

Mix all the ingredients together and chill.

Quick Tortellini Appetizer

For a quick appetizer, prepare a package
of frozen tortellini, toss with a tablespoon
of olive oil and serve with your favorite dips.

DIVAS WITH DICE TIP:

Sometimes it can be rather hard to hear over all the chatter and good times so we have a cow bell to indicate the round is over. We also have our very own Diva (a special dice "doll") that travels around the room. Every time you roll a Bunco you get the Diva. At the end of the game whoever has the Diva gets a special surprise. Our Diva is very fashionable and has been known to change her attire based on the time of year. For example, during the March of Dimes campaign, she wore a "With your help, there's hope" T-shirt to help promote the cause.

DRUNKOBABES
MIDLOTHIAN, VIRGINIA

Chocolate Martinis

1½ ounces dark crème de cacao
1½ ounces Godiva chocolate liqueur
1 ounce vodka

Stir all the ingredients together and serve.

Note: These martinis are also tasty with milk or half-and-half added, in whatever proportions you desire.

ABOUT THE DRUNKOBABES

Our Bunco group started up in January 2008. We had such a good time at a New Year's Eve party that we decided we needed to get to-gether more often and our Bunco group was born. We meet up once a month, usually on the third Saturday of the month and everyone takes a turn hosting (although we're pretty informal about the turn-taking). We have slowly morphed into having "themed" nights—Cinco

Recipes 321

de Mayo (with killer blue margaritas), St. Patrick's feast, wine and cheeses, grill nights (complete with s'mores in a fire pit), and chocolate for Valentine's Day—just to name a few.

Our newest bit of fun is a traveling pig. The pig arrived at the January hostess's house with a poem telling about his life and why he has run away from his farm to our Bunco group. The end of the poem instructed the members to "provide new text." So, on the pig has traveled, going to a new member's house each month, complete with a new poem or story! We are saving the poems that get written and have put them in a plastic sleeve so they don't go missing. The pig is DEFINITELY a highlight of our get-togethers!

LITTLE ROCK BUNKO BABES
LITTLE ROCK, ARKANSAS

Ice Cream Heath Bar Dessert

20–24 ice cream sandwiches
1 bag of mini Heath Bars, crushed
⅔ cup Amaretto
1 small container of Cool Whip

In a 13x9-inch baking pan, position the ice cream sandwiches on their sides. Squeeze them in tightly. If you use a different size pan, adjust the number of sandwiches.

Place in freezer for a few minutes to reset.

Pour the Amaretto lightly over the ice cream sandwiches. You can use slightly more or less, depending on how strong you want it.

Sprinkle most of the Heath Bar pieces over the top and press in lightly.

Top with the Cool Whip, flavored with a bit more Amaretto to taste.

Sprinkle top with remaining Heath Bar pieces and "dust."

Freeze until firm.

Remove from freezer 30 minutes before serving.

LITTLE ROCK BUNKO BABES TIPS

Never look a monkey in the eye.

Always serve alcohol.

Always RSVP.

Always pass to the right, AND

ALWAYS play it like you mean it.

BUNCO MAMAS CALIENTES
MELBOURNE, FLORIDA
(This is my mother's group!)

Cuban Mojitos

Yield: one serving. Repeat recipe
to make as many as you like.

Mint leaves, to taste
Juice from 1 lime
1 teaspoon powdered sugar
2 ounces white rum
2 ounces club soda
Crushed ice

Place the mint leaves into a tall glass and squeeze the lime juice over it. Add the powdered sugar, then gently crush the mint, lime juice, and sugar together. Add crushed ice. Stir in the rum and top off with the club soda. Garnish with a mint sprig.

Salud!

Bunco Mamas Calientes Super Secret Quiche

Recipe courtesy of Carmen Palacios

Step 1. Get in car and go to grocery store (Publix is my favorite).

Step 2. Go to Bakery section and pick up 2 quiches from selections available.

Step 3. Drive home.

Step 4. Remove from box and heat according to directions.

Step 5. Place warmed quiche on platter. May garnish with parsley or basil leaves.

Delicious!

ABOUT THE BUNCO MAMAS CALIENTES:

We are a group of retired ladies from different Latina backgrounds who gather on the last Tuesday of the month. We meet at ten a.m. and start with brunch. Then we play several rounds of Bunco and break up around one p.m. or whenever we run out of gossip.

Once a month we invite our husbands to play with us for Couples Bunco. We usually play on a Friday evening and do a dinner buffet. We aren't sure who loves playing more—us or our husbands!

TALLAHASSEE BUNCO BROADS
TALLAHASSEE, FLORIDA

Bunco Broad Slushie

This slushie mix is our signature drink.
It's guaranteed to please!

1 cup water
1 cup sugar
1 large can pineapple juice
2 liters 7-Up or Sprite
1 can frozen orange juice concentrate
1 can water (using the above OJ concentrate container)
2½ to 3 cups vodka
1 small jar of cherries (drained, no stems)

Heat sugar and 1 cup of water on stovetop until sugar is dissolved. Cool completely.

In a large bowl, mix together the remaining ingredients.

Add the cooled sugar water to the pineapple juice mixture and freeze in Ziploc gallon freezer bags. Remove the bags from the freezer 2 to 3 hours before serving so consistency is "slushie."

ABOUT THE BUNCO BROADS:

This is my own Bunco group! We play the first Wednesday of the month from September to May. We don't play in June and July because so many of us are out of town for summer vacation. In August, we plan a "Bunco organization" meeting (usually at Debbie's house). We catch up on everything that's happened over the summer and plan the coming schedule.

December Bunco is always special. For the past several years we've either adopted a family or donated our Bunco money to local groups who collect toys for children. Last year, we bought infant items to donate to Tallahassee YoungLives, a nonprofit group that helps teen moms build better lives for themselves and their children.

Bunco isn't just about rolling the dice and winning prizes. It's also about building relationships, being part of the community, and of course, having fun!